Billionaire Unreachable

THE BILLIONAIRE'S OBSESSION
Wyatt

J. S. SCOTT

Billionaire Unreachable

Copyright © 2023 by J. S. Scott

All rights reserved. No part of this document may be reproduced or transmitted in any form or by any means, electronic, mechanical, photocopying, recording, or otherwise, without prior written permission.

Cover Photo by Wander Aguiar Photography
Proof Editing by Michele Ficht

ISBN: 9798364357694 (Print)
ISBN: 9781951102951 (E-Book)

Contents

Chapter 1	1
Chapter 2	10
Chapter 3	19
Chapter 4	27
Chapter 5	36
Chapter 6	43
Chapter 7	53
Chapter 8	60
Chapter 9	67
Chapter 10	76
Chapter 11	84
Chapter 12	95
Chapter 13	102
Chapter 14	110
Chapter 15	116
Chapter 16	122
Chapter 17	129
Chapter 18	138
Chapter 19	145
Chapter 20	153

Chapter 21	159
Chapter 22	166
Chapter 23	174
Chapter 24	181
Chapter 25	187
Chapter 26	194
Chapter 27	199
Chapter 28	205
Chapter 29	212
Chapter 30	220
Chapter 31	228
Chapter 32	235
Chapter 33	241
Chapter 34	249
Chapter 35	256
Chapter 36	263
Epilogue	269

Chapter 1

Shelby

"Are you really doing okay, Shelby?" my cousin, Kaleb, asked with a frown. "I know you always tell us that you're doing fine, but you've been there in San Diego for over a year now, and I'm still not completely buying it. I don't think any of us are."

I looked back at the beloved faces of my three male cousins and my Aunt Millie on my computer screen.

Am I really fine?

Maybe…not completely.

Things were definitely getting easier here in California, but I couldn't say that the events in my history still didn't haunt me.

There were parts of me that were still a little broken and might stay that way for the foreseeable future, but I was surviving better than I was a year ago.

That was something, right?

I tried hard not to worry my family with my bullshit.

I was thirty-five years old, and my cousins and my aunt had been there for enough of my past drama.

I was also normally an optimist, which had gotten me in trouble at times, and I really wanted to believe that I could stop thinking about my former life sometime soon.

I looked at Kaleb's image and nodded slowly, trying to convey to him that I was okay.

While I was close to everyone on my computer screen, I'd developed a special bond with Kaleb over the last several years. He could read me a little better than his brothers and Aunt Millie because I'd opened up to him more than I had with the rest of my family.

The five of us had been meeting via video conference every Saturday afternoon when we could all get free for a little over a year now, ever since I'd relocated from Montana to San Diego.

I wasn't sure whether it helped my loneliness or if it made it worse to see the people I loved on a computer screen. There were still times when I felt guilty every time I saw them because my mistakes had hurt them, too, but they had never judged me. It was more likely that I was the one who couldn't get over it.

They all *wanted* me to be okay after everything that had happened in Montana, so I tried to tell them what they needed to hear.

My three cousins, Kaleb, Tanner, and Devon, were busy billionaires who ran a diversified multinational holding company.

The three of them were like older brothers to me.

Their mother, my Aunt Millie, was like a parent to me, too. She was now comfortably retired.

None of them needed to hear about how lonely and lost I'd been since I'd moved to San Diego.

Besides, things *had* gotten better for me recently. I was making new friends, and my head was on straighter now than it had been a year ago.

I took in the four concerned faces on my laptop screen and plastered what I hoped was an upbeat smile on my face. "I'm good," I insisted. "My food blog is still growing, and I do as many events here as possible. It's nice to be able to work for myself."

"We aren't just talking about your businesses," Tanner scoffed. "We want to know if you're really happy there in San Diego now."

Happy?

I wasn't entirely certain I even remembered what real happiness felt like anymore, but I was more…content.

Realizing they were more interested in my personal life than my career, I said, "I'm going to a barbecue at Tori Montgomery's house later. I have some friends here now. Things *are* getting better. I promise."

That much was true.

Becoming friends with Tori Montgomery was probably the best thing that happened to me in San Diego.

After a year of being alone in a city that wasn't familiar to me with no real friends, I was grateful that I'd finally met someone as genuine as Tori.

"You met her at Chase's wedding, right?" Devon questioned.

"Yes," I confirmed.

I owed Kaleb for that profitable catering job he'd gotten me by recommending my services to a friend here in San Diego a few months ago. Not only had it helped my dwindling bank account, but it had introduced me to several female friends I now valued.

Being the caterer and chef for the wedding of a powerful billionaire here in California had been extremely good for business. I'd been offered several other profitable gigs I probably wouldn't have gotten without that event on my resumé.

"So you finally met Wyatt in person," Kaleb mused. "Did you figure out that he isn't really an asshole?"

I had to force the smile to stay fixed in position after that question.

My aunt's face suddenly lit up as she questioned, "Did you like him, Shelby? He's such a nice boy."

I tried not to visibly cringe as I thought about Tori's oldest brother, Wyatt.

Shit! That's the last person I want to talk about right now.

And *only* my Aunt Millie would refer to a man like Wyatt Durand as a *nice boy*.

My brief encounter with Wyatt at his younger brother Chase's wedding hadn't exactly gone well, and it had done nothing to convince me that I was wrong in my previous assumptions about the guy.

Wyatt Durand *was* an arrogant jerk, but that wasn't something I was going to tell my cousins or my aunt.

They all thought the man walked on water.

Wyatt and Kaleb had been friends since college, and the two of them were still tight even though they lived in different states.

"I didn't exactly mingle. I wasn't a guest," I said jokingly. "I was the hired help at that wedding. I didn't really talk much to the groom or his older brother."

That wasn't exactly a lie. The groom, Chase Montgomery, had been the man who hired me and worked out the basic menu, but the women had gotten involved in most of the details. I'd talked to them more often than I'd spoken to Chase. And my one and only discussion with his older brother hadn't lasted for more than a few minutes.

"You got friendly with Tori, Savannah, and the rest of the Montgomery women," Kaleb pointed out.

"They were really nice," I said honestly. "Everyone pitched in to help pull that wedding off quickly, and I talked with all of them fairly often. We all had the chance to get to know each other a little before the wedding."

Wyatt hadn't helped with the wedding planning. He'd simply loaned out his extravagant waterfront mansion in Del Mar for his brother's reception.

Yes, I'd had a private encounter with Wyatt after all the guests at the reception had left, but it was nothing I wanted to discuss with my family.

He was just as arrogant and snobby as I'd imagined he was a year ago, when he'd refused to meet me on a blind date that Kaleb had tried to set up.

Hell, he was probably *worse* than I'd envisioned back then.

It was truly a shame that a man that attractive could be such a total asshole.

However, to be entirely fair, I hadn't exactly been nice to him, either.

"Well," my aunt mused. "I think you should get to know Wyatt better. He's a very eligible bachelor, and he's been completely charming every time we've met. He's also attractive, not to mention wealthy and accomplished."

I wanted to strangle my three cousins as they all grinned.

They were probably happy and relieved that their mother was turning her matchmaking tendencies toward me instead of them for a change.

"I think it's very unlikely that we'll run into each other again, Aunt Millie," I said firmly.

My aunt was a bulldog when she set her mind on something, and I didn't want her to assume there was even a possibility that anything would ever happen between Wyatt Durand and me.

Not only did we *not* like each other, but he was also an outrageously wealthy billionaire who owned Durand Industries, the most successful luxury product and high fashion business in the world.

I was a working-class chef.

Under normal circumstances, our paths would never cross again. We didn't exactly live or work in the same world.

Thank God!

"You might meet up again in the future," Aunt Millie considered thoughtfully, obviously unwilling to give up hope. "You're getting close to Tori Montgomery, and she's his younger sister."

I rolled my eyes in frustration, and then sent a pleading look to each of my male cousins.

Unfortunately, none of them wiped the grins off their faces or even *tried* to help me out.

Traitors!

Kaleb winked at me, and I got the sudden urge to smack the smile off his handsome face.

"Don't get your hopes up," I cautioned my aunt. "It's unlikely we'll bump into each other, and Wyatt Durand isn't my type."

He was probably more into high-fashion models and the gorgeous women in his industry.

Everything that I...wasn't.

I was a female who was as tall as some men at five foot nine, and even though I had the height of a model, I certainly didn't have the willowy body of a model. I was a chef. I liked comfort food, and I had the curvy body of a woman who really liked to eat.

I'd also inherited my father's red hair, and it made me stand out, but not always in a good way because it was curly.

My best feature was probably my green eyes, but they hardly made up for all of my other not-so-attractive traits.

I was pretty content with who I was and my physical appearance most of the time, but being rejected by someone like Wyatt Durand had made me evaluate every flaw I had for months after he'd adamantly rejected the idea of us meeting up a year ago.

Maybe that was one of the reasons I disliked him so damn much.

I'd already been down on myself a year ago, and not even close to recovering my confidence.

The last thing I'd needed back then was some arrogant asshole reminding me of everything I wasn't by flatly refusing to meet me in person.

Kaleb was the only one who knew that Wyatt had turned down a possible date with me over a year ago, and he'd apparently kept that knowledge to himself.

If anyone else in my family knew, they wouldn't be encouraging me to cozy up to a guy who had already rejected me.

Well, except for Kaleb, who was really close to Wyatt, and still insisted that his good friend wasn't a bad guy.

"If you're going to Tori's barbecue, won't you see Wyatt there?" Tanner asked.

"Wyatt is apparently out of the country," I informed my family.

I definitely wouldn't have agreed to go to Tori's place this evening if there was even a chance I'd run into Wyatt Durand again.

I'd deliberately avoided him since my friendship with Tori had developed, and I planned on doing so in the future.

I could be friends with Tori *without* seeing her arrogant, unpleasant older brother.

I felt a twinge of remorse when I saw the wistful look on my aunt's face as she replied, "That's too bad. Will there be anyone else who's single there?"

I snorted. "You're not being very subtle, Aunt Millie. As far as I know, it's just couples, and I'm not looking for single guys right now. Maybe you should work on your sons instead."

My cousins all shot me a disgruntled look, and I smiled sweetly back at them. I didn't have a single bit of sympathy for any of them after they'd refused to rescue me from my aunt's matchmaking attempts.

Aunt Millie shook her head. "They're hopeless. All three of them. Not one of my single sons are interested in settling down. But maybe they'll meet someone nice at the annual picnic. Most of the town will be here. You will be here this year, won't you, Shelby?"

I sighed, even though I'd already known that subject would come up in this virtual conversation. We were already well into summer, and the event wasn't that far away. It was always held in September, after the summer heat, but before the cold weather started.

I hadn't seen my aunt in person since the first of the year. Not since we'd gotten together here for the holidays.

My cousins had brought Aunt Millie to San Diego for Christmas and New Year's. They'd rented an enormous house here so we could spend the holidays together, but I hadn't set foot in Montana since the day I'd left.

I'd skipped the annual Remington picnic at my aunt's ranch to avoid the gossip last year.

God, I still missed Montana sometimes.

It was still home because I'd grown up there with plenty of happy memories, despite the nightmare that occurred later.

I missed my cousins and my Aunt Millie.

I missed the ranch, and I really missed the small town of Crystal Fork.

Unfortunately, I could never go back there for good.

Things would never be the same.

I couldn't change what had happened there, and those fond childhood memories would probably forever be clouded by my more recent history in Montana.

"It's not news here anymore, Shelby," Kaleb informed me in a gruff voice. "People have moved on, and your friends have been asking about you. Everyone who cares about you wants to see you. Especially the four of us."

I looked at the hopeful faces on my computer screen, my heart aching as I answered, "I'll…think about it."

If the talk had died down, maybe there was really no reason to avoid going back to Montana now for a visit.

Will it really be that painful anymore? I can't avoid Montana forever.

"Say the word," Devon said earnestly. "One of us will come and get you. Maybe all of us will come and drag you back here for the party."

I shook off my negative thoughts and smiled at my family, knowing my cousins would happily fly to San Diego in one of their private jets to drag me back to Montana for Aunt Millie's annual event. Considering their vast financial resources, it would be a pretty easy task for them.

My cousins hadn't grown up with private jets and helicopters at their disposal, but they'd been outrageously wealthy for years now. I should probably be used to their billionaire lifestyle, but I wasn't.

It was still hard to believe that the guys I'd always seen as annoying older brothers were worshipped like gods in the business world.

"I said I'd think about it," I reminded them firmly, not completely certain that I was ready to go back home, even for a visit.

Tanner grinned. "You know that's as good as a *yes* to us."

Kaleb, Devon, and my aunt nodded eagerly in agreement.

God, they looked so hopeful that it made me want to cry.

That was the moment I knew I *was* going to end up going to Montana for the annual picnic.

The event was important to my Aunt Millie, and it was a tradition for many people in my hometown.

There was no way I could disappoint the only family I had, and I had to rip the Band-Aid off those Montana wounds sooner or later.

Everyone who mattered to me still lived there.

"You're all impossible to argue with," I accused lightheartedly.

"We'd never know that you feel that way," Kaleb teased. "You're stubborn enough to argue with us all the time. You just don't win all that often."

"Because you all gang up on me," I complained with a laugh. "Well, except for Aunt Millie. She always tries not to take sides."

"That's not why we always win," Kaleb said drily. "It's because you're much too sweet to not forgive all of us before we really deserve it."

My aunt sent me a loving smile as she said, "We've all missed you so much, Shelby. It will be nice to have you here again. You have no idea how lovely it will be to see your face in person instead of on a screen."

I swallowed hard, trying to clear the lump in my throat.

She had no idea how much I wanted to see their faces again in person, too, or how much I looked forward to a very big and familiar hug from all of them.

Even though I was finally making some friends in San Diego, it had been way too long since I'd felt like I was home and surrounded by people who loved me.

Chapter 2

Shelby

"I think you just made enough food to feed an entire army," Tori Montgomery commented as I put the things I'd just prepared for a tomato roasted mac and cheese dish into the oven. "Now sit and have a glass of wine with me, Shelby. Just watching you makes me tired. All I did was chop a few things and pull ingredients out. I have no idea how you think of such creative side dishes. If you weren't here, the meat would be tossed on the grill without those fancy marinades and sauces. I would have thrown some corn and potatoes on the grill with the meat, opened canned baked beans and called it dinner."

I turned and smiled at Tori as she took a seat at her kitchen island and downed a sip of her wine.

I was done with all of the prep for the barbecue, so I joined her at the island, picking up the glass of wine she'd poured for me a few minutes ago.

Nothing I'd done in the last hour had been a chore for me.

Making food for less than ten people was pretty much a breeze compared to the work I'd done in the past as a chef.

I shrugged. "I like feeding people well."

Tori snorted. "And we love eating the food you make, but I didn't invite you here to work."

I knew that.

It had been me who had suggested that I do some prep and make some side dishes and sauces I'd been working on.

"It wasn't really all that much work," I explained after I swallowed some wine. "Cooking isn't just work for me. Creating new dishes is a hobby. You know that food is my passion, and it's not like we're feeding a massive crowd of people. You also have an amazing kitchen that makes it fun to cook."

Torie Montgomery lived in a gorgeous, waterfront mansion in La Jolla, a place I could only imagine owning in my wildest dreams.

Torie lifted a brow as she gave me a thoughtful glance. "Then maybe you need a few new hobbies. I don't mind cooking sometimes, but I'll never be as comfortable or as happy as you are in a kitchen. At least we have our love of hiking and the outdoors in common. What else do you do for fun when you're not cooking? Do you still miss Montana?"

I sighed. "Mostly, I think I just miss being closer to my family. And having a horse available when I want to ride. It's hard to compare living in Montana to San Diego. They have different advantages and disadvantages. I doubt I'll ever get used to not having cold weather or snow at Christmas or the view of the night sky that you can only get in Montana. But there are good things about not being stuck indoors all winter because of the brutal weather. There's also a lot more opportunity here for me in my profession."

"Have you ever thought about opening your own restaurant?" she asked curiously.

I swallowed the lump in my throat, reminding myself that I was trying to forget the mistakes I'd made in the past.

I'd tried hard not to ruminate about all of my failures, but I wasn't quite there yet.

"Been there, done that," I confessed. "It didn't work out. I think I much prefer experimenting with recipes and blogging about the results. With all of the work for catering available here, I can manage to make a decent living without working fifteen hour days every single day like I did when I had my own restaurant.

I'd opened up a lot to Tori, but there were things she still didn't know. Not because I didn't trust her, but because there were things I just didn't talk about with anyone. Most of them were a painful part of my history that I really wanted to forget.

Maybe I still believed in being positive, but I didn't exactly look at the world through rose-colored glasses anymore because I'd been burnt pretty badly by past events.

I couldn't be the same woman I'd been back when I'd started my own restaurant in Montana, and maybe it was better that I wasn't the same person. I'd been blissfully idealistic and ignorant.

"Your blog is incredible," Tori replied. "I think your focus on elevated comfort food with some fresh, healthier ingredients is genius. I've tried several of the ones that can be prepared in less than thirty minutes. Cooper and I loved them, and they're so easy to make after working a long day. Sometimes I just don't feel like spending a ton of time in the kitchen in the evening."

I smiled at her. "Then I've done my job. The whole reason for that blog was to make things easier for people who are really busy or who work long hours. Keeping dinner simple and delicious is a lot cheaper than delivery. Don't get me wrong, I love ordering from an app when I just don't feel like cooking myself dinner, but I've always had to stay on a budget. I might love feeding people, but cooking for just me at dinnertime isn't as much fun as cooking for other people, either."

Tori shrugged. "I can understand that, but I guess I'm really lucky. I've never had to worry about money or a tight budget. I ate out a lot when I was working for the UN and only feeding myself. I don't mind cooking something at home now that I'm married to a guy I can't wait to see every evening." She grinned as she added, "Cooking isn't one of Cooper's many talents, but he's always more than happy to clean up if I make dinner."

"I'd take that deal in a heartbeat," I told her enthusiastically. "Doing cleanup duty is the worst part of cooking for me."

I could easily see Cooper Montgomery trying to help Tori—even if he was a filthy rich guy with a very large corporation to run. It was obvious that he adored his wife and would want to lighten her load in any way possible because she had a busy schedule, too.

"Don't you dare try to lift a finger once dinner is over," Tori warned. "The guys are getting cleanup duty tonight. Taylor, Harlow, and Vanna will be here in a few minutes. They wanted to help with dinner. Okay, so maybe we're all just going to end up drinking wine together until the guys get here. Because of you, everything is pretty much prepped and done, but our husbands don't need to know that. If you don't mind, we'll let them all think we slaved over a hot stove for hours to help you."

I laughed, loving how close all of my friends were to their spouses and how they worked as a team—most of the time.

Maybe it should feel uncomfortable for me to be the lone person at this get-together who *wasn't* a billionaire, but Tori, Taylor, Harlow, and Vanna weren't pretentious. I'd discovered that it really didn't matter if we came from different worlds. They all had the same insecurities and issues that any other woman had.

As a member of the prestigious Durand family, Tori had been extremely wealthy before she'd met Cooper Montgomery. But she'd chosen to work hard as a linguist for the UN, and now she worked at a local university. She'd never been the least bit interested in working in the Durand luxury brands empire that her older brothers ran together.

Taylor, Harlow, and Vanna all had their own careers, too, and none of them had come from enormous wealth.

I'd met all of their husbands, and I doubted that any of them would have to be forced to do dishes. They were all genuinely nice guys, and extremely protective of their wives.

I knew that Hudson, Jax, Cooper, and Chase would try to make me feel comfortable, even though I was the only single, budget conscious person here.

Strangely, these casual dinners were always fun for me because *everyone* made me feel like I was part of their tribe.

I was starting to realize that my loneliness here in San Diego had essentially been *my* fault.

When I'd first arrived in California, I'd pretty much lost my ability to trust anyone except my family, and friendship wasn't easy without some level of trust.

Luckily, I'd finally met an amazing group of people who made me feel at home in their group.

"Thank you," I said quietly.

Tori raised a brow. "For what?"

"For having me here tonight. For befriending me. For introducing me to your friends so they could be my friends, too. It means a lot to me."

She shook her head. "Don't thank me. I don't think you realize how much you give to people, Shelby. I can't think of anyone who *wouldn't* want to be your friend. I'm the one who feels grateful that you wanted to be my friend."

Before I could answer her, Tori reached for her phone as it vibrated on the counter.

Her face lit up as she looked at me apologetically. "Sorry. I have to answer this text."

I waved my hand, encouraging her to answer, letting her know it was no big deal.

Her thumbs flew over the screen as she typed, apparently having a text conversation with someone she knew well. By the time she put the phone down again, her genuine smile was radiant.

"Wyatt's coming," Tori announced happily. "He just flew in from France. I'm excited that you'll finally get the chance to meet him. The minute I told him that food was going to be available, he invited himself over. My brother never turns down an opportunity for a dinner that he doesn't have to pick up from a takeout place."

I swallowed the sip of wine that I'd nearly choked on after she'd mentioned Wyatt.

Oh, God, how am I going to get out of here now? I prepped all of the food. I have to be here to finish it.

I felt panic well up inside me, and I really hated myself for wanting to flee just because Tori's older brother and I were going to run into each other again.

"What's wrong?" Tori asked, her tone concerned.

Dammit!

Obviously, I hadn't done a very good job of hiding my feelings from her.

Unfortunately, Tori had probably seen my distress written all over my face. My cousins had always told me that I was a horrible poker player because they could read what hand I had by looking at my facial expressions.

I wasn't exactly terrified of Wyatt or anything, but I really didn't want to spend any time breathing the same air he did.

He'd made his opinion of me pretty clear the last and only time we'd met face-to-face.

"Nothing is wrong," I replied, not sure how to handle a delicate situation like this one.

I valued Tori's friendship, and she adored her two older brothers.

I could hardly tell her that while I was really fond of Chase, I really didn't want to share space with Wyatt.

"I call bullshit," Tori said drily. "I can tell by the look on your face that something changed the moment I told you that Wyatt was coming to dinner. You don't want to meet him?"

I sighed. Tori was way too intuitive. I wasn't going to bluff my way out of confessing the truth anymore. "We've…met. He doesn't like me," I admitted. "And the feeling is mutual. I'm sorry. I'll try to cut out of here early."

"No, you won't," she argued adamantly with a frown. "You prepared most of this dinner. You're not leaving early, and I want you to stay. I didn't even realize you two knew each other."

"We don't," I rushed to confirm. "Not really. I've only seen him in person once. After Vanna and Chase's wedding reception."

She folded her arms across her chest as she sent me a probing look. "Well, I can see that Wyatt didn't make a great first impression on you. Spill it. What happened?"

I shrugged. "Nothing earthshattering. Honestly. The entire exchange lasted all of five minutes or so. Your brother isn't exactly talky, and I was really tired from working all day. It wasn't a big deal, Tori."

"I'm still not buying it," Tori said patiently. "He said something that pissed you off, which isn't unusual for Wyatt. You're not the kind of woman who would dislike someone for no reason."

I let out an exasperated breath. "He's your brother, Tori."

She nodded. "Which means I know just how much of an ass he can be sometimes. What did he say?"

"He thought I was intruding on his privacy because I was in his kitchen eating my dinner after everyone had left," I said honestly. "Normally, I probably wouldn't have been bitchy to him, but he just rubbed me the wrong way that night. I should have just dropped my food and left. It was his house, and he was indirectly my client. The reception venue was his home."

"Wyatt rubs almost *everyone* the wrong way at first," Tori answered. "He never opens his home to anyone, much less a crowd of people for a wedding reception. I'm sure he was probably a jerk. Did he say something horrible?"

I shook my head. "I just...overreacted. I was probably even ruder than he was that night. His arrogance set me off. He can be a little abrasive."

I'd thought about that brief interaction many times since it had happened four or five weeks ago.

Wyatt *hadn't* said anything horrible or unforgivable.

He was just a man with a really...bad attitude.

It wasn't like I didn't know how to handle that. I'd been working in the service industry for a long time.

Tori snorted. "Abrasive is a nice way of saying he comes off as extremely rude sometimes. I know Wyatt. I know he's not the guy who most people see on the surface. But I'd be hard-pressed to convince anyone else who doesn't know him well that he isn't a major jerk. I'm glad you stood up to him. Please don't let his attitude scare you away. I know you're not that easily intimidated."

I wasn't.

Not usually.

"It's not just his attitude," I confessed reluctantly, knowing I needed to tell Tori the whole story. It was apparent that Wyatt had never said a word about it to his family, but she was bound to find out eventually, and I'd rather she heard it from me. "You know my cousin and Wyatt have been friends for a long time, right?"

"Kaleb? Yes, I know," Tori confirmed. "They've been close since college."

I took a slug of my wine before I continued, "When I first moved to San Diego over a year ago, Kaleb tried to set me up on a blind date with Wyatt a month or two after I arrived because I didn't know anyone here. Your brother adamantly refused. Maybe that shouldn't have hurt my feelings—"

"Of course it hurt your feelings," Tori interrupted.

"I wasn't eager to do the blind date thing, either," I rushed to explain, not wanting Tori to misinterpret the reasons I'd gone along with the whole idea of a blind date in the first place. "I wasn't looking for a romantic relationship with anyone, but I thought maybe I could make a friend here in San Diego who was close to Kaleb. I would have refused myself if Kaleb and Wyatt weren't so close, but I was really missing my family in Montana. I wasn't expecting a gorgeous billionaire to be attracted to me romantically, but I agreed to meet Wyatt to see if we could be friends. Kaleb trusted Wyatt, so I had no reason not to trust him, too. Your brother…didn't agree to meet up with me. I never got the chance to tell him that all I was interested in was a possible friendship."

Finding myself a man in San Diego hadn't even been on my radar at the time.

It still wasn't.

The last thing I wanted was to date anyone.

All I'd wanted was to see a friendly smile from a person that Kaleb liked and trusted.

"I don't think that refusal had anything to do with *you*," Tori said thoughtfully. "I have a feeling he was reluctant because you were related to a good friend. Wyatt doesn't really…. date. He hasn't had anything that I'd call a serious relationship since he got out of the military years ago. My brother is a workaholic. He should have met up with you though. He trusts Kaleb and he should have trusted his judgment. Wyatt's reaction to the offer was pretty thoughtless, but I honestly don't think he ever thought that your feelings would be hurt. Underneath that cool and aloof exterior of his, he really does have a heart. Give him a chance, Shelby. If you do, he'll eventually grow on you."

I highly doubted *that,* but Tori was my friend, and I didn't want this kind of awkwardness with one of her brothers. "It's fine. It happened a year ago, and he never really said anything personally hurtful after the reception."

I might not like Wyatt Durand, but he *was* Tori's brother, and I *did* like everyone else coming to this dinner.

How difficult could it be to tolerate the annoying man for one evening?

Chapter 3

Wyatt

My stomach growled as I pulled into the driveway of my sister's home.

I'd skipped lunch on my flight back from Paris, and I was starving.

I'd also been in nonstop meetings for the last two weeks, and maybe I wanted to see some friendly faces of people who wanted nothing from me but my presence at a casual meal.

Okay, so maybe I *had* invited myself to this get-together, but a guy had to eat, and it was a lot better for my digestion to do it while I was talking to people who didn't want a piece of me for business reasons.

I wouldn't stay long.

I never did.

When I could actually make the time for my sister's casual dinners with family and friends, I usually had other obligations to handle later that evening.

I could only hang out long enough to eat dinner and touch base with my family and friends.

I was also curious to hear about the mission that Last Hope had done in my absence, and since every person at the dinner tonight knew about or was a fellow volunteer for the hostage rescue organization, we could speak openly.

I knew that the latest mission had been successful. The hostage had been rescued without incident. Not that I expected it would go any differently, but I still wanted to know the details.

I hated it when an operation happened and I wasn't here to take part in it from our San Diego headquarters.

Especially when it had been volunteer members from my previous Delta Force team who had completed that flawless op out in the field.

It wasn't that I didn't trust every single person involved in Last Hope, but I'd been there to watch my team's six for years, just like they'd watched mine.

I didn't like it when they were running a rescue, and I wasn't there to monitor it personally.

I exited my black, F-150 Limited and shrugged out of my suit jacket, tossing it in the back before I locked the truck.

Maybe my truck wasn't the vehicle of choice for a lot of guys who had the money to buy any car on the planet. But there was no way I was going to suffer by contorting my extra-large frame into a seven-figure vehicle just for the prestige of driving an expensive sports car.

I was a large man who needed more shoulder, leg, and head room. I also wasn't into status cars that were as uncomfortable as hell to drive every day.

Occasionally, when I had the time—which was almost never—I liked to find remote areas to just chill out, camp, and fish. At times, I liked to get out of the city, and those pricey sports cars didn't cut it on dirt roads.

I also liked my damn space and comfort when I was driving in traffic on a daily basis.

As I walked to the door of Tori and Cooper's home, I rolled up the sleeves of my dress shirt.

I guess I could have made a stop at home first to change.

But my empty stomach had been in control, and I'd wanted to get to this barbecue before all the food was gone.

Hudson, Jax, Cooper, and Chase could put away enough food that would usually feed a dozen people, and I wanted my share.

"Wyatt!" Tori exclaimed as she opened the door and instantly threw herself into my arms with a delighted shriek. "I'm so glad you're home."

Generally, I wasn't a hugger or a touchy-feely kind of guy, but my little sister was the exception.

I wrapped my arms around her, lifting her feet off the ground as I returned her embrace.

Tori was the only female who ever embraced me unconditionally, even when I was an asshole, which was most of the time.

I realized that she had a husband now who watched out for her well-being. Yeah, I trusted Cooper Montgomery, but I'd been Tori's protector long before he had taken on that job. I'd always taken that responsibility seriously, and my big brother instincts hadn't lessened just because Tori was married.

Hell, I'd almost lost my baby sister not once, but twice, because she'd been kidnapped in the Amazon on two separate occasions.

I was grateful that she was happy, healthy, and still alive to hug my ornery ass.

"Where's the food?" I asked gruffly as I released her.

She grabbed my arm and I allowed her to pull me inside as she chattered, "We have plenty of food. My friend is here. She made enough incredible food to feed the entire neighborhood. Everything is still warm. Grab a plate."

My stomach rumbled as I arrived in the kitchen and inhaled some of the most mouthwatering scents I'd ever experienced.

After years of MRE's in the military, anything edible that *wasn't* ready-to-eat meals that mostly tasted like crap got my attention.

I appreciated good food, but despite the fact that I had plenty of money to buy the best cuisine, I rarely did.

My schedule was too damn busy to take the time to eat at good restaurants, and my own culinary skills were extremely limited.

"Who's the friend?" I asked, distracted by all of the dishes that filled every space on the large kitchen island.

Granted, I was disappointed that there was apparently an outsider at this gathering, which would keep me from getting the details of our latest Last Hope mission, but I still wanted to eat.

Tori slapped me on the arm playfully as she handed me a plate. "Shelby Remington. You've met her. She was the chef at Chase's wedding. Load a plate and come outside by the fire pit with us. And don't forget to take some of that caramel apple cake with cream cheese frosting. It's ridiculous. You're lucky that we left any of that for you."

I didn't move to dish up my food.

I just stared at my sister before I asked cautiously, "Shelby Remington? Do you mean Kaleb's cousin?"

Fuck! The woman was a sharp-tongued menace.

Kaleb had always claimed that his beloved female cousin was the kindest female on Earth, but I'd seen no evidence of that during a brief encounter with her after Chase and Savannah's reception.

Tori had told me that she and Shelby still kept in touch, but I hadn't expected to see her *here.*

My sister always limited these casual barbecues to family and close friends so everything was relaxed, a way to blow off steam in a trusted environment.

Tori's face fell as I frowned, which made me feel slightly guilty, but I shrugged off that momentary twinge of remorse.

What in the hell had possessed her to invite *that woman* to this dinner?

"Please be nice," Tori said in a pleading tone. "She said you two got off to a bad start when you met at Vanna and Chase's reception, but she's my friend, Wyatt."

We got off to a bad start?

That was putting it mildly.

Okay, so maybe I *had* jumped the gun by assuming that she was an unwanted intruder the night of the reception, but she'd insulted me several times, and she'd swilled a tumbler of my best whisky, dammit. Right before she'd high-tailed it out of my place like she didn't want to spend another second in my company.

"She's an annoying, bad-tempered, sarcastic woman with no filter," I grumbled.

Tori rolled her eyes. "No, she's not, but I'm sure it was disconcerting to find a woman who didn't fall all over you."

Fall all over me?

Not only had she *not* fallen all over me, but she'd also irritated me like no other person—male or female—ever had.

Nobody had ever ignored me or needled me the way she had, and I hadn't particularly liked her sarcasm directed toward me, even though I was a master at it myself.

"Please," Tori said again in that cajoling voice she knew I couldn't refuse.

I forked a perfectly cooked steak and dropped it on my plate. I then started taking some of everything on the island until my plate was so full that I couldn't fit anything else on it.

It was hard for me to say no to Tori. She knew that, and right now, she was taking advantage of one of my few weaknesses.

"No promises," I said vaguely.

Honestly, my cooperation was going to depend on Shelby Remington's attitude.

If she was as surly as she'd been the evening of Chase and Vanna's wedding reception, all bets were off.

All I really wanted to do was eat in peace, and leave as quickly as possible.

"Go and eat," Tori insisted as she cut what I assumed was a piece of that irresistible cake for me and put it on a smaller plate. "The chair right next to Shelby's is available."

I stared at my little sister suspiciously. "Are you trying to set me up?"

It wouldn't be the first time.

She rolled her eyes at me. "No, I'm not setting you up. But it would be nice if you got to know her since she's my friend. I think everything that happened between the two of you was a misunderstanding.

She told me about the blind date thing a year ago, but only because I forced her to cough up that information. Refusing to meet her after she'd already agreed to meet you was kind of a crappy thing for you to do. She was new in town, Wyatt. She didn't have any friends here. She didn't have any ulterior motives. All she wanted to do was meet up with a friend of Kaleb's."

Fuck! I'd really hoped that Tori hadn't been informed about *that* incident.

I put my loaded plate down on the counter and ran a hand through my hair in frustration. "Kaleb didn't tell me that she knew he was attempting to hook us up. I thought he'd asked *me* first, so I nixed the idea right away. I didn't know he'd already asked Shelby."

Tori looked at me with a puzzled expression. "Why would he ask you first? She's his cousin, and they're really close. Of course he cleared it with her before he asked you. You hurt her feelings, Wyatt. I really don't blame her for being a little standoffish and short with you when the two of you finally met in person."

"Short?" I protested. "She called me a superficial asshole and indicated that she thought I was conceited. For some strange reason, she seemed to think I refused to meet her because of the way she looked."

Tori shot me an accusatory look. "She's gorgeous, and any guy would have to be an idiot to refuse a date with her, but did you do it because you didn't think she was attractive? That's the reason most guys refuse a blind date, which does make them superficial and stuck up."

"I had no fucking idea what she looked like," I said grumpily. "We'd never met. Not even when I visited Montana to see Kaleb and his family. I was never around when she was, and all I'd ever seen was pictures of Shelby with her cousins when she was nothing more than a child. I have no intention of getting romantically involved with *any* woman. I'd rather not lose my mind like all of my friends and my brother. She was better off never meeting me at all. I don't have a romantic bone in my body, Tori. You know that."

"She was no more interested in romance than you were. So you were afraid of jeopardizing your friendship with Kaleb?" she queried. "And you don't find her...unattractive?"

Fuck, no. Shelby Remington was beautiful. Statuesque and gorgeous, with large, flaming red curls that looked softer than silk and a curvy body that had made my dick twitch the moment I'd seen her. However, I wasn't about to share those little details with Tori.

Truthfully, Shelby Remington's audacity had challenged and surprised me, which hadn't happened in a long time. Sure, it had been somewhat annoying, but it had also intrigued me...at first. Before she'd ran away like she couldn't tolerate another moment in my company. But I wasn't confessing *that* to Tori, either.

My little sister was always insistent that I just hadn't met the right woman yet, and I didn't want to encourage her to keep making that incorrect assumption.

If Tori knew that Shelby had stood out from other women in any way to me, she'd jump all over that information.

I shrugged. "I was mostly worried about my friendship with Kaleb. But it was for her own good, too. I'm a jaded asshole who spends most of my time working. What female wants to deal with that?"

"All she wanted was a friend," Tori said softly.

"Yeah. Well. I'd suck at that, too," I informed her bluntly. "I've never been friends with a woman."

I'd spent the majority of my adult life in special forces in the military, many of those military years leading Delta Force missions with the same guys over and over again.

I knew zero about being there for a female when she needed me, and even less about how a woman's mind worked in general.

That was a lesson I'd learned a very long time ago, and I wasn't eager to try and fail at it again.

"You have a little sister, and I'm also a female. You've always been there for me when I needed you," Tori reminded me gently.

"Sisters are different," I retorted firmly. "You're family. There's no romance involved."

"Oh, Wyatt," Tori breathed out softly. "You're much more compassionate than most of the world sees."

I picked up my loaded plate, stacked the dessert on top, and then snatched a napkin and silverware. "I really hope you don't feel the need to share that opinion with anyone else because it's bullshit," I told her unhappily as I strode toward the patio door.

Luckily, Tori only saw a small portion of the man that I was and always would be.

She didn't know the man who could kill someone without a second thought when it was necessary.

She didn't know the person who had always put duty first and personal relationships last.

She also didn't know the cutthroat businessman who did what he needed to do and almost never looked back at the destruction in his wake.

Tori only knew the big brother who had been there to protect her for as long as she could remember.

She only saw the guy I wanted her to see, and I was oddly grateful that she didn't know what I was capable of outside of that little sister bubble.

At least there was one woman on the planet who *didn't* think I was an asshole, and I really wanted to keep it that way.

Shelby

"I'm sorry that I called you a superficial asshole," I blurted out as I watched Wyatt devour his food like he hadn't eaten in a very long time. "I don't know you, and it wasn't fair for me to say that."

The tension between me and Wyatt Durand was thick enough to cut with a knife. It had been since the moment he had taken the seat beside me about ten minutes earlier.

We were all sitting around the enormous firepit, and there were several conversations going on, but the silence had been deafening in this particular area.

Wyatt hadn't said a word to me, even though we were sitting so close to each other that our bodies were almost touching.

Done with my own dinner, I took a huge slug of my wine as I watched him, waiting for him to respond.

I'd finally decided that the strain between the two of us was too much.

Okay, maybe it didn't matter to Wyatt.

I couldn't read him at all.

But it had been way too much *for me.*

I wasn't used to sitting this close to someone in complete and utter silence.

Maybe I didn't make friends as easily as I used to, but I was generally polite and friendly.

Dammit! Maybe I wouldn't be so uncomfortable if he didn't look and smell so incredible.

Maybe he was an intolerable jerk, but he smelled like hot sex and sin, and he was annoyingly attractive.

He looked a little tired, and he was obviously hungry, but it didn't detract from his animal magnetism or the way I reacted to that overwhelming aura he seemed to emanate from every pore of his powerful body.

Wyatt Durand was tall, probably a few inches over six feet, and the man was built like a tank. All muscle and brute strength. Strangely, I didn't find that unappealing. In fact, it had me squirming in my chair rather uncomfortably.

His short, black hair was slightly disheveled, and judging by the stubble on his face, he hadn't shaved in a while. But I supposed I'd probably look the same way if I'd just done a very long, international flight. Surprisingly, those small imperfections were a sexy look on him, too. I much preferred the man who didn't look as perfect or as foreboding as he had at Chase and Savannah's reception.

The sleeves of his crisp, white, and probably very expensive dress shirt were rolled up, and I was unexplainably fascinated by the strong muscles in his forearms.

He didn't look nearly as buttoned up or arrogant as he had last time I'd seen him.

Still, he reeked of power, strength, and irresistible, alpha male. The fact that I suddenly found those traits overwhelmingly alluring was probably beyond dangerous.

We were sitting way too close for me not to notice things I hadn't when we were in his kitchen.

I hated it, but I could hardly move away from him without someone catching the fact that my close proximity to Wyatt unnerved me.

My breath caught as he finally turned his head to look at me, his dark gray eyes pinning me to my chair.

"Your assessment was correct," he finally answered with a careless shrug. "There's plenty of people who would agree with you."

His penetrating stare probably should have prompted me to flee as quickly as possible, but it didn't. Because there was almost no distance between us, I could see that there was something in his gaze that was more self-mocking than conceited right now.

"I still shouldn't have said it," I mumbled.

"I think I was more put out that you downed a glass of whiskey that I'd poured for myself," he replied drily. "After that long reception, I needed it."

Amused, I shot him a small smile. "I think I needed it more than you did. It was a long day. Two of my crew called in sick right before the reception. I was working with a short staff, and I wanted to do a good job for Chase and Vanna."

"Mission accomplished," he commented. "The food was amazing. No one would have ever known that you didn't have a full staff. I'd definitely know that you cooked this dinner tonight, too, even if Tori hadn't shared that information already. It's fantastic. Possibly even better than the food at the reception, which I didn't think was possible."

Warmth spread over my body at his compliment, and I softened just a little toward Wyatt Durand.

"You like it?" I asked. "What's your favorite? I was testing out some new side dish recipes."

He put his empty plate on the side table. "I've never had mac and cheese like yours, and I have no idea what you did to that steak, but it's the best I've ever had. Honestly, everything was great. I haven't had a dinner like this one in a long time, and I haven't gotten to the caramel apple cake yet."

"That's new for me, too," I said conversationally. "It's an old recipe of mine with a new twist. Try it. I'm looking for honest opinions."

I knew I'd get a blunt opinion from Wyatt, but I was totally open to constructive criticism. It was my job to pay attention to feedback on my food and to correct anything that wasn't quite right.

Most of the tension in the air faded as I watched him grab the cake and shovel a large bite into his mouth.

The rapturous look on his face as he chewed said it all.

If nothing else, this infuriating man and I could definitely bond over food.

He loved to eat, obviously.

And I loved to cook things that made people happy.

He didn't say a word as he finished his dessert.

When he finally put the empty dessert plate on top of the larger one on his side table, he turned to me and grinned.

The smile transformed his usually grim expression, and it was one of the most beguiling things I'd ever seen.

Who knew that Wyatt was actually capable of smiling?

"Also one of the best things I've ever eaten," he informed me. "Where in the hell did you learn to cook like that?"

I shrugged. "I've been cooking most of my life. You might already know that my Aunt Millie is an amazing cook. She taught me everything she knew when I was young. Then I went to culinary school in Chicago, and I stayed there for years, working my way up in a Michelin-star restaurant until I was a head chef."

He surveyed me with those mesmerizing eyes as he asked, "What did you do after that? I think Kaleb once mentioned that you opened your own place in Billings, and that it was a huge success."

Maybe I should have been ready for that question. Kaleb used to brag about my successes all the time. I answered as briefly and as vaguely as possible. "I did, and it was, but in the end, it just…didn't work out. I left the restaurant in Chicago to move back to Montana. I missed my roots and making simpler comfort food. As you can probably tell by looking at me, I appreciate heartier food. *Shelby's* was a restaurant that celebrated elevated comfort food, just like I made for dinner tonight.

I held my breath, hoping he wouldn't ask any questions that I didn't want to answer.

His eyes roamed over me, and I squirmed under his assessing gaze. "There isn't a fucking thing wrong with the way you look," he said in a deep voice that wasn't meant to be sensual, but it was to me.

I released the air from my lungs, glad that he'd gotten distracted by another subject.

I sent him an exasperated look. "Please. You don't think it's obvious that I like to eat what I cook. Isn't that one of the reasons that you refused to meet up with me a year ago?"

"I had no idea what you looked like, Shelby," Wyatt answered shortly. "I've only seen pictures of you and Kaleb as children. I didn't want to do a blind date because I am, in fact, an asshole, and you're the beloved cousin of one of my best friends. I didn't want you to be disappointed, and I had no desire to have a romantic relationship with any woman. Still don't. I had no idea that he'd already cleared the idea with you, so I also didn't know that my refusal would hurt your feelings."

He hadn't apologized, but I realized that what Wyatt had just said was probably as close to an apology as he ever got.

His answer had surprised me, and I gaped at him, unsure of exactly what he was saying.

He really didn't know what I looked like?

I supposed that could be true.

It wasn't like Wyatt went to Montana often, and when he had, his visits had been extremely brief.

There was probably no reason to think he'd seen a recent picture of me before that proposed meeting over a year ago.

I'd probably jumped to that conclusion because of my own insecurities.

"I only agreed because I wanted to make a friend in San Diego," I shared openly. "I didn't want a romantic relationship, either. I didn't know anyone when I first got here to California. Initially, I came here for a chef position that a friend from Chicago had offered me. By the time I relocated and was ready to start the new job, she'd accepted another position in Tokyo and was ready to leave. I saw her for one day and then she was gone."

"And the new job?" Wyatt asked in a curious tone.

I sighed. "The restaurant went out of business a short time later. I could have gotten hired somewhere else, but my blog was really growing, so I decided to do gig work with some people I met while I was working at that restaurant. I wanted to work harder on my blog. I was tired of working for other people, and the pay wasn't great at the restaurant."

"Did I hear you say something about your blog?" Tori asked from her position several feet away. "It's amazing, Wyatt. Don't let her tell you anything else. Her following is fantastic. I just wish she'd start doing videos. I'd love to see her actually making some of her recipes."

Because Tori had spoken so boisterously, everyone seated around the fire pit was shooting me a speculative look. I explained loud enough for everyone to hear. "I have the equipment to video now, but the kitchen in my apartment isn't large enough or updated enough for that. It's tiny. The videos will have to wait until I can get a place with a nicer kitchen."

"You can use mine," Tori offered. "Cooper and I are both gone all day."

"Or ours," Savannah said. "I work at home most of the time, but I'm always up for company."

"Mine is available all day, too," Taylor added.

"You could come to our place," Harlow said enthusiastically.

I looked from one woman to another, flabbergasted that every single one of them was willing to let me use their kitchens.

I hadn't known any of them that long.

I shook my head slowly. "I appreciate all of the offers, but I couldn't intrude—"

"Not necessary," Wyatt cut in matter-of-factly. "I'm willing to make a deal with Shelby. One that would benefit both of us. She can cook and video at my place if I get to eat what she cooks for dinner. I also just lost my dog sitter for the sad excuse of a canine that Jax foisted off on me a few months ago. I'd be willing to pay Shelby to come to my house to entertain that animal and cook during the day."

"I told you that it's only temporary," Jax explained. "The veteran who was supposed to take Xena had to move and couldn't have a dog in his new apartment. We don't have space for her anymore at the training center. She's an excellent companion dog, and I'll find her a new owner. Give me another month or two. She likes you, even if the feeling isn't exactly mutual yet."

"She's a pain in my ass," Wyatt grumbled as he looked at me. "Are you interested?"

Interested?

God, I'd cooked for over fifty guests in that glorious kitchen of Wyatt's.

It was a chef's dream kitchen, and it would be perfect for my videos and photos. It would be an amazing opportunity to extend my blog.

And it did sound like the agreement would be advantageous for both of us.

Obviously, Wyatt could easily hire a private chef for himself, but apparently hadn't for some reason.

I wouldn't feel like I was taking advantage if he was getting something out of the deal, too.

"I don't want you to pay me if we make this deal. I'd be benefiting enough," I said hesitantly. "I love dogs. I've had several shelter dogs, but I can't have one in my apartment here. And I'd be happy to leave what I cook on video for your dinner every night. Is Xena aggressive?"

"Oh, God, no," Tori drawled. "She's the sweetest little French bulldog you've ever seen. I've worked with her at the training center. It's not usually a great breed for service dogs, but we came across her at the shelter, and we knew she'd make a good companion dog for the right person. She's just a little...stubborn. We don't have anyone who just needs a companion dog at the moment. Most of the people waiting need a dog with special skills, but we'll find placement for Xena. We just need a little more time."

I knew that Cooper and Tori worked with Jax as volunteers at his training center for service dogs for veterans.

I was also aware that the place occasionally got a little crowded when they had a high demand and a lot of dogs in training at the same time.

"She's not sweet," Wyatt argued as he fixed his disgruntled gaze on his sister. "She snores louder than a full-grown, male human, and she passes gas like one, too. She also has allergies, which means she needs special medications and even special shampoo. That dog is more high-maintenance than any human I've ever met. She obviously has a bladder the size of a pea because she wants to go outside a thousand times a day. You also neglected to tell me that her breed has separation anxiety. She whines every single morning when I leave."

"Lots of breeds have separation anxiety," Jax muttered. "And she wouldn't be having separation anxiety if she wasn't already attached to you."

"She's a mess," Wyatt griped. "And I don't want her to be attached to me. You called in a favor that I owed you. You knew I couldn't say no."

"She's a sweetheart," Tori said defensively. "And it's not like you can't afford to hire another dog sitter. Or you could try her in doggie daycare."

"She wouldn't like it," Wyatt said unhappily. "She's needy. She prefers one-on-one attention."

I looked from Wyatt to Tori. My friend winked at me, obviously trying to convey the fact that no matter how much Wyatt complained, he still had some compassion for the canine.

I turned my head toward Wyatt again as I said, "I can't believe you actually have a…Frenchie."

I heard Jax snicker, and Wyatt instantly shot him a fuck-you look, which made me instantly regret my words.

I hadn't meant for the comment to seem rude, but I'd peg Wyatt as the type of guy who'd prefer a dog that would rip someone's face off. Not a sweet Frenchie that couldn't stand it when he left the house every day.

However, it was obvious that Wyatt Durand actually had some humaneness for the small animal, despite all of his complaints.

"She's not my dog," Wyatt rumbled. "And I will pay you. I'll be getting both a chef and a dog sitter. All you'll be getting is a video and some pictures in a nice kitchen. That's hardly fair. And you haven't met the pain in the ass canine yet, either. You might decide to quit after your first day with her."

I smiled at him and was disappointed when that smile was met with a stony, emotionless expression. "I'm sure she'll be fine with me. How soon do you need someone to sit with her?"

For one shining moment, I'd started to see Wyatt Durand in a different light.

He'd acted like he was interested in me as a person. He'd been curious about my history, and had even complimented me on my skills as a chef.

No matter how much he complained, he obviously tried to meet the needs of the small animal under his care.

And then, he'd snapped back to the cantankerous man I'd met after Chase and Vanna's reception.

Apparently, he had the social skills to act like a decent person, but those tendencies were fleeting.

Does it really matter? He's offering me an opportunity I can't resist. It's a business arrangement.

"Tomorrow?" he asked coolly. "Xena has been staying in a suite at a dog resort while I was gone, but I'll have to pick her up tonight."

I had to try hard to keep a neutral expression on my face because I definitely wanted to laugh.

He's keeping a dog he supposedly dislikes in a suite at a doggie resort?

Since I had no catering gigs scheduled until the following week, I had no reason *not* to accept.

I didn't have to like the guy. I'd worked for several really unpleasant, arrogant, male bosses in the past. My occupation was male-dominated, and some of those men were total jerks. I really wouldn't have to spend much, if any, time in Wyatt's presence.

And just like that, Wyatt Durand and I were making plans for this mutually beneficial arrangement to start the very next day.

Chapter 5

Wyatt

"What in the hell possessed you to offer Shelby your kitchen and a dog sitting job yesterday?" my brother Chase asked as we sat together in my office at Durand Industries the next day. "Everyone else offered, and there isn't a single one of us who would have minded helping Shelby out."

Chase and I had been preparing for an important meeting the following week, and I'd tried to keep our attention focused on that task this afternoon.

However, now that we were finished, I should have known that I wasn't going to be able to avoid that inevitable question.

The problem was, I had no idea how to answer.

Chase knew me.

He knew my habits.

He also knew that I valued my privacy.

My home was the only place where I could relax and not have to deal with the constant demands on my time.

Having someone come in and out of my house as a dog sitter during the day was one thing. I didn't like it, but it was a necessary inconvenience.

Letting someone actually use my refuge as a video location was something else entirely.

Hell, Chase didn't even know the rest of the deal. I'd actually insisted on Shelby staying and working at my place even after she was done with her cooking videos so Xena had less time alone in the house. She didn't think what I was paying her was justified for just a few hours a day, so I'd used that separation anxiety excuse to give her more hours.

I sure as hell wasn't about to tell my brother about that.

It would make him even more suspicious than he already was right now.

I looked up from my computer and shot my younger brother a don't-ask-me-why-in-the-fuck-I-did-something look, hoping he wouldn't ask any more questions.

Unfortunately, my brother knew me, and he wasn't the least bit intimidated by the warning glare.

He simply lifted a brow when I didn't respond. "There must be some reason you did something so out of character," he prompted.

"I needed a dog sitter for that psychotic canine that Jax needed off his hands for a while," I said gruffly. "I'd also like to eat something other than takeout. The situation works for both of us."

For some reason, I'd sensed that Shelby wasn't about to be persuaded to use someone else's kitchen without being able to provide something for that person in return.

She'd been in the process of refusing all of the other offers, so I'd tossed one out there that she'd probably accept.

I was a man who made it a point not to squander any opportunities, so I'd swooped in to reap the benefits of a mutually beneficial agreement with Shelby.

Was something like that unusual for me?

Probably.

But I still didn't regret making that offer. I'd solved my dog sitting problem and secured what I knew were going to be some very good dinners in one small action.

Two problems solved with very little effort.

Chase shot me a skeptical look. "It's not like there are no other dog sitters in San Diego."

"I'm sure there are plenty of them," I said drily. "But they don't cook like Shelby Remington. Just drop it, Chase. You can't possibly think I did it to be a *nice guy*. When has that ever happened?"

I'd gotten a glimpse of a different side of Shelby Remington yesterday, which had probably fueled my interest in making that agreement.

She was obviously a hard worker, and she was definitely intelligent. She'd lost her job almost immediately after she'd arrived here in San Diego, yet she'd managed to pivot to make that situation work to her advantage.

Maybe there was more to this woman than I'd initially assumed.

She'd also been…nice, which was a welcome change after the way we'd met the first time.

"Tori told Savannah about the whole blind date thing," Chase admitted. "And about the run-in you and Shelby had after our wedding reception. Are you sure this offer doesn't have anything to do with the fact that you once hurt Shelby's feelings?"

Fuck! I should have known that my sister wouldn't keep that info to herself.

She was growing way too close to Shelby, and Tori had a tendency to share too much information with Chase's wife, Savannah.

"That had absolutely nothing to do with it," I said irritably. "I never knew I hurt her damn feelings, and she did call me a superficial asshole after the reception."

Chase smirked. "So she actually told you off?"

My body tensed as I remembered that brief encounter. "Yes," I said stiffly.

"What was that like?" Chase asked conversationally. "It's probably been a while since anyone has stood up to you except for family."

I hadn't liked it. At all.

I was used to people never questioning me or calling me on anything, and I liked it that way.

"It was ridiculous," I snapped. "I might be an asshole, but I didn't do the things she accused me of doing. She thought I turned down the opportunity to meet up with her because she wasn't my physical ideal, which is asinine. I had no clue what she looked like, but I knew she was Kaleb's cousin. He sees Shelby as more of a little sister than a cousin. I wasn't interested in being set up with *any* female, much less a woman who means something to one of my friends. I don't date. I don't do romantic relationships. My relationship with Kaleb has always been solid and valuable. My refusal had nothing to do with the way she looks. Hell, she's beautiful, but she definitely isn't the sweet woman that Kaleb made her out to be."

"Actually," Chase mused. "She's probably exactly the type of woman that Kaleb described. You just never got a chance to see that side of her before you pissed her off. Shelby has three cousins who are billionaires, but from what I understand, she's never accepted anything from them but their affection. You know that Kaleb, Tanner, and Devon would happily set her up so well that she'd never have to work if she was willing to accept their help. She could be living in luxury. Instead, she works her ass off to make a living herself. Maybe I don't know her that well, but I find it pretty admirable that she refuses to benefit from her cousins' successes. I'm also in awe of the fact that no matter how busy she is making a living, she's making the time to volunteer her cooking skills in a soup kitchen in the downtown area. A place that serves a lot of military veterans and elderly people who don't have enough money to eat. All things considered, I think she *is* the sweet woman that Kaleb and his brothers adore."

Despite my surprise, I tried to keep my expression neutral as I confessed gruffly, "I didn't know about all that."

I'd already figured out that Shelby was stubborn, and was obviously determined to make her own living, despite the fact that there was a lot of money in the Remington family.

Her apparent disinterest in the family money intrigued me, but I'd been unaware of the fact that she used her talents to help feed people who couldn't afford to eat.

Chase shrugged. "Maybe you would have realized that she wasn't like the other women you've met if you would have agreed to meet up with her a year ago. I happen to think she's a woman worth knowing."

"I wouldn't know," I said tersely. "She...doesn't like me."

"You might try being nicer to her," Chase suggested. "No offense, but you do come off as a major jackass most of the time. Tori and I know you. We can see right through that bullshit, and maybe that cold, unknowable façade works well in business for you, but it doesn't serve you all that well in your personal life."

"I don't have a personal life," I growled. "Durand Industries is my entire life."

"Whose fault is that?" Chase questioned. "We don't have to give Durand all of our time or energy anymore. I admit, it was difficult when we had to travel back and forth to Paris all the time, but our permanent headquarters is here in San Diego now. Our travel is more limited. Yeah, I know we're needed here in the office sometimes, but you don't have to be here sixteen hours a day. We have very competent staff who can handle some of the things you still insist on doing yourself. Maybe you're willing to give your entire life to this company, but I'm not anymore. I have a wife that I look forward to seeing every night. I love this company as much as you do. Dad built Durand into the powerhouse it is today, and I want to maintain the same ethics and quality that he did. But Savannah is my priority now, and I almost lost her not so long ago."

"I don't expect you to sacrifice your life to Durand," I protested.

I wanted my brother and sister to be happy. Much as I couldn't even begin to understand their obsessions with their spouses, that kind of life seemed to suit both of them.

As the eldest Durand, I'd promised my father many times that if anything ever happened to him, I'd look out for my siblings, and I'd kept that vow to the best of my ability.

They were happy, and I was finally content with the knowledge that I'd kept that promise to my dad.

"I know that," Chase shot back at me. "But I want you to know that I don't expect you to give up your life for Durand, either. It's not necessary."

I shot my brother a withering gaze. "Has it ever occurred to you that maybe I don't want the same things you do?"

Chase grinned back at me, completely ignoring the look of annoyance on my face. "Nope. I think you want more, but you don't believe it exists. And the reason I know that is because I felt the same way not so long ago. I was happy investing most of my time and effort into Durand, too. So, are you attracted to Shelby?"

Since I wasn't about to tell my brother that the woman made my dick hard whenever we were in the same space together, I responded carefully, "I'm extremely attracted to her food and the fact that she doesn't seem to mind watching that demon dog living at my house right now. That's it, Chase. Let it go. Not everyone wants to live a life obsessed with someone else's well-being."

I was a selfish bastard, and I knew it.

I wasn't capable of the kind of tender emotions my siblings had.

I was a realist.

A cynic.

The most unromantic male on the planet, and I was perfectly okay with that.

I signed off my computer as I added, "Now, if we're done here, I think I'll head out and make sure that Xena - The Warrior Princess didn't make my new dog sitter quit on her first day. That would completely ruin my day since I've been looking forward to eating whatever Shelby decided to cook today."

Chase glanced at the clock and back at me with a surprised expression. "Are you seriously going to leave the office at four-thirty in the afternoon?"

I raised a brow. "Aren't you thinking about heading out yourself very shortly?"

My brother rarely stayed at the office after five anymore, so he had no reason to look at me like I was doing something wrong.

Truth was, I did want to check on my house and make sure disaster hadn't struck on Shelby's first day.

Number one...I did want to keep Shelby as a dog sitter. Yes, I could hire another dogsitter, but the vetting process was a pain in the ass since there were very few people I was willing to trust with access to my home.

Number two…I'd missed lunch, I was starving, and I wanted to see what she'd cooked today.

And number three…it seemed that I had a rare inability to concentrate well this afternoon.

I wasn't sure I'd be able to focus until I'd satisfied my curiosity, and I saw no reason that I couldn't go home a little early now that our meeting prep for next week was done.

"I leave at five now, but you're usually the last person to take off at night," Chase mused suspiciously. "Don't get me wrong, I'm glad you're taking off at a reasonable hour, but that's never happened before."

Fuck! Was I always that predictable?

I stood, picked up my jacket from the back of my office chair, and shrugged into it.

"I'd like to make sure that Shelby is going to remain my dog sitter after meeting Cujo for the first time," I grumbled.

Chase chuckled. "Xena isn't exactly an attack dog. If Shelby can handle problematic horses that weigh over a thousand pounds, I'm pretty sure she can deal with a twenty-five pound Frenchie that just wants a little more attention."

I frowned as I looked at Chase. "She worked with horses?" I asked.

"Yeah. She grew up helping her father train horses with all kinds of issues," he replied. "She mentioned it at a barbecue we had while you were in Paris."

I nodded and turned to leave, wondering why I was annoyed that my brother seemed to know far more about Shelby Remington than I did.

Chapter 6

Shelby

I laughed at Xena's antics as she cuddled up next to me on the floor, her head coming to rest against my thigh. She snuffled, and after acting like she was looking for the perfect position, she looked like she was settling in for a long nap.

I rubbed her belly, and she let out a satisfied sigh.

I'd let her come to me and get closer to me on her terms today.

While she could be a handful, she was also the sweetest, most adorable dog I'd ever seen.

She had a pretty, cream-colored coat with a black snout and dark, soulful eyes that she had no problem using to her advantage when she wanted something. Her huge ears had black tips that made those oversized ears look even larger and more noticeable.

Xena had happily hung out with me in the kitchen while I'd made a cooking video, a task that had taken me a while since I wasn't used to the equipment or cooking in front of a camera.

Yeah, maybe I'd spoiled her a little by giving her small pieces of cooked chicken, but I'd made her work for it with obedience.

She'd obviously been well-trained by Jax's canine center, and any stubbornness she had was simply fear and uncertainty.

She was a shelter dog that had been taken in for training.

While Tori didn't know much about her history, it was pretty clear that Xena hadn't had a secure home in a while.

Honestly, all the adorable canine needed was a routine and clear expectations to be obedient and joyful.

She already had a sweet temperament.

Her occasional stubbornness felt more like confusion and a lack of guidance to me.

"Are you all worn out?" I crooned to Xena as I continued to rub her belly, an act that appeared to be putting her to sleep.

I'd kept her frequent walks short since Frenchies didn't have a high exercise tolerance, especially on a very warm day like today. But we'd played plenty inside in the air conditioning, and she had a ridiculous amount of toys.

I suspected that those toys hadn't come with her from the center.

Wyatt had apparently tried to appease her by buying every toy in the pet store.

Xena also had a very large closet designated only to her doggie treats, medicines, and special items for her allergies.

For a guy who insisted that he resented Xena's presence in his home, Wyatt didn't seem to hesitate to give his small companion everything she could ever want or need.

I looked at the clock, knowing it was probably about time for me to leave.

I'd gotten a lot accomplished today.

Wyatt and I had agreed that I'd arrive at around ten in the morning so that Xena wouldn't be alone for too long. He fed her and took her out before he left for work, and she'd been napping in her bed when I'd come in earlier.

I'd confirmed that I was willing to stay until around four-thirty or five when I didn't have a catering job to do in the evening.

Apparently, Wyatt worked pretty late most of the time, so there was probably no chance we'd ever run into each other, which was fine with me.

Really, he was paying me an absolutely stupid amount of money to be here with Xena. I was pretty much doing my own work while I was here, and this sweet little dog was more of a bonus than a hindrance. I wouldn't even need to take any more side gigs at the moment unless I really wanted to do the event.

The Frenchie needed some attention, but she also loved to nap. A lot. Which meant I had a lot of time to work on monetizing my blog.

I'd already uploaded my video for today, and I'd even had time to do a little work on the cookbook I was compiling.

Being here, in this amazing waterfront mansion, staring at the stunning views of the water, wasn't exactly a hardship. I hadn't gone upstairs because I had no reason to be there, but I was sure it was just as large and as beautiful as the main floor. And I was truly grateful to be working in a kitchen like Wyatt's.

It still amazed me that the man never cooked, yet he had a chef's kitchen with so many cooking accessories and high-tech gadgets available.

I closed my laptop and gathered the cord, moving away from Xena slowly so I didn't disturb her sleep.

It was time for me to leave.

I still needed to stop downtown at The Friendly Kitchen to prep some meals for tomorrow.

The soup kitchen was small, probably smaller than the area needed to serve people who weren't getting good meals on a daily basis. I wished I could do more there, but it felt good to be cooking for people who really appreciated the meals.

I put my computer on the kitchen counter and went to gather my purse and my keys from a table near the door.

I let out a squeak of surprise as Wyatt Durand suddenly came barreling through the front door.

"Oh, my God!" I exclaimed as I put a hand against my pounding heart. "You scared me. I wasn't expecting you to come home this early."

"Everything okay?" he asked as our eyes met. "I wanted to see how your first day went with the psycho dog."

Xena yipped in the living room, obviously awake and excited by the sound of Wyatt's deep voice.

The dog came bouncing out of the living room and danced excitedly at Wyatt's feet, whining like she hadn't seen him in years.

I was shocked when Wyatt actually picked Xena up carefully and gave the dog the affection she wanted.

This man is such a fraud. There's no way he doesn't like this dog.

He didn't even flinch when the Frenchie licked his face.

I gaped at him when he casually returned her to the floor.

"She really does adore you," I said, bemused.

"She adores anyone who feeds her," he scoffed as he walked into the kitchen. "How did it go today?"

I yanked myself out of my confused state and followed him, putting my purse and keys next to my laptop. "Everything was fine. Xena is an adorable and well-trained dog. I think she just gets a little anxious sometimes. She probably hasn't had the easiest life."

I tried to hold back a smile as I watched the Frenchie prance into the kitchen with her tug toy in her mouth. She stopped next to Wyatt expectantly.

He frowned down at her. "Not now," he told Xena. "I just walked in the door."

Judging by Xena's behavior, Wyatt had played tug with her many times before, and she usually got her way when she wanted to play.

The dog dropped the toy at his feet and whined.

A small laugh escaped my lips before I could stop it.

Wyatt shot me an annoyed look and then glanced back at the dog like he had no idea what to do with her now.

I took pity on him, scooped up the tug toy, and carried it back to the toy basket near the front door. I lifted the basket onto the table where she couldn't reach it, pulled out a squeaky toy, and tossed it toward the living room.

Xena trotted toward the toy, snatched it, and carried it happily into the living room so she could play with it by herself.

"Sorry," I muttered as I walked back into the kitchen. "I meant to move that toy basket earlier. You probably shouldn't leave it where she can get to it. For now, you should probably initiate play when you want it and cut her off when she's tired out. She has toys, like that squeaky, that she'll happily play with by herself if it's a bad time for you to play tug. Xena knows all of her commands. Just be firm when you want her to stay or go to her bed. She'll do it. Give her love and affection when she does the right thing. You can give her a treat as a reward after she does what you want her to do if you want, but don't lure her into behavior with a treat in your hand all the time. She'll learn not to pay attention to you unless you have food in your hand."

"Easy for you to say," he rumbled. "She looks at me like she's going to die if I don't give her a treat."

I smiled at him. "Because she knows you're easy and you'll give in to those big, dark eyes of hers. She's adorable, but you'll have to put your foot down with her. At least until she learns who the leader is in this house. Don't fall for that starving dog look. You know she's very well fed. She responds well to affection and praise. Praise her when she's doing things right. She's smart, Wyatt. She'll only be naughty if you let her. If you keep correcting her consistently, she won't run you in circles. She'll pick up the rules of the house pretty fast if they're consistent."

"I don't think she likes rules," he said wryly as he shrugged out of his suit jacket. "She's a holy terror. If I piss her off, she turns her back on me and blows me off."

A ridiculous giggle escaped my lips, and I immediately slapped my hand over my mouth. "Sorry," I said contritely. "But you have no idea how amusing it is to watch a powerful billionaire get played by a harmless Frenchie."

He shot me a look that should have terrified me, but it didn't.

Wyatt might be grumpy, but he wasn't the least bit dangerous.

Any guy who could be played by a sad doggie expression had to have *some* redeeming qualities.

He raised an arrogant brow. "Do you think this is funny?" he asked in a growly tone.

"A little," I confessed.

The big, powerful CEO who commanded thousands of people at a gigantic, powerhouse corporation was obviously helpless when it came to disciplining a stubborn little dog.

How could that *not* be amusing?

The problem was, it also melted my heart just a little. Wyatt wasn't exactly the hard man one saw on the surface, but he wasn't what I'd describe as friendly, either.

My smile disappeared as our eyes met and clashed.

God, why did Wyatt have to be so heart stopping gorgeous?

We were maybe a few feet from each other, but I could still smell his masculine scent, an aroma that made my heart skip a beat.

Wyatt Durand was a little overwhelming, and it wasn't just his height and his massive, muscular body that made my head swim.

When those gorgeous gray eyes weren't cold and frosty, they radiated with an intensity that took my breath away.

I felt like he could see what I was thinking, which was more than a little bit ridiculous, but it still scared the hell out of me.

"F-food?" I stammered as I broke eye contact with him.

I couldn't look into those mesmerizing eyes of his for long without thinking about hot sex, tangled sheets, and multiple orgasms.

Not that I'd ever really experienced any of those things personally, but Wyatt was a guy who could make a woman fantasize about all of those things.

I couldn't say I really *liked* him, but all that raw masculinity screwed with my head and my body.

"Something smells good," Wyatt commented in a deep, fuck-me baritone that was almost impossible to ignore.

He oozed testosterone, and my female hormones were responding accordingly.

Dammit!

I'd never wanted to hop into a bed with a man I didn't even like, and the fact that just seeing Wyatt or hearing his voice could make me this edgy was unnerving.

Desperate to stop thinking about Wyatt Durand and sex, I strode over to the fridge and started pulling out the food I'd cooked earlier.

Food, Shelby! Just focus on the damn food, and for God's sake, don't look into his eyes.

"Red beans and rice, sour cream cornbread, and banana pudding," I told him as I motioned for him to sit at the island. "Sit. I'll heat it up for you."

I could feel him watching me as I dashed around the kitchen, but he sat as requested at the island and rolled up the sleeves of his dress shirt. "You made all of that in your video today?" he asked huskily.

I shrugged, hating myself for wishing that I wasn't dressed in an old pair of jeans that hugged my generous ass too tightly, and a simple, green, cotton shirt. My hair was pulled back in a snug ponytail, my usual style, especially when I was cooking. "Just the red beans and rice and the cornbread," I confessed. "I made the pudding for you. It's a no-bake, easy recipe. I thought you might like it. It's sort of a thank you for letting me use your amazing kitchen."

The pudding had been quick. It was really nothing more than layered custard, fresh bananas, and vanilla wafers that was topped with whipped cream. But I thought that Wyatt might appreciate it since he seemed to have a fondness for dessert.

"You made that dessert just because you thought I'd like it?" he questioned, his tone slightly confused.

I put a heaping plate of food in front of him, cut a large piece of cornbread, and put it onto a smaller plate. "You don't like bananas?" I asked as I put the smaller plate with cornbread beside the red beans and rice.

"I like just about anything that has sugar in it, and I do like bananas," he informed me. "I guess I'm just not used to anyone doing anything nice for me for no reason unless they're family."

His comment had been matter-of-fact, but it still made my heart squeeze inside my chest.

Really?

How was it possible that people hadn't done just about anything to please a man like Wyatt Durand without getting paid for it?

He had to have women tripping all over themselves to make him happy, right?

Maybe he did have some hard edges, but he *was* a very rich, powerful, and very attractive guy.

I thought about his comment for a minute, comparing things my cousins had told me with what Wyatt had just said.

"So everyone usually wants a piece of you, but they don't offer you anything in return?" I asked.

He shrugged and started to devour his food. "Pretty much. Not unless I pay them to do something. Payment is generally expected, especially when you have as much money as I do."

How many times had I heard that from Kaleb, Tanner, and Devon? *Too many.*

And I still found it incredibly...sad.

I had no idea why people thought that wealthy individuals wanted for nothing and that they wouldn't be grateful for thoughtful gestures.

People were all the same, no matter how much money they had. Everyone appreciated a little kindness sometimes. For no reason at all.

"I wanted to make it for you," I told him honestly as I crossed my arms over my chest. "Is that a problem for you?"

Shit! Maybe I'd made him uncomfortable. I was here for a purpose. I was getting paid for watching his dog. It was entirely possible that he didn't want spontaneous gestures of gratitude from someone who worked for him.

I grabbed a glass, went to the fridge, and got him some ice water.

My actions were automatic. It had been my job to take care of people and their food for years now, and it was a hard habit to break, even when I wasn't in a work environment.

As I put the glass down beside his plate, he reached out and snaked his fingers around my wrist firmly, but not tight enough to be painful. "Shelby?" he said in a gruff voice as he stopped eating and gazed at my face.

Without thinking about it, I met his eyes again because his voice was so damn compelling that I couldn't stop myself.

"Yes?" I said breathlessly, my skin burning from his simple touch.

"I didn't say I had a problem with it," he clarified, his eyes blazing with a fierceness that I didn't understand. "I just said that I wasn't used to it."

I nodded slowly, too captivated to answer.

He released me as he asked, "Are you planning on sitting your ass down to eat? I don't expect you to serve me. I just asked for you to leave me the food."

I blinked as I emerged from my lust-filled stupor.

Holy shit! I really hated the way this man affected me.

He was a bad-tempered, sexy, enigma that I really wanted to figure out, but I didn't dare.

I shook my head. "I had something earlier, and it's hard for me to stop serving people. It's an ingrained instinct after working so long as a chef."

"I'm willing to share that banana pudding," he informed me.

For just a moment, I was tempted.

Really tempted.

I really wanted to get to know him better. I suspected that there was more to Wyatt Durand underneath his very guarded exterior. I wanted to put those puzzle pieces together, but I also knew getting to know the man beneath the mask was not going to be easy. I wasn't sure I was up to the task because I was so ridiculously attracted to him.

He doesn't really want me to stay.

I knew he was probably just trying to be nice because I'd done something extra for him.

Is Wyatt really the type of guy who would be polite?

Um…probably not, and if I couldn't figure out his motivations, I definitely couldn't stay.

"I have to run," I said cheerily. "I volunteer at a soup kitchen and I need to prep some food tonight. Enjoy your dinner."

I grabbed my stuff and hightailed it out of Wyatt's kitchen so fast that he never had a chance to respond.

This is just a temporary job.

A mutually beneficial arrangement.

There were reasons why I didn't date, and why I couldn't even contemplate a relationship with any guy right now.

Not that I thought that *he* was lusting after *me*.

Hell, maybe he felt sorry for me because he'd hurt my feelings a year ago.

There was no way Wyatt was interested in me, and I had no business thinking about my temporary boss in relationship to multiple orgasms and sexual bliss.

I was nothing to him except a convenient chef and dog sitter rolled into one, and my life would remain much simpler if I never forgot that a man like Wyatt Durand, even if I had no intention of dating anyone, was way out of my league.

Chapter 7

Wyatt

"How are things going with Shelby and Xena?" Tori asked as we both sat in the meeting room at Last Hope headquarters downtown.

My sister looked as tired as I felt right now, but she was still here after running a long rescue with us that had required a linguist.

Cooper was in our mission room messing with a piece of equipment that he'd wanted installed as soon as possible, even though it was almost two am.

Everyone else had left a few minutes ago.

It had been a long night, but my guys in Michigan had run a flawless operation, as usual, and the hostages were safely on their way back home.

The volunteers from my old Delta Force team really deserved hazardous duty pay for the things they did for Last Hope, but I knew they would neither accept it or want it.

They were motivated to rescue as many people as possible for reasons that had nothing to do with money.

Nevertheless, I was damn happy they were Last Hope volunteers because they took on some of the rescues that others might hesitate to accept.

Hopefully, they'd get a very long rest before they were called on to do another op. Sometimes we could go months and months without a rescue mission, and there were others to perform some of the ops. We'd just had a run of really complicated hostage situations in the last few months, and our Michigan team was our go-to team when we knew shit was going to hit the fan.

I looked up from the notes I was writing on the laptop in front of me.

Marshall, our Last Hope leader, insisted on us documenting operations only on the protected computers at headquarters, a place that had more security features than The Pentagon.

I shrugged as I finally answered, "You'd probably know more than I do about how Shelby is doing. I haven't seen her since her first day last week."

For some fucking reason, that irritated the hell out of me.

Shelby had run out of my house like her ass was on fire…again, even though I'd actually invited her to stay this time.

I guess, because she'd done something nice for me, I'd forgotten that she really didn't like me.

I went home every night to a fairly well-behaved mutt and the tantalizing scent of food, but I'd never run into Shelby again.

Hell, I'd even cut out early from the office again…twice, but she'd been just pulling out of my driveway both times.

She'd waved and smiled, but she'd kept on going.

Shelby Remington had basically blown me off, but I always felt her presence there when I got home.

She left instructions on how to heat the food, and left me notes about Xena, but never anything personal.

Not that I really *wanted* to know anything about her personal life.

It was none of my business how she spent her time or what was happening in her life.

But it was slightly annoying that she never bothered to talk to me in person.

I hated myself for actually watching her cooking videos just to see what she'd left for me that she hadn't cooked that day for work.

And damned if it didn't make me feel good when I noticed something on my menu that hadn't been in her video that day.

Jesus! I had no idea what was wrong with me, but I really needed to stop giving a shit about the nice things she did for me that she didn't have to do.

I'd told myself a couple of times that my behavior was pathetic, but I was always compelled to do it again the next day.

"Shelby said that Xena is settling in well at your place. Is everything else okay?" Tori asked inquisitively.

I glanced down to see Xena sleeping peacefully, her head on top of my foot.

That couldn't be comfortable, but the neurotic dog didn't seem to mind.

Her continual snoring seemed to verify that she was perfectly relaxed in that odd position.

"Great," I informed her curtly. "Cujo is more cooperative, and the food is fantastic. The arrangement is working out well on my end."

"Don't give me that businesslike response. I'm your sister. Remember? I'm not an employee. Using your kitchen has helped Shelby a lot, and I know she's grateful. She's starting to amass an even bigger following because of the videos. She's struggling a little with the technical stuff, but Cooper is doing everything he can to help. She's grown so fast over the last year, and she's had to learn the technical, business, and advertising parts of this business really quickly. I honestly think Shelby would rather spend more time in the kitchen testing recipes than wrestling with the other things."

"Can't she hire someone to help her?" I asked. "She never asked me. Cooper is a pro with tech, but I might know more about advertising."

Tori shot me a stunned look. "I don't think she can really afford to pay anyone quite yet, but I'm sure she's thinking about it. Would you help her out? I think her biggest struggle is monetizing her work more. She's big enough to be earning a lot more than she does right now. I doubt she'd be comfortable asking you. You are the guy who wanted nothing to do with her a year ago."

Christ! Why did Tori constantly feel like she had to remind me about what I'd done a year ago?

"I...might," I said noncommittally. "Hell, she's nice to me, regardless of the fact that she thinks that I'm an asshole. I suppose it wouldn't be that much of an effort to give her some advice."

Tori folded her arms over her chest as she accused, "You...like her. Admit it. She's not the woman you thought she was when you dropped into my barbecue. I think you're starting to realize just how nice she really is and how appreciative she is for anything someone does for her."

"I didn't say that I actually liked her," I corrected. It wasn't like I actually saw her enough to know whether or not I liked her. "I just said that she's nice to me for no reason at all. That's...unusual."

"Is it really that hard to accept that's just the way Shelby is, Wyatt? She does thoughtful things for me all the time. I'm a billionaire married to another billionaire, and she treats me like a normal friend. Why do you think we've become such close friends? She's the kind of person who just wants to make people happy, and she doesn't expect anything in return. Maybe that's rare in the world we grew up in, but people like that do exist."

Fuck! I already knew I *was* going to help Shelby Remington. I had some kind of strange urge to make her life easier if I could. "What does she need?"

"Help monetizing her blog more without making those advertisements completely annoying to her followers," Tori replied. "I think she's worried that if she puts in too many ads that it will take away from the purpose of the blog. Cooper has already helped her with her tech questions on the videos." She hesitated before she added, "You're a decent guy, Wyatt, even though you might not think so."

I raised my hand to stop her. "Let's not get carried away. I have my own motives for wanting her to be successful. Maybe I just want her to keep cooking every day at my place. I haven't eaten this good in a long time."

Tori shot me an exasperated look. "You're so full of crap. You could hire a personal chef and another dog sitter if you wanted to, but you trust Shelby. Don't deny it. You wouldn't give her free rein in your home if you didn't. What are you going to do when we find a home for Xena?"

I narrowed my brows. "Celebrate?" I suggested. "Enjoy my peace every night instead of dealing with a doggie temper tantrum when I won't play tug with her? The dog is a damn diva."

"But she adores you," Tori pointed out. "And I think you'll actually miss her when we do find a permanent home for her."

"I wouldn't go that far," I said drily. "Although I have to admit that she's improved since Shelby's been with her."

It was evident that Shelby reinforced the dog's training during the day.

I'd used the tips that Shelby had given me, and that consistency had improved Xena's behavior.

The mutt wasn't exactly a demon dog anymore, and I *almost* tolerated having her around now.

I watched as my sister reached for her cell phone after it vibrated on the table.

"Who is it?" I asked as Tori's expression grew pensive.

"Shelby," she told me distractedly. "I told her a little earlier that I was still awake, and to text me when she got home. She had a catering job tonight that she went to after she left your place, and then she went to The Friendly Kitchen to prep food. She usually walks to the soup kitchen because it's pretty close to her apartment near the Gaslamp. I know that San Diego is a fairly safe city, but I don't think it's safe in any big city for a woman to walk alone this late at night. I just wanted to know that she got home safely."

The worried expression on Tori's face bothered me more than I wanted to admit.

My sister had been a solo world traveler who had always taken precautions when she'd traveled, but despite her attention to possible dangers, she'd still ended up kidnapped, raped, and nearly killed in the Amazon jungle.

I wouldn't say that Tori was anything close to paranoid, but it made sense that she worried about her female friends.

Tori knew better than anyone that anything could happen to a woman alone, no matter how careful that female was about her safety.

"She was working in the soup kitchen this late?" I asked. "It's after two."

She'd started working at ten this morning at my house, and she was still working?

"The event she did tonight ran late," Tori explained in a troubled tone. "She went to The Friendly Kitchen after the job. She's home now, but someone broke into her apartment. She said everything is fine, and the police are there, but I don't like it. I think Cooper and I should swing by there to make sure she's okay. Maybe have her pack some things and stay with us. I think it would be safer until they figure out what happened."

"She should never be walking by herself this late at night," I said as I stood up, suddenly wider awake than I'd been a few minutes ago. "And it's Friday night. Things get a little rowdier because people get extremely drunk on the weekends."

Cooper strode into the room as I picked up Xena and put her leash on.

"Ready to go?" Cooper asked Tori.

"I've got this," I told my sister. "You two go home and get some sleep. Text me Shelby's number and address. I'll make sure she's safe."

"It's not far from here. It shouldn't take you long to get there," Tori commented as she started texting me the information. "Please text me, and bring her to our place if she needs a place to stay."

Fuck! I hated that anxious expression on my little sister's face.

"Where is Wyatt going?" Cooper asked curiously.

"Thank you, Wyatt," Tori said with a yawn before she started to explain to Cooper where I was going.

I didn't wait for Tori to finish explaining things to her husband.

I wanted to get to Shelby.

I had to see for myself that she was okay, and that she was in a safe environment.

Someone had breached her home, a place where she was supposed to be safe.

And what in the hell was she thinking when she'd walked home from The Friendly Kitchen?

She was a volunteer at the soup kitchen, and I was sure that no one expected her to be working there all alone this late at night.

I really hated the thought of her walking alone after dark through streets filled with drunken, idiotic males.

Or worse yet…down darkened streets where no one was around.

I'd seen the very worst of humanity, and I knew that anything could happen in any location when a woman made herself vulnerable.

Every muscle in my body was tense as I thought about Shelby walking downtown this late at night.

In the dark.

Alone and exposed.

Fuck! Maybe I shouldn't give a damn, but I did, and my instincts were impossible to ignore right now.

"We'll make sure everything is secure here," Cooper called out from the meeting room. "Just go. Let me know if you need anything."

Obviously, Tori had already told him where I was going and what had happened.

I let myself out of Last Hope headquarters without saying another word, more uptight than I'd been in a very long time.

Shelby Remington needed someone to watch her gorgeous ass, and since Kaleb wasn't around to do it, I'd just decided that I was the guy who was going to make damn sure that she stayed safe.

Chapter 8

Shelby

I rubbed my hands over my upper arms, trying to make the goosebumps on my flesh disappear.

The police were dusting my apartment for fingerprints and any other evidence they could find.

I waited outside. I was finished with the police interview, which I was certain hadn't helped much.

I was just as clueless as the police were as to exactly why this had happened.

"Shelby?" A deep voice sounded from behind me. "Are you okay?"

I startled because I was so damn edgy and turned around quickly.

Wyatt?

What was he doing here?

The tension that had invaded my body started to relax as I saw that his expression was filled with something that looked like concern.

He was dressed casually in a pair of jeans and an older, gray, Army T-shirt, a casual look that made him temptingly approachable.

Just the sight of him made me relax because his strong, muscular body was only a foot or two away.

So solid.

So powerful.

And so damn reassuring that my eyes filled with tears.

Dammit! I hated how vulnerable I felt at the moment.

Maybe this incident shouldn't make me feel so violated.

People got burglarized every single day.

But this situation just felt so…personal.

"I'm fine. Just a little shaken up, I guess. What are you doing here?" I asked Wyatt, my voice vibrating with uncertainty.

I had no idea why he'd shown up, but I was actually glad that he was here.

Maybe he wasn't the most pleasant person in the world, but every instinct I had was telling me that he was safe. That he was trustworthy. And at the moment, I desperately needed someone I trusted.

When he held out his arms in a wordless invitation, I flew into them like I was in a hurricane and he was the only solid shelter available.

He wrapped his powerful arms around me and held me as the tears I couldn't hold back started to leak from my eyes.

"You're not fine," he said huskily next to my ear. "Your whole damn body is shaking."

Wyatt felt good.

He smelled amazing.

And even at my height, Wyatt Durand towered over me and made me feel a lot more secure than I had a few moments ago.

It was my uneasiness that was making my body quake uncontrollably.

I wasn't a woman who scared easily, but I was still trying to understand why this had happened to me.

If it was a normal burglary, I doubt it would have upset me very much, but it had been far creepier than a regular break-in.

"Everything is going to be fine, Shelby," Wyatt said in a low, soothing voice as he stroked a comforting hand up and down my back. "Do you want to tell me what happened?"

I nodded as the tremors started to subside.

I pulled away from him, knowing I was being ridiculous, and swiped the tears from my face. "I'm sorry, but this whole thing is just so freaky that it creeped me out."

I briefly explained what had happened as he listened intently and patiently.

He didn't say a word as I told him that someone had broken my bedroom window, and had stolen nothing except some lingerie from my dresser.

My place had also been vandalized, but the damage had been limited to pictures of me.

"Let me check with the police and see if they need anything else from you. I'm taking you home with me. You can't stay here," he insisted.

"We just wrapped up," an officer said from behind me. I turned around to face him, Wyatt's reassuring hand on my back as he continued, "Here's a card with a number you can call. We'll be in touch. Just be cautious. If this is a fetish crime, this person could be dangerous. It could be some drunk kids having what they consider fun on a Friday night. But it could be personal, and there are some sick people out there."

I reached out and took the offered business card. "Thank you," I answered robotically. "Can I go inside to get a few things?"

I wasn't going to refuse Wyatt's offer to spend the night at his place.

If I didn't, I'd never sleep. My bedroom window was broken. Prank or not, the weirdness of the incident had me pretty shaken up.

The officer nodded, and I stepped back inside my apartment while Wyatt continued to chat with the police.

The shock of finding my apartment burglarized and vandalized had worn off a little, but the hair still stood up on the back of my neck as I saw the smashed pictures of my cousins and myself scattered around the small living space.

Who in the hell dislikes me so much that they feel the need to destroy my pictures?

Was it personal or was it someone who had randomly decided that it might be fun to wreak havoc on a Friday night to shake up a stranger?

I stood there for a few minutes, racking my brain to think of anyone who could have done this.

But I came up...empty.

I'd only been in San Diego for a little more than a year, and I hardly knew anyone here. Most certainly not someone who would want to do me any harm.

I moved into my bedroom, shuddering as I saw the broken window and the dust from the fingerprint search on my dresser drawers.

I shook off the tingle of unease that slithered down my spine and pulled out a suitcase. Distracted, I wandered into the small bathroom to get what I needed and then returned to the bedroom to start filling the bag with more things than I probably needed for the night.

I didn't even second-guess my decision to stay with Wyatt. He might be cranky, but he wasn't dangerous, and he was Tori's older brother. I was sure that his instinct to hug me when I was upset came from many years of comforting his little sister in the same way when something bad happened to her.

"Pack heavy so we won't have to come back here for a while," Wyatt instructed as he walked into the small bedroom.

"But I'm only spending the night with you," I reminded him.

"More than one night. It's going to take time to get the window fixed, and probably even longer to catch the perpetrator," he answered firmly. "Just pack what you need for a while."

I added more stuff to my suitcase, unwilling to argue.

I was emotionally wiped out, and all I wanted to do was flee this apartment for now.

What had once been home was now kind of a scary place. I could almost feel the negative energy in the small apartment. Maybe I was just still shocked about the burglary, but I no longer felt comfortable in this space.

Wyatt's eyes scanned the room, like he was taking in every detail. He pulled the curtain back and focused on the broken window.

"The front door was still locked," I explained as I started to close my suitcase. "Whoever it was came in and out of that window."

He nodded. "They broke it just enough to unlock it and get the window up enough to enter. I can understand why they came in this way. It's the best entry point since it's dark and further away from the other apartments. It's also ground level, an end unit, and pretty low to the ground. It wasn't difficult for someone to get in and out this way without being seen. Your front door faces the street. That would be a lot more noticeable to anyone passing by, and suspicious to other renters coming home or leaving. Were any of the lights on inside the apartment?"

"Just a small kitchen light that I leave on so I can see once I get inside at night," I answered. "Do you think they knew no one was here?"

Wyatt nodded. "I think so. Maybe that breaking glass wasn't heard by other residents, but this place is small. You would have heard that glass breaking, and whoever broke in would know that you'd be able to hear it and call the police. It's more likely the perpetrator knew that you were gone."

"How would they know that?" I asked, my heart pounding hard at the thought of a stranger or strangers coming in and out my bedroom window late at night. What if I *had* been here? "My car is in my parking spot."

"They could have been watching the apartment and saw you leave or it's possible they've been watching you," Wyatt said tightly. "And we need to talk about this habit you have of strolling around the downtown alone in the middle of the night, but we'll discuss that later."

I sighed as Wyatt picked up my suitcase. "I wasn't alone for the entire trip. I ran into one of my neighbors after I left The Friendly Kitchen, and we walked home together. How is it that you know so much about criminal behavior?"

"I'm not an expert on criminal behavior, but I know a lot about finding the best access to enter a building. Military experience. Trust me, Shelby, we are going to figure out who did this."

I could tell by the dismissive tone of his voice that he wasn't going to elaborate on that military experience right now.

I knew very little about Wyatt's military career, but Tori had told me that he'd gone into the Army right after college.

"Obviously, I do trust you," I informed him as I followed him toward the front door, grabbing my purse and my keys on the way out. "I'm going home with you in the middle of the night."

He turned, and our gazes met and held until I felt breathless.

I couldn't tell exactly what he was thinking, but those gorgeous eyes were far warmer than usual as he said solemnly, "I won't let anything bad happen to you, Shelby."

I nodded slowly, believing exactly what he said.

I had no idea how I knew that Wyatt's words were like a vow, and that he'd never break his word, but I felt the sincerity in that promise.

For some unknown reason, he gave a damn what happened to me. I could sense it.

He might act like he was cold, calculating, and grumpy sometimes, but the way that he'd held me in my moment of panic was telling.

He wasn't a jerk. Not when someone really needed him.

Granted, he was solemn and serious, but he hadn't said a single sarcastic word to me, and he hadn't brushed off my fear.

"Thank you," I said, my voice little more than a whisper.

He didn't respond. He just jerked his head toward the door, indicating that he wanted me to exit.

He remained silent as I locked the door, but I could feel his comforting presence right behind me.

When I finished locking up and turned around, he took my hand, his eyes scanning the area as we walked to the curb.

I wasn't surprised when he opened the door of a big, black truck. I'd seen him a few times coming in and out of his driveway when I was leaving.

I wasn't sure what I'd expected a California billionaire to drive, but it wasn't this type of vehicle.

Then again, with his height and bulk, would he really fit comfortably into a small, high-performance sports car?

I smiled for the first time in hours as Xena greeted me with an excited whine.

"Hello, sweet girl," I crooned as I slid into the front seat and pulled Xena carefully onto my lap.

I rubbed the canine's belly as Wyatt tossed my suitcase in the back and then got into the driver's seat.

"You brought her with you?" I asked curiously.

"I was already...out," Wyatt said carefully. "I had Xena with me. Tori told me what happened. I was close to your apartment. I didn't want to take the time to drop Xena at home."

Out?

Seriously?

What in the world had he been doing with his Frenchie in tow at this time of night?

Since Wyatt hadn't elaborated, I forced myself not to ask that nosy question.

For some odd reason, I already sensed that I wouldn't get a completely honest answer, and he didn't owe me any kind of explanation.

Tori had told me that he didn't have a serious relationship with anyone, but it was still possible that he'd been with someone nearby when Tori had told him what happened.

I reminded myself that Wyatt Durand's sex life was none of my business.

He was getting me away from my apartment right now.

I felt a whole lot safer with him than I did at home.

At the moment, those were the only things that really mattered.

Chapter 9

Wyatt

"What exactly did you do in the military?" Shelby asked curiously as she shifted to a different yoga position on the mat in my home gym.

When she'd asked if she could join me in the gym this afternoon while I did my daily run on the treadmill, I'd agreed because she said yoga helped her relax.

We'd both been exhausted by the time we'd turned in early this morning, so I'd slept later than usual, and then we'd taken care of some things that had to be done because of the break-in.

I'd told her that I was hitting my home gym because I'd missed my morning run outdoors. Running outside in the heat of the afternoon in the middle of the summer would be idiotic. She'd politely asked if she could come and do some yoga.

It had seemed like a harmless request at the time.

I'd had no real reason to refuse, other than the fact that I usually liked my solitude while I was running or working out.

I'd pushed my normal routine aside because Shelby did need to relax after what had happened the night before.

Saturday was usually an office day for me, but I'd blown that off, too.

Even though her basic demeanor was calm and collected now, I could still see a flicker of fear in her eyes when she was talking about the break-in.

Now, watching that curvy body bend like a pretzel into a new position, I wished to hell that I'd adamantly refused her request to come into the gym with me.

Fuck! It wasn't like she was garbed to entice a man.

She was dressed like a sensible woman who just wanted to be comfortable in the gym.

Yoga pants.

An oversized T-shirt.

Hair in a ponytail.

No makeup in sight.

Doesn't fucking matter.

I still wanted to nail her against the wall.

Or on the floor.

Or anyplace in the goddamn room.

I wished that I'd gone for a long run outdoors before it had gotten ungodly hot, but I hadn't wanted to leave her alone in the house earlier.

So here I was, late on a Saturday afternoon, trying to keep my head on straight while I fantasized like a complete idiot about all the things I could do with a woman *that damn flexible.*

Okay, not just *any* woman.

Just. Her.

I wasn't going to try to convince myself that I hadn't been attracted to her before, but things had gotten increasingly difficult since she'd thrown herself into my arms last night.

I'd actually *felt* those lush, generous curves against me.

I'd also inhaled the enticing, faint scent of strawberries and vanilla in her hair.

That had been all it took to make my dick snap to attention, and I'd gotten very little reprieve from my condition since the moment I'd touched her.

Yeah, it was supposed to be a comforting embrace only, but I was a goddamn guy who wasn't related to her, and it had nearly killed me.

"I'm sorry. Was that an intrusive question?" she asked hesitantly.

I quickly pulled myself out of my lust-filled thoughts. "No," I denied, feeling guilty that I'd been too busy watching her to answer her question.

She'd asked me what I'd done in the military.

Generally, I'd give some vague or blatantly untrue answer to someone I didn't know well.

I'd admit to being in the Army if someone asked. It was the easiest and most general explanation.

I might, in special circumstances, admit that I was in special forces if someone actually needed to know.

However, being a Delta Force operator wasn't something I talked about with anyone outside of my Last Hope circle and my family. There was no point in revealing that detail in the first place. I couldn't talk about anything classified. Which, when you were in a unit like Delta Force, was almost *everything*.

I knew the details of my military history wasn't something that Tori would tell Shelby. None of us hid the fact that we'd once been in the military. Because she was proud of our service to our country, my little sister wouldn't hesitate to tell people that Chase and I had served. But she'd never out the specifics. Tori was a member of Last Hope, and she was good at keeping quiet about the things she knew about any of the member's former military careers.

Oddly, I felt like this was one of those special circumstances when I could share that I'd been in special forces with Shelby. I wasn't sure exactly why I felt that way, but she was vulnerable right now, and the last thing I wanted to do was tell her a blatant lie.

It also might make her feel better to know that I didn't lack the skills or knowledge to protect her if needed.

I sensed Shelby wasn't the type of person who would babble about something that I'd prefer to keep quiet.

"I spent most of my time in special forces," I explained. "But that's not something I broadcast to many people."

She raised her head to look at me, a surprised expression on her beautiful face. "Wow. I didn't know that. I'd never tell anyone, Wyatt. So you were a badass?" A heartbeat later she added, "Wait! I shouldn't have asked that. Special forces is secretive, right? Thank you for everything you did for all of us. Even though I have no idea exactly what you went through, I'm sure it was dangerous. I'm glad that you're safe."

Fuck! Kaleb had been right. Shelby *was* sweet.

Optimistic and upbeat.

Ridiculously grateful for almost everything.

And way too nice to give a shit about a guy who was currently ogling her curvaceous, flexible body instead of focusing on his daily run.

On top of that, she thinks I'm a badass, which I'm...not.

"I'm not a badass. Never was," I confessed. "I was simply part of a great team that could accomplish some difficult missions together. One man is nothing without the rest of his team."

She sent me a gorgeous smile before she dipped her head down again and mumbled, "Then you were a team of badasses, and just watching you run like that makes me feel completely exhausted and woefully out of shape. How much longer are you going to kill yourself with that punishing pace?"

I grinned. I was actually slacking today. I normally pushed myself a lot harder on a daily run. I wasn't quite as fit as I'd been when I was active duty, but staying in shape remained a habit that was ingrained in me during my years in the military.

Maybe I didn't work out in the field anymore with Last Hope like my team in Michigan did, but there was always a chance that something could go south on a rescue operation. Even if there was only a slim chance of that happening, I wanted to be prepared to go after the guys in the field if necessary.

I also didn't want any thanks from anyone for my military service. I was simply doing the job I'd needed to do, the work I'd signed up for voluntarily. I was used to staying anonymous. Delta Force was a very covert unit. Very few people even knew what we did, and we liked it that way. But hearing those sincere words from Shelby's lips was…different.

Hell, if she wanted to see me as some kind of special forces hero, I was okay with that, even if it wasn't true.

"I still have a couple more miles," I told her.

She moved again, changing positions fluidly until her shapely ass was in the air. Her head was down almost to the ground, and her palms were flat on the mat.

"And you've barely broken a sweat yet," she grumbled. "I think I'm exercising when I walk a mile or two. You're ridiculous."

My grin grew wider. I couldn't remember the last time that someone had dared to call me ridiculous, but because she'd actually meant it as a compliment, it was hard to be offended.

Honestly, I'd rather run another ten miles than to try to bend my body into some of those unnatural positions she was managing to do effortlessly.

"If it makes you feel any better," I said. "My body doesn't bend in any of those positions you're doing right now. It looks painful."

"I'm used to it. It actually helps with stress and to keep me limber. I spend a lot of time doing physical work when I'm cooking for a large event. Those side gigs can be grueling. Sometimes I don't sit down or stop for twelve or fourteen hours, and I'm not in my early twenties anymore. I also carry a little more weight than I did when I was younger. I eat far more of my own cooking than I should, and all of those carbs show on my ass and my hips," she finished dryly.

"They look pretty damn good from where I am right now," I said huskily before I could stop myself. I hated the fact that she saw anything about her body that was worth criticizing. "How old are you now?"

"Thirty-five," she answered without hesitation. "And I feel every bit of the mileage I've put on this body over the years. But I can hardly complain considering all the physical things you had to do in the military. You're Kaleb's age, right?"

"Forty in a few months," I confirmed grudgingly. "Kaleb was a year behind me. We met on the campus."

She snorted. "You're in pretty damn good shape for your age, grandpa."

"Smartass," I shot back, even though I really didn't mind her teasing me about my age because it was also a backhanded compliment.

I wasn't sure why I cared what she thought, but I did.

Generally, women weren't all that physically attracted to me, and they certainly weren't drawn to my not-so-charming personality.

They were attracted to my wealth and power if they could get past their hesitation because of my size, my overly serious, sarcastic demeanor, and my lack of charisma.

Chase had always been the charming, handsome, and magnetic Durand brother, and I'd never been envious that my brother had a way with women.

My younger brother and I just had different personalities and physical appearances, which was actually an asset to me since Chase was better with people than I was. Always had been.

I was a loner, and I usually preferred it that way.

Strangely, I didn't dislike Shelby's playful attitude. I couldn't remember the last time a woman had joked around with me like this, and I actually liked the fact that she felt comfortable enough with me to do it.

Very few women did.

Shelby Remington had never been intimidated by me, which, if I was being honest, had captivated me from the first time we'd met. She wasn't afraid to tell me exactly what she thought. She was refreshingly honest, which was new and different for me.

Okay, so maybe I hadn't enjoyed being raked over the coals for my presumed arrogance, but at least she'd said exactly what she'd thought at the time.

She moved into what looked like a more comfortable, seated position before she asked, "What would you like for dinner?"

"You need to do another video?" I questioned, starting to feel the miles I'd burned up.

"Not tonight. I'll just cook for us."

No, she fucking wouldn't! Shelby worked too hard to be cooking when it wasn't necessary.

"How about you take a break, and I'll take you out for dinner," I suggested, surprising myself with that offer.

She turned her head toward me and smiled so broadly that I could see a very small, very adorable dimple in her right cheek, which wasn't exactly a flaw. Unfortunately for me, it made her even more attractive.

"Are you trying to take me out for that dinner you rejected over a year ago?"

She was joking, but I felt a small twinge of guilt anyway.

"What if I am?" I challenged before I could think about my response. "What if I said that I might regret turning down the opportunity to get to know you a long time ago?"

Why in the fucking hell had I just admitted that out loud?

Was the exercise depriving my brain of oxygen right now?

This female was dangerous. I needed to stop blurting out exactly what I was thinking before I considered the repercussions of those words.

"Then I'd probably admit that I don't really think that you're a superficial asshole anymore," she said earnestly. "In fact, I think I misjudged you, Wyatt."

"You didn't," I warned her. "But I'd still like to take you out for dinner anyway. You don't have to cook when it's not necessary for your job, Shelby."

"I don't really mind doing it, but I think I'll take you up on that offer. Honestly, I could go for takeout and an earlier night than last night. I'm a little tired. I didn't sleep very well," she confessed. "I guess I'm still trying to understand why someone would break into my apartment just to destroy some of my pictures, and steal the only two really nice sets of underwear I had."

She looked so forlorn that I wanted to tell her that I'd give her my credit card so she could replace her missing lingerie, but I managed to keep my mouth shut this time.

"Were you afraid last night?" I asked with a frown. "I have a state of the art security system. No one is getting into this house without me knowing about it."

She looked so bereft and confused about the burglary that it would probably tug at my heartstrings if I actually had a heart.

Shelby shook her head. "No. I felt safe here and not as incredibly creeped out as I was at my apartment. I guess I'm still just trying to understand why it happened in the first place. I can't think of a single person here who would want to do something like that, Wyatt. It makes no sense to me."

I decreased my speed, and started my cool down. "We'll figure it out, Shelby. Try to put it out of your mind for a little while, and give your brain a break for one evening. I know an expert who can help investigate this. I'll also put my security on your tail when you have to go somewhere."

If Marshall couldn't dig up any information on this situation, then the details were unfindable. The man had connections everywhere, from the top levels of the government to the darkest of locations.

"You'd do that for me?" she asked with a puzzled expression on her face. "Do you think it's really possible that someone is watching me?"

Hell, yes, I thought it was entirely possible that she had a stalker. Fetish crimes didn't just happen for no apparent reason, and my gut was telling me that this wasn't a bunch of kids that did it out of boredom. The destruction of her pictures wasn't random. Someone had methodically found every picture she was in, and had made damn sure that photo was destroyed.

I was also starting to think that there was very little I wouldn't do to make sure this woman was safe.

Maybe I didn't know her well, but I sensed that Shelby Remington wasn't generally high strung, and for some damned reason, it irked me to see the worry etched into her expression.

"I'm just trying to cover all of the bases," I said, unwilling to see her stress anymore over a possible psycho who might be following her. If she actually did have a stalker, that bastard wasn't going to get anywhere near her. "And yes, I'd do that for you. It's not a big deal to dig for information or to put some of my security on your tail."

"You really are a good guy, Wyatt," she said, her tone genuine and sweet.

"Don't start thinking that I'm something that I'm not just because I want to keep you safe, Shelby," I cautioned more harshly than intended. "You're Kaleb's cousin. He'd do the same for me."

Her face fell, and her disappointed expression made my gut ache, but I couldn't take my words back.

They were, after all, the truth, and after almost forty years of being an unfeeling jackass, it was very unlikely that I was ever going to change.

Chapter 10

Shelby

"That's probably the best Thai food I've ever had," I told Wyatt honestly as he made himself a drink after dinner. "I didn't even know that little restaurant existed until tonight. I'm glad you decided to order there."

Honestly, I was pleasantly surprised when Wyatt had suggested delivery from a small, casual, hole-in-the-wall place that he swore had fantastic Thai food.

He hadn't been wrong.

Then again, he'd grown up in San Diego, and considering his love of food, maybe it wasn't surprising that he'd sniffed out every place in San Diego that served fantastic food. Even the small, not particularly fancy, family owned establishments, which, in my opinion, usually had the best food.

I didn't quite know what to think of Wyatt Durand anymore.

He swore he was an asshole, and at one time, I would have completely agreed with him.

Yet, he wasn't the man I'd thought he was after we'd had that angsty meeting after Chase and Savannah's wedding reception.

There was a whole different guy behind that mask of indifference and cynicism he wore most of the time.

I'd seen it.

I was benefiting from Wyatt's kindness in so many ways right now.

I didn't believe for a single moment that Wyatt was letting me stay at his home and under his protection because he was one of Kaleb's best friends.

It wasn't necessary for him to personally be this supportive just to help a buddy.

His perception of himself didn't match the actual kind man that I knew existed, but I wasn't quite sure…why.

I had to admit that he hid the real Wyatt Durand quite well. So well that probably very few people could really see through all of his bullshit.

But I did.

He might be a guy of few words, and yeah, the words he did utter were generally derisive, but his actions were far different from the misanthropic statements that came out of his mouth sometimes.

I had to wonder if anyone else except his family had ever noticed that while Wyatt said one thing, his actions often belied his words.

Maybe he'd always been and always would be gruff and pessimistic.

Maybe he'd never be a smooth talker.

Maybe he'd always be more than a little rough around the edges.

Call me crazy, but there was something that was actually endearing to me about this man who spewed bullshit, but actually did have a good heart.

He obviously didn't wear that heart on his sleeve. In fact, he hid it so well that I wasn't exactly sure if *he* knew that he had a heart.

I watched him from my position on the living room sofa as he poured himself a whiskey at the bar.

We'd eaten at the kitchen island, and I was so full that I felt like my stomach was going to pop.

He shrugged. "I've been going to that place for decades. It was one of my father's favorites. But they usually close pretty early, so I rarely get home in time to order there." He held up an empty whiskey tumbler with a sardonic smirk. "Should I pour you a glass of your own this time?"

I smiled as I shook my head, instantly recognizing that he was reminding me of the time I'd thrown back his tumbler of good whiskey after the wedding reception. "No, but thank you. I don't usually down a tumbler of someone else's whiskey in one gulp. That was a special circumstance. You pissed me off, and I was having a bad night, but I wouldn't refuse a glass of wine if you have one."

"I have quite a few bottles," he informed me. "Chase is a wine connoisseur. Do you have a preference?"

"Anything that isn't incredibly dry is fine," I told him, and then watched him as he selected a bottle, expertly removed the cork, and poured some into a wine glass.

For a guy as big as Wyatt, he managed to move with fluid, confident motions that were surprisingly graceful.

I had to wonder if those almost stealthy movements were a product of his former military career.

The fact that he'd been a special forces operative had been astonishing to me at first. He had, after all, been the heir apparent to the Durand empire when he'd been in the military.

What guy that obscenely rich wanted to risk his life on a daily basis going on dangerous missions?

But the more I talked to Wyatt and got to know him a little better, the more sense it made to me.

He wasn't hung up on the money he had or the power he could wield. I was certain of that, even though he was guarded about his motives for everything at all times.

He cared about people and the rest of the world, no matter how much he tried to convince me otherwise.

Men who didn't give a crap about people didn't offer a shoulder to cry on to a woman who was confused and upset about her apartment getting broken into.

They also didn't offer to open their home to give that woman a safe place to stay.

And they certainly didn't risk their lives doing dangerous missions with special forces when they could be living an opulent life.

Wyatt might care from a distance, but he *did* care. He just didn't show those emotions to the world.

I probably understood that inclination because I was once that wary and distrusting myself.

"Thanks," I said gratefully as he handed me the glass of wine and then sat on the opposite end of the sofa.

Wyatt's cell started to ring before I could say anything else, and he pulled it out of the pocket of his jeans with a frown. "Kaleb," he said as he looked at his phone.

"I spoke to my family a little earlier about what happened. He's probably still worried," I said with a sigh.

I'd hesitated to tell my family about the break-in because I knew they'd be concerned. But in the end, there was really no other way for me to explain why I was staying with Wyatt, and that detail wasn't something that he was going to hide from Kaleb.

Wyatt nodded as he answered. He put the phone on speaker and dropped the cell on the coffee table in front of us before he said gruffly. "Hey, Kaleb. What's up? Shelby is here, too."

I listened as Kaleb answered. "I just wanted to check in and see how things are going. Is everything okay? If Shelby needs me, I'm jumping on my jet. I can be there in a few hours."

"I told you that everything was okay earlier," I reminded Kaleb.

"Some asshole broke your bedroom window just to pocket your underwear, Shelby," Kaleb said angrily. "This isn't nothing, and it wasn't just a burglary. If you don't want me to come there, then come home. You'll be safer here."

"I'm not running away from my obligations here just because some jerk tried to intimidate me," I said firmly.

"She's perfectly safe here, Kaleb," Wyatt said soberly. "I have a friend whose trying to dig up more information as we speak. And I have good security here. Better than yours."

That was probably the truth since people in Crystal Fork rarely even locked their doors. My cousins weren't stupid, and they all had basic security systems. But the environment in small town Montana was probably a lot safer for my cousins than it was for the Durands here in San Diego.

Not to mention the fact that my cousins went out of their way not to draw much public attention to themselves. The Durands worked in a higher profile industry.

"But she'd be further away from whoever did this," Kaleb replied impatiently.

"Maybe," Wyatt answered grimly. "But maybe not. If someone was bold enough to break into her house to steal her damn panties, does it really matter what location she's in? They had to have known that she wasn't home."

"Are you saying someone is stalking her? Watching her every move. Shelby should be with her family right now, Wyatt," Kaleb insisted irritably. "She's alone there."

"She's not alone," Wyatt argued. "She has me and a multitude of friends who care about what happens to her. She'll stay here and have my security watching her when I'm not around. Shelby will never be unprotected. I promise you that, and you should know by now that I don't break my word."

I took a deep breath and let the testosterone fly.

Kaleb might not be here physically, but the male hormones buzzing around in the room were still getting pretty thick.

I was used to it.

I'd been raised with three male cousins who were all as stubborn as ornery mules, and they argued like this all the time.

They'd also tried to run my life most of the time, but had never succeeded.

I'd learned that it was only worth speaking up when things got totally out of hand. My cousins loved me, and they were worried, which was why Kaleb was blowing off steam with Wyatt right now. But in the end, I was going to do what was best for me, no matter what the bullheaded males in my family decided.

"Fuck!" Kaleb cursed. "I don't like this, but you know I trust you, Wyatt. You know what you're doing. You were special forces for a long time. I suppose if I have to trust anyone with Shelby's safety, I'm glad it's you."

"Every friend she has is married to a guy who was in special forces," Wyatt told Kaleb in a confident, reassuring tone that I'd never heard before. "Every one of those guys will be watching out for her."

I gaped at Wyatt, shocked to discover that Hudson, Jax, Cooper, and Chase had all been special forces, too.

I'd known that all of them had been in the military at one time, but Tori, Taylor, Harlow and Vanna had never mentioned their connections to special forces.

Then again, I hadn't really known them for all that long. It was possible that their husbands didn't really want many people to know about their previous connections to special forces. Wyatt certainly didn't.

"You told me that earlier, and I'm not doubting any of your abilities to keep her safe," Kaleb grumbled, obviously already aware of a fact that I hadn't known. "But it sucks to be this far away from Shelby when something like this is happening. We're family, and our family sticks together when bad shit happens."

"I'd feel the same way if this was happening to Tori and I wasn't in the same city with her," Wyatt commiserated. "But you'll have to trust me for now. We've got this. There's nothing more you can do that we aren't already doing."

"Do I have a choice?" Kaleb asked drily.

"No, you don't," I cut in calmly, knowing it was time to remind Kaleb that I was a grown adult and had been for a very long time. "It's my decision to stay for now. I'll keep you all informed, but I have too much going on right now to run and hide from whoever did this. I can't exactly go offline and hide out. Blogging is my main income now. We don't even know if someone is really stalking me. It could just be some kids doing a high school prank of some kind."

"Nothing strange like this has happened before," Wyatt pointed out. "And Shelby doesn't know of anyone who would want to harm her."

"There is someone who'd like to harm her," Kaleb muttered vehemently. "But the bastard is in prison."

I swallowed hard. That wasn't something I'd expected Kaleb to announce.

Wyatt shot me a disgruntled expression as he asked huskily, "Who exactly would that be?"

Shit! Shit! Shit! I really didn't want to go there.

"It doesn't matter," I said in a rush. "He *is* in prison, and I don't think he had anything to do with this incident."

"Fuck!" Kaleb mumbled. "I'm sorry, Shelby. Wyatt doesn't know? I guess I shouldn't have assumed that he did. I thought you'd tell him because he's trying to help investigate this, and you're obviously comfortable staying with him."

"Nobody here knows yet," I said, my comment barely audible.

It wasn't like I was trying to hide my past from my friends. I just hadn't had an opportunity to tell Tori and my other female friends yet.

And Wyatt? There was probably *never* going to be a time when I'd feel comfortable pouring out the details of how stupid I'd been or the mistakes I'd made in Montana.

I'd been trying like hell to leave all of that behind me.

It wasn't like Wyatt and I were close enough to be sharing our deepest secrets with each other, but he was helping me. I had planned on telling him later this evening, at least the parts that he needed to know to help his friend investigate.

I looked at Wyatt, and when our eyes met, I nearly flinched at the intensity in his molten gray eyes as he drawled smoothly, "Shelby and I will talk about it as soon as we get off the phone. Is this guy a danger to her? Is it possible that he convinced someone to do this even though he's in prison."

"Doubtful," Kaleb commented. "He's in a federal prison with a high level of security. I'm not saying it's impossible, but it's probably unlikely."

Without breaking eye contact with me, Wyatt replied, "It's definitely something I'll check out."

I made the appropriate responses over the next few minutes as the three of us continued to talk, but my eyes stayed locked on Wyatt's because his fiery gaze wouldn't allow me to look away.

My stomach flip-flopped as I wondered what kind of reaction I was going to get once he was off the phone.

I released a tremulous breath as we ended the conversation.

"Do you want to tell me what that was all about?" Wyatt asked in a modulated tone right after he disconnected the call. "I can't force you to trust me, but I can't thoroughly investigate unless I know what I'm dealing with in your past."

He was right.

I knew he was right.

I probably should have already mentioned my past.

But just the thought of talking about my stupid mistakes with someone like Wyatt Durand turned me inside out, and it brought back every insecurity I'd been trying to hide for years.

I took a deep breath before I spoke. "The man who's in a federal prison isn't just a guy who hates me. He was also…my husband."

Chapter 11

Wyatt

Every muscle in my body was tense as I tried to absorb the information that Shelby had just blurted out.

Married? She's fucking married?

"It would have helped if you'd shared the fact that you had a husband," I said tightly.

"My ex-husband," Shelby corrected, her normally upbeat, cheery voice more subdued and lifeless at the moment.

My muscles relaxed slowly as I realized that she was no longer married to a criminal.

Thank fuck!

Hell, I hadn't really liked the idea that she was married to *anyone*, much less a goddamn felon.

"Tell me. It's important that I know everything," I encouraged in a softer tone because it was obvious that whatever happened was upsetting her.

"Justin and I were married for a little less than a year," she continued flatly. "I filed for divorce as soon as I learned that he had a gambling addiction, and that he'd stolen the life savings from a lot of people, including some of my friends in Crystal Fork. God, at one time, I considered myself lucky that I'd married a man who was a successful financial advisor. A guy who supposedly helped other people secure their financial futures. I was working so many hours in my restaurant that I never knew what he was doing. The signs were probably all there, but I was too exhausted and too naïve to see them. I thought we'd have the perfect life. He took care of the money, and I worked hard for that happily ever after. It never happened, Wyatt. I was the stupidest woman on the planet. I let it happen. I trusted his integrity completely until the moment the authorities came and dragged him away in handcuffs. I was married to a man I never really knew at all. We met in Billings at my restaurant. He swept me off my feet with pretty words that had no meaning to him at all. And I was stupid enough to marry him."

My gut ached as I saw the pain in her eyes and heard the vulnerability in her voice.

Christ! Maybe a sociopath had duped her, but she wouldn't be the first highly intelligent person who had fallen for a con.

"You are not stupid," I growled. "He was obviously a good con man."

"Or maybe I was just easily duped," she said wistfully. "He was considerate and kind before we were married, and he said all the right things. But once I had that ring on my finger, he flipped like a light switch. Nothing I did was right anymore, and he undermined my confidence little by little. He was subtle at first, with small digs about my appearance, but he got meaner the longer we were married. He didn't get physical until the day he was arrested. He smacked me pretty hard before the police could get the handcuffs on because he thought I was the one who had turned him in. God, I *wish* I had been smart enough to realize what he was doing. I wish I had caught on sooner, but I didn't."

Anger coursed through my veins, a genuine fury like I hadn't felt since my sister Tori had gotten kidnapped.

He fucking hit Shelby?

If the son of a bitch wasn't in a prison where I couldn't get to him, I'd probably take his fucking head off myself right now.

"Did Kaleb know?" I asked, my voice graveled and rough.

She shook her head. "That he smacked me? No. I felt like such an idiot that I didn't tell anyone that he actually hit me during the arrest, but it came out during the trial. My family eventually knew everything, and all of Crystal Fork knew, too. His arrest and prosecution was always in the news. Every. Single. Day. Unfortunately, it was big news in Montana, and it tainted my family by association. Obviously, there was speculation by the public that I was involved, even though it was made clear that I wasn't going to be charged, and that I was cooperating completely. Looking back at it now, I'm not sure how it took an arrest and almost eleven months to realize that I was being manipulated. Somehow, Justin knew exactly what to do and say to make me feel like everything was all my fault, so I kept on trying to fix things. In hindsight, I think the only reason he married me was to find a few more victims."

Son of a bitch! I suspected that she didn't tell anyone that he'd hit her because Kaleb would have felt the same way I did. My buddy had probably wanted to hurt the bastard for everything he'd done to Shelby, and the hell he'd dragged her through.

In fact, I was certain that Kaleb and his brothers had needed to hold themselves back every damn time they saw Shelby's tormentor in the courtroom.

"How is it possible that I never knew about any of this?" I questioned aloud, even though I probably already knew the answer to that question.

Kaleb and I were close, but we could sometimes go months without talking to each other because we were both busy, and Kaleb's sense of family loyalty ran deep. It wasn't likely that he'd share any of Shelby's secrets with someone who was a stranger to her if he didn't have to do it.

I'd heard the remorse in his voice for even mentioning her marriage to me because Shelby hadn't told me about it herself. I could tell that he felt like shit for bringing it up without talking to her first.

Besides, there were things that Kaleb didn't know about me, either, and we'd known each other a long time.

He had absolutely no idea that Last Hope existed, which was a big part of my life. He knew that Chase and the Montgomery brothers had a history in special forces now because I'd wanted him to feel better about Shelby staying here in San Diego. But he didn't know about Last Hope. Not because I didn't trust him, but because our existence just wasn't shared with anyone who had no real ties to the organization.

"We didn't talk about it outside of our family," Shelby said, her voice sounding completely defeated. "My cousins and Aunt Millie were never particularly fond of Justin in the first place. All of them thought everything had moved too fast, and they were right. We got married at the courthouse, and there was never a real wedding. After he was arrested, I was already humiliated and beaten up emotionally, and it seemed like everyone in Montana was talking about it. It probably wasn't big enough news for the rest of the country, but it dominated the news in Montana."

I nodded, hating the hell that she'd been through simply because she'd married the wrong man.

In the grand scheme of things, it wasn't just the fact that he hit her that was so fucking wrong.

The prolonged verbal abuse and manipulation was probably even worse for her psyche than getting hit as he was being taken away in handcuffs. Getting through the trial had probably been brutal, too.

How in the fucking hell had she gotten through all that and still managed to maintain such a positive attitude? I had no idea why she wanted to do anything nice for anyone after that nightmare.

"What happened once he was arrested?" I asked succinctly, still wanting to kill the asshole who had broken the trust of a woman like Shelby.

"I had to testify and provide as much information as I could to get him convicted," she replied. "I *wanted* to help the authorities. I sold *Shelby's* and gave up the proceeds in the settlement. I gave up everything Justin and I had. All I wanted was enough to live until I could get a job. I felt so horrible that he'd scammed money out of people who had worked their asses off to secure their futures. The gossip about the whole situation was rampant during the trial and after it was over. I came to San Diego to try to start all over again once everything was wrapped up in Montana. I couldn't live there anymore."

Fuck! She'd obviously come to San Diego almost destitute because she'd given all of her money to try to pay victims back. She could have tried to negotiate more since the marriage was short and she wasn't involved. She could have kept her restaurant, too, because it was how she made her living, but she…hadn't.

She'd also been friendless here, which I tried not to think about because I'd refused the opportunity to become someone she could trust after everything she'd been through.

Okay, so maybe I *hadn't* wanted a blind date, but as she'd already told me, what she'd really wanted and needed was a friend.

I would have been better than nothing, and had I known what she'd been through, I sure as hell wouldn't have refused.

I was an asshole, but maybe not *that* big of an asshole.

Of course, it would have helped if Kaleb had given me more information about Shelby, but I understood why he hadn't. "I'm sure Kaleb would have helped you financially—"

"No!" Shelby interrupted fiercely. "Yes, all of my cousins would have stepped in to help me without a second thought. They didn't know that I lost everything. I didn't share the financials of the case with anyone. You can't tell them, Wyatt. It was my mistake, my problems to deal with on my own. It was bad enough that people gossiped about my whole family, and they supported me emotionally, which helped me get through that nightmare."

I very much doubted that Kaleb wasn't somewhat aware of just how much Shelby had lost. He was a brilliant guy. He would have made it his business to know. However, there wasn't much the Remington brothers could do if Shelby refused their assistance.

Christ! She was stubborn, but there was part of me that admired the way she'd pulled this off on her own. She'd fought her way back, and had managed to support herself in an expensive city by being creative. Her tenacity was praiseworthy, but I couldn't shake my displeasure about the fact that she'd been alone with no one to talk to, and no one to help her, during what was probably the worst period of her life.

I felt like I'd been sucker punched in the solar plexus when I saw tears leaking from Shelby's beautiful emerald eyes. The breath left my body because I knew she was in pain, and there wasn't a damn thing I could do or say that would really help her.

We didn't know each other that well, and judging by the way she'd quickly swiped away her tears, she didn't want anything she might consider pity or sympathy.

Between the break-in and the retelling of a very painful period in her life, she looked wiped out, but I wasn't quite done with my questions.

I figured I might as well get it all over with because I really didn't want to see her cry again.

"Are there any other pissed off boyfriends or previous husbands in your past?" I asked drily.

She snorted. "No, thank God! Justin was my big mistake, and I have no desire to repeat it. I'm perfectly content without a man who would undermine my self-confidence and make me feel like I was nothing."

"You're not nothing, and it wasn't your fault, Shelby," I rasped. "You can't beat yourself up for trusting someone who wasn't worthy of that trust. Most of us have done it at least once in our life."

She shot me a dubious glance. "I doubt it's ever happened to you."

She was wrong.

"I did. Once," I admitted reluctantly. "But this isn't about me. Right now, we need to figure out who broke into your apartment."

I had no idea why I'd confessed to being duped myself. Maybe because I could still see the pain in Shelby's eyes, and I didn't want her to think she was the only intelligent person in the world who had gotten conned.

"There is no one else who hates me that much," Shelby said soberly. "And like Kaleb, I think Justin is an unlikely suspect."

I shrugged. I'd have Marshall investigate the possibility. I had no doubt that he had the connections to investigate the lead, even in a federal prison. "Then we'll have to wait and see what my friend, Marshall, and the police can find out. In the meantime, you're staying with me until we figure this out. I promised Kaleb that I'd protect you, and I will."

She lifted her brows. "Don't you think that's a little bossy and presumptuous?"

"No," I stated rigidly.

"It is," she corrected. "But I'm not going to argue with you about it right now because it makes sense. I'm fine with taking precautions at the moment. I'm still a little uneasy. But it's not like I can stay with you forever. I have to work, and I have to live my life, Wyatt. I have an apartment and things I'll need from that apartment, eventually."

"You can stay here for as long as it takes to catch the perpetrator, and that could take a while," I informed her. "I'll get you whatever you need from your apartment. You're not going back there anytime soon. I think you also need to think about whether or not you want to live there again at all after what happened. Once this is resolved, I think you should consider moving to a safer area."

She shot me an exasperated look as she answered. "That area is safe. The break-in was unusual. Where would I move to? Del Mar? La Jolla? Coronado? Rancho Santa Fe? Normal people don't live in those locations, Wyatt. I'm a chef, not an executive. San Diego is expensive. I have to live somewhere practical and affordable."

"You're a goddamn Remington," I said irritably.

Her cousins, who obviously adored her and worried about her, were three of the richest men on the planet.

I knew Kaleb, and he'd probably offered to buy her a place many times since she'd moved here.

"A Remington from the poorer branch of the family," she said patiently. "That was true even before my cousins became richer than God. My father was a horse trainer with very little land, and my mother was a teacher. Kaleb's parents owned a sizable ranch that produced a lot of income, and my Aunt Millie was a very successful artist. I wasn't deprived. I loved my childhood. I don't even think I realized that we were tight on money when I was a kid. But when my parents died in a car accident when I was a teenager, and my aunt and uncle took me in, I grew up fast. I knew my parents hadn't been able to save a dime because I saw their will and their lack of assets. Luckily, I wasn't interested in an Ivy League college, even though my aunt and uncle would have happily paid for it. Culinary school was my dream, and my remaining family supported that dream. They made it happen for me, and I'll always be grateful for their help. I'm not sure what would have happened to me if my aunt and uncle hadn't taken me in like I was their own child, but I didn't expect them to support me forever. I love my family dearly, but it wasn't my aunt and uncle's responsibility. I wasn't their child, and they had to put three of their own boys through college. I wanted to make my own way in life. My parents didn't have a lot of money, but they had incredible work ethics, and they raised me to be self-sufficient."

I studied the adamant expression on Shelby's face for a moment, surprised by what she'd revealed.

Kaleb had never mentioned the fact that Shelby had lost her parents at such a young age.

Hell, there was so much I didn't know about this woman, but with every word she spoke, my admiration grew.

I'd grown up privileged, so I had no idea what it was like to worry about making ends meet every month.

I'd always known that I was probably never going to want for anything, and that Chase and I would someday take over my father's luxury brand empire.

"I didn't know about any of that," I told her. "Kaleb has always talked about you a lot, and I always knew how proud he was of your accomplishments."

"Just like I was proud of him, Tanner, and Devon," she said with a shrug. "We've always supported each other. They're as close as brothers to me, and just as annoying sometimes. If I allowed it, they'd take over my life and make everything easy for me. But that's never what I wanted. All I needed was their love and emotional support, and I've always gotten that."

It surprised me that there didn't seem to be an envious bone in this woman's body, nor did she seem to expect anything except love from her ultra-rich family.

She was fucking…grateful. And sincere. And goodhearted.

Maybe she thought she'd lost her ability to trust anyone, but she still had faith in humanity even after all the struggles she'd experienced in her life.

She went out of her way to try to make life better for other people. How in the hell had she maintained her upbeat attitude and kindness? I was financially privileged.

My father taught me good morals and values.

Still, the darker things and people in the world had made me jaded and distrusting of almost everyone except my family.

"So, do you consider yourself…happy?" I asked curiously.

She smiled at me, and that damn adorable dimple dented her cheek just a little as she answered, "Yes. Most of the time. When I'm not dealing with the drama of having some jerk break into my apartment. I have a good life. I love what I do. I guess maybe I'm lonely sometimes without my family nearby, but I'm grateful to have Tori, Taylor, Harlow, and Vanna as friends now."

Grateful.

There was that word, that feeling that I didn't really understand…again.

There was something about Shelby that made me want to protect her beautiful ass and make sure she never knew another moment of uncertainty and pain in her life.

Ever.

I couldn't say that I was accustomed to feeling that way with anyone except my family, but it was a gut instinct that I couldn't ignore.

Shelby deserved better than the painful shitshow she'd gotten from her ex-husband.

A lot better.

"What about you, Wyatt?" Shelby queried softly. "Are you happy?"

She asked that question like she was genuinely interested, which was puzzling to me.

Everyone assumed I was ecstatically happy because I had enough money to buy anything I wanted.

I couldn't remember if anyone outside of my family had ever asked me that question.

"I'm obscenely rich," I answered gruffly.

"Money doesn't buy happiness, silly," she said with a light, joyful laugh.

Maybe I should be offended because she'd called me *silly*, something no one in my world would dare to utter.

But coming from her mouth, the word almost sounded like an endearment, so I let it pass.

"Maybe not," I conceded. "But it doesn't hurt."

"Do you like the work that you do at Durand?"

I shrugged. "It was my legacy, and I want to run the company in a way that would make my father proud. There are aspects of it that I enjoy and some that I don't."

"Just like any profession," she pondered. "I can't say that I love doing some of the cleanup after the cooking, but you have to take the good with the bad when you enjoy what you're doing."

"Exactly," I agreed. "So tell me what would make you happier than you are already?"

Fuck! I had no idea why I'd asked her that question, but I was suddenly and uncharacteristically obsessed with Shelby Remington's happiness for some damn reason.

Hell, if anyone deserved happiness, it was her.

I picked up Xena while I was waiting for Shelby's answer because she was begging for some attention. I already knew that the needy monster wouldn't stop whining until she got exactly what she wanted.

I put her on the sofa beside me, which immediately made her settle down.

Shelby shot me a grin as she rubbed the canine's belly. "Not happening. I'm not going to tell you. You didn't really answer *my* question yet."

I scowled at her, but her smile just became a little more mischievous.

She wasn't the least bit daunted, and I knew she wasn't going to talk until she got an answer.

Cheeky woman.

"I'm as happy as I can be," I replied vaguely.

I would be happier if I could get this woman in my bed, naked, willing, and screaming my name because she was having the best orgasm of her life.

I didn't want to admit to myself just how badly I wanted Shelby Remington. It was distracting, and almost nothing distracted me.

Just being in the same room with her made my dick hard, and that little problem seemed to be getting worse and worse instead of better.

Forget about it! She's not the kind of woman you can fuck without some kind of commitment, asshole.

For once, I actually ignored that warning voice in my head because those cautionary words just weren't helping anymore.

Somehow, Shelby was getting under my thick skin, and if I let her get any closer, I wasn't completely sure I'd want to let her go anytime soon.

Chapter 12

Shelby

"What's wrong, Ted? You didn't like the stroganoff today?" I asked as I stopped strolling around the small dining room at The Friendly Kitchen to talk to one of the regulars.

I didn't know every single person who used the facility, but I knew some of the regulars who used the soup kitchen often. Ted hadn't been using the facility for long, but he came here almost every day.

Wyatt had convinced me to be cautious, so I'd agreed to start doing all of my volunteer work here during the day.

Because Wyatt had asked, I'd also turned down any catering gigs for now, which had made it easier for me to shift my volunteer hours.

In many ways, I enjoyed that change.

I got to spend more time with the people who used the soup kitchen instead of just doing the prep work.

I now came to The Friendly Kitchen in the afternoon Monday and Tuesday to prep and cook. After that, I was able to spend a little time during the early dinner hour to check on the diners to see how they liked the food.

After listening to all of Wyatt's reasons for doing so, I'd also decided to give up my apartment because it was the reasonable thing to do.

I was never going to live there again. I'd need to find a new place once we sorted out what had happened with the break-in. Even if we could figure out who the perpetrator had been, I'd always feel uncomfortable there because of what had happened.

We'd put a lot of my things into storage, and I was now saving a ridiculous amount of money by not having to maintain an apartment while I was hanging out somewhere else.

That needed to end soon.

I couldn't stay with Wyatt forever. I'd already been at his house for over two weeks, and the police had zero leads on the case. Although he never seemed to mind my presence, I felt guilty for freeloading at his place.

I could find an apartment with a better kitchen that would work for me.

Really, between the ridiculous wage Wyatt was giving me for dog sitting—which he refused to stop paying—and the money coming from my increased efforts with my blog, I didn't need what I'd made for catering events.

I was also getting close to finishing my cookbook, which I hoped would be successful now that I was getting more name recognition.

Financially, I was doing well because my blog was becoming even more popular and profitable every day. Wyatt was helping me monetize it in ways that wouldn't compromise the quality of the blog, which had helped me a lot.

He'd been so much more than generous with his time in the evenings, and he was patient.

Little by little, communication had become much easier with Wyatt, and he seemed more comfortable dropping some of his bullshit when we were alone together.

I could feel the presence of Wyatt's security personnel around me. They were posing as diners, but they were apparently good at blending into any environment. No one else even seemed to notice them.

Luckily, nothing weird had happened since the burglary, which was making me relax a little more every day.

"I liked it," Ted finally answered with a frown. "I guess I'm just not that hungry today."

I sat down in a vacant chair across the table from him, my heart aching for this big man who had apparently spiraled down in the world so quickly.

Nobody knew a lot about him, but it was common knowledge that he'd lost his entire family—his wife and three children—in a car accident not so long ago.

He'd started drinking, and from what I understood, he'd lost his job.

I could empathize with his loneliness and his sorrow, and I could certainly relate to losing a family to a tragic accident.

I reached out and took his hand as I said, "I could make you something else. You didn't eat much."

His eyes went to our joined hands, his expression sad and hopeless. "I don't want anything else. I just want my family back."

"I know you do," I said gently. "And I wish I could give them back to you. I lost my parents in a car accident. I know it's not the same thing, but I know a little about how difficult it is to get over something like that."

He looked down at his nearly full plate, and he asked in a desperate voice, "How did you get through it?"

"It was hard at first, but I knew my parents would want me to have someone else in my life who loved me. I was lucky. I had family. Do you have anyone, Ted?"

"No other close family," he said, his voice cracking with emotion. "But I've met a few people at the shelter who are nice to me. They were military at one time, too."

"I didn't know that you were in the military," I mused.

He nodded, but didn't raise his head. "Got out a long time ago, but it's still nice to talk to some guys who understand what that life was like."

"Fred told me that he gave you a referral for free counseling. Have you had a chance to meet up with someone there?" I asked curiously.

Fred was one of the volunteers who came here daily and had been donating his time to The Friendly Kitchen since the day it opened years ago. He knew the regulars much better than I did. The man also knew every free service available in the city to help the people who came here.

"Not yet," Ted answered. "I'm not sure I really want to talk about it right now."

I understood that. Everyone grieved at a different speed and in their own way. There had been a time when I'd wanted to ignore my parents' deaths, but I'd eventually been ready to see someone to talk about losing my parents.

My Aunt Millie had never pushed on me to face the truth until I was ready.

"Do you still have that information available in case you start to feel like you're ready?" I questioned softly.

"It's at the shelter," he confirmed.

I squeezed his hand. "Good. I think you'll know when you're ready."

"Do you think so?" he asked hopefully.

"I know so," I reassured him. "Be patient with yourself. You've been through a lot and you've lost a lot."

"Thanks, Shelby," he said as I let go of his hand so I could get up and check on other diners.

I smiled at him and nodded as I pushed the chair I'd been sitting in closer to the table. "Let me know if you need anything else, Ted."

He picked up his fork. "I'll just eat this. It really is good."

Contentment settled over me as I watched him start to eat his food, and I moved on to chat with other people in the dining room.

Small steps, Shelby. Be happy with small steps forward.

Volunteering here could be frustrating at times.

What we were doing at The Friendly Kitchen didn't seem like enough when so many people were suffering, many of them veterans and the elderly, but it was *something*.

Aunt Millie used to remind me that I couldn't change the world overnight.

I'd learned to celebrate my smaller accomplishments when it came to volunteer work.

It felt good to be doing whatever I could do with the skills I had to help others who didn't have the luxury of an amazing family or a decent job that paid well when things went to hell for them.

I was chatting with a woman and her three kids when my phone vibrated in the pocket of my jeans.

I stepped away and smiled when I saw the text.

Wyatt: *Do you want me to bring home dinner?*

It was early. He probably hadn't left the office yet, but he was still thoughtful enough to think about handling dinner so I didn't have to do it.

People could say what they wanted about Wyatt Durand, but he really wasn't a heartless jerk.

Maybe he wanted people to believe that he was, but I'd gotten more than a glimpse of his kinder side, and I was getting so used to his gruff exterior that I could easily blow it off.

Yeah, okay, so maybe he wasn't exactly warm and fuzzy, but he was a decent man, just like my cousins were underneath their bullshit.

Because I'd been married to an asshole who had been a good con man, I'd learned that everything you see on the exterior meant next to nothing.

Me: *No need. I did a video today. I just need to warm up the food. I'm heading back to the house soon.*

Wyatt: *Make sure my security is on your ass when you do.*

Me: *Yes, sir.*

Wyatt: *I'm not even going to consider that you might mean that seriously. You're never that compliant! You're mocking me.*

I was, and he knew it, but only in a good way.

The man really needed to learn to mellow out.

Me: *You're Wyatt Durand. Do you think I'd ever dare to mock you?*

Wyatt: *In a fucking heartbeat. Everything go ok today?*

My heart tripped when I thought about how many times he'd asked me that since the break-in.

The guy was busy all day, with people constantly wanting a piece of him, and he was already doing so much for me.

It still amazed me that he even had time to think about me during his workday, but he did.

He checked in with me frequently when we weren't together.

Me: *Everything is fine.*

Wyatt: *Good. Keep it that way.*

A laugh escaped from my lips, and I reached up a hand to cover my mouth before people around me started to wonder what I was laughing about.

But that comment was so…Wyatt.

Strangely, I always seemed to be the only person who noticed that his grumbly and abrupt comments weren't really all that foreboding.

Me: *I'll do my best. I hope you're having a good day.*

Wyatt: *I made a lot of money for Durand. That makes it a good day.*

I rolled my eyes. He was never going to convince me that he was completely financially driven, no matter how hard he tried.

Me: *Does it?*

Wyatt: *Of course. But it will be even better when I'm sampling whatever incredible dishes you created today.*

Me: *It feels great to be wanted only for my food.*

I was joking…sort of.

There was a hesitation before he replied.

Wyatt: *Do you want me to tell you that I'm looking forward to seeing you, too?*

I nibbled at my bottom lip.

We'd spent a lot of time talking in the evenings. Getting to know Wyatt Durand was like peeling an onion. It was a slow and difficult process, but with each layer I uncovered, I got to like him even more, which was probably dangerous. I was already so physically attracted to him that it was difficult not to think about how desperately I wanted to climb into his lap and explore that enormous, muscular body of his.

I'd also been more honest with him about myself than I had been with anyone in a long time.

So yeah, maybe I did want to hear that he was looking forward to seeing me and not just my seafood gumbo.

Wyatt: *Shelby?*

I straightened my shoulders, reminding myself that I had to be realistic. Wyatt and I would never be in a romantic relationship of any kind. I didn't expect him to be attracted to me like I was to him, but would it really hurt for him to tell me that he wanted to see *me*?

We'd formed some kind of weird truce or friendship. I wasn't sure exactly what it was on his side, but it was something.

Of course, it wasn't the same as my incessant desire to strip off all of his clothes and beg him to fuck me, but it wasn't…nothing.

Wyatt: *OK. You win. I don't really care what you made for dinner today. I'm looking forward to seeing you tonight, goddammit!*

I snorted quietly as I saw his irritated response because I hadn't answered right away.

For Wyatt, that was almost a declaration of devoted friendship or something.

Me: *Thanks. I'm looking forward to seeing you, too. Later.*

I put my phone back into my pocket and got ready to head back to Del Mar.

I was so satisfied by Wyatt's text that I might just have to make his favorite dessert for him tonight.

Chapter 13

Wyatt

"Nobody can figure out anything about this break-in," I told Shelby reluctantly a few nights later. "I've put the best people I know on the situation, but there's not even a suspect."

I went to pour myself a glass of whiskey as Shelby tapped away on her computer at the kitchen island.

I knew she was working on her cookbook, something she did often after dinner.

I'd finally decided that I had to be upfront with her, even though I hadn't wanted to tell her that I couldn't fix this situation, a fact that was frustrating as hell.

I was the head of one of the most successful corporations in the world. I also helped to successfully rescue hostages in dire situations.

And I still wasn't capable of discovering who in the hell had broken into Shelby's apartment.

Marshall had come up empty so far, so there was really no other option but to keep looking. Shelby was in contact with the local authorities and they didn't have a single lead, either.

"Then we'll just have to let it go," she said as she looked up from her computer and watched me at the bar. "It's not your fault, Wyatt. You tried, and I appreciate everything you've done. It must have been a prank or a one-time event. I can live with that."

"I can't," I said hoarsely. "I don't like the fact that someone did something like that to you, and we can't catch the bastard."

It haunted me that someone had possession of and could touch something so intimate that belonged to Shelby. And I couldn't even consider the possibility that the perverted fucker could be jacking off with those items while he thought about her.

I'd definitely developed one hell of a protective instinct toward Shelby, but it was far different from the way I wanted to protect my family.

It might be an unwelcome proclivity, but it was something I couldn't control.

And fuck knew I'd tried.

"Nothing else has happened," she contemplated. "I'm not even really nervous or that creeped out anymore. I can't let one person's actions control my life forever, and I'm going to have to find another place to live."

"Not. Now," I said in a graveled voice. "There's no reason why you can't stay here longer."

"Do you really want me here?" she asked in a skeptical voice.

Did I want her here?

Hell yes, I wanted her here. I wouldn't have insisted that she stay if I didn't. It wasn't completely out of concern for her safety anymore, either.

Somehow, I'd also gotten used to her being here, *and* I actually liked it.

Granted, it was torture because my balls were blue, but I didn't want her to leave. Christ! I must have masochistic tendencies that I never knew about before her.

I didn't crave my solitude anymore.

I also didn't mind Cujo being here, either, or the fact that the damn dog was snoring loudly on a bed in the living room right now. She was well-behaved and not nearly as needy since Shelby had gotten here.

The two females in my home had turned my world upside down, but I wasn't exactly complaining about it.

In fact, I didn't want to even think about Shelby going anywhere. My home would be much too quiet, and my hellion canine would probably go into a temper tantrum over the loss.

"Yes, I want you to stay." Amazingly, those words hadn't really been all that hard to say.

She sent me a genuine smile that made my gut ache.

"Then I'll stay for a while since I haven't found another place with a kitchen that will work for me yet," she said gently. "Maybe until after I get back from Montana?"

Okay, that would work…for now. I could convince her to stay longer once she got back from that annual picnic in Montana.

"I'm sure you got an invite to the picnic," she mused.

I nodded. "I did. I always do, but I've never been able to make it. It's at a really busy time of the year for Durand Industries. All of the fall collections are usually coming out around that time. I'd like to go, but I have some important meetings that week that have been scheduled for months. There are some executives flying in from around the world. I can't get there for the picnic, but I'll come pick you up so I can see Kaleb and his family."

"I'd love that, and I know my family would love to see you, too," she said with a happy sigh. "Kaleb is sending his jet to come pick me up for the trip there."

I looked at the contented expression on her face, my chest tight.

Fuck! What in the hell was wrong with me?

I downed half my whiskey in one gulp, and went to sit beside her at the breakfast bar.

I was slightly alarmed that I'd automatically poured her a glass of wine that she liked without even thinking about that action. I set it on the breakfast bar and pushed it toward her.

I wasn't sure when it had become my mission to make sure that I anticipated Shelby's wants or needs, but that was another damn compulsion I couldn't seem to control.

"Can I ask you a question?" she queried hesitantly as she closed her laptop and then took a sip of her wine.

I sent her a wary glance. She was normally never shy about asking anything she wanted. "What?"

"You said that someone duped you once. I was just wondering what happened. I'm assuming it was a female."

"It was," I replied reluctantly. It was part of my history that I rarely talked about with anyone.

"Tell me," she cajoled softly. "You know about every stupid thing I did in my past. I'm certainly never going to judge. Or is it still painful?"

It wasn't.

Not anymore.

But the effects of that experience had probably helped shape my views on life and romance.

Since Shelby had always been open with me, I answered, "It was a long time ago. While I was still in the military. Her name was Simone. We were together for several years. They say it's always hard for a special forces guy to keep a girlfriend because our missions can be long and frequent. Sometimes we're gone more than we're at our assigned base in the States. I thought I'd beat those odds. That I'd found a woman who really cared because she'd put up with my absences for years. I was planning on proposing to her once I returned from a particularly long op. Hell, I even had the ring in my pocket when I got home. I came home from that deployment and found her in our bed with one of my friends, which explained why she was so patient all the time. She had at least one backup guy when I wasn't around."

I heard Shelby gasp before she said angrily. "She was a fool. God, I'm so sorry she hurt you, Wyatt. You must have really loved her if you were together that long."

I shrugged. "I thought I did. I thought she felt the same, but when she realized I was never going to take her back, she told me it was all about my money. We had a really nice place off base, I gave her a nicer vehicle than I had myself, and she had access to my money and my cards to buy anything she wanted. Shopping was her favorite hobby, but I figured she deserved whatever she wanted since I was gone more than I was home. When I told her to move out, she said she'd enjoyed spending my money, but that she could never love a cold bastard like me."

Shelby reached out and laid her hand on my forearm. "So now you probably think that no woman will ever care about anything except your money? She was wrong, Wyatt. God, I'd really like to bitch slap that woman into the stratosphere right now. She actually had a good guy, and she threw you away? She cheated on you while you were off somewhere serving our country? Unbelievable. She was the cold one, not you."

I tried not to grin at Shelby's indignation over a woman who had burned me years ago, but I was only partially successful.

I certainly wasn't going to remind her that she hadn't liked me at all a month or two ago.

I had no idea what I'd done to warrant her passionate defense, but I liked it.

One of the many things that I liked about Shelby was her unwavering support of family and the people she considered friends.

I shrugged. "It happens fairly often. My mistake was thinking that it would never happen to me. But she was right about one thing. I am a cold bastard. About the only thing I really have to offer *is* my money."

"I hate it when you say things like that," she mumbled, sounding annoyed as she turned her chair to look at me directly because I was sitting sideways at the breakfast bar. "Because it's not true."

Amused, I requested, "Then please enlighten me, because most people find me highly unlikeable with no redeeming traits."

"I don't," she said emphatically. "Okay, so maybe I got the wrong impression of you at first, but I think you're just wary and cynical because you've been hurt pretty badly before. Not to mention the fact that you didn't exactly see anything uplifting in all the years that you were in the military. You're honest. You say exactly what you're thinking without much of a filter, but I'd rather deal with someone who tells the truth than someone who lies. Cold bastards don't help a woman they barely know, and they certainly don't spend valuable free time trying to give them business advice."

I lifted a brow. "Has it ever occurred to you that I might have ulterior motives for doing those things?"

She shook her head, her eyes still glued to mine. "Nope. What other possible reason could you have for being nice to a woman like me?"

Jesus! She really was clueless. "You've honestly never considered the possibility that I might be attracted to you and all of these so-called nice things I'm doing might be a ploy to get you into my bed?"

Suddenly, she burst into laughter, breaking our eye contact. "You're joking, right?" she said as she recovered.

I grimaced as I questioned, "Why did you immediately assume that?"

"Because I'm…me. And you're Wyatt Durand, an incredibly hot, brilliant billionaire. Women like me wouldn't even be on your radar. I'm a curvy female who rarely wears much makeup, and my regular attire is mostly old jeans and a T-shirt because I work in a kitchen most of the day. You work in high-fashion and luxury products. You see gorgeous supermodels every day. I'm not your type."

Okay. That answer really pissed me off. Shelby's body was perfect, and she didn't need a ton of makeup because she was naturally beautiful.

In fact, she was so fucking hot that I had to get myself off on a daily basis so I didn't lose it with her.

I was a guy who had never understood why any woman needed to starve themselves to the point that they looked like a skeleton, even though I was in the fashion business.

Personally, I'd never found that attractive.

Obviously, her ex had screwed with her head so well and cut down her self-image to the point where she still hadn't gotten over it.

"First," I said irritably. "You obviously have no idea what I do all day. I don't see models very often. I'm not a designer. My work is far from glamorous. Most of my time is spent in a conference room with middle-aged or elderly bald men. All of them just as eager as I am to make their business endeavors more successful. Second, you have no idea what my type of woman is or might be. I've never been attracted to a supermodel. And third, you get my dick hard every damn time I look at you. It seems that I have a weakness for gorgeous redheads with curvy bodies who think I'm an asshole."

Fuck! I knew this topic was dangerous, but I was going there anyway.

It fried my ass to listen to the most beautiful woman I'd ever seen toss out self-deprecating comments that couldn't be further from the truth.

I understood that she'd been manipulated and made to feel like she was nothing, but Shelby Remington was something. Probably the most incredible woman I'd ever known.

In reality, *she* was way too good for *me*, and I knew it, but it didn't stop me from wanting to claim her anyway.

My balls were bluer than a damn Smurf's from being this close to her day after day, and until tonight, she'd never given me any indication that she might be as attracted to me as I was to her.

But tonight, right at this very moment, I thought I could see lust in those stunning eyes of hers, and I was ready to find out if this unholy attraction went both ways. For some reason I didn't completely understand, I couldn't help myself, even though I knew I'd be screwed if it did.

I actually enjoyed seeing the surprised expression on her face when I slammed a hand on both of the armrests of her chair, effectively keeping her from going anywhere until I was finished *explaining*.

"Wyatt!" she squeaked, her emerald green eyes staring at my lips before locking with mine.

Oh, hell yes, she wanted me, and that knowledge made me happier than I'd been in a very long time.

She licked those plump, tempting lips of hers, which only made my dick harder, if that was even possible.

Christ! Nothing was going to stop this interlude except a natural disaster or her reluctance to continue.

"Wyatt," she said again, this time in a needy whisper as her eyes turned liquid with desire.

I leaned forward, waiting for her to protest, but she didn't, which sealed her damn fate as far as I was concerned.

"Don't ever tell me that you're not my type again," I growled right before I did what I'd been tempted to do since the very first time we'd met.

Chapter 14

Shelby

Wyatt kissed the same way he did everything else—with absolutely no hesitation and with so much power that I gasped into his mouth with shock as those skilled lips began to devour mine.

His embrace was hungry and sensual, and it made me feel things I'd never experienced before.

Need.

Longing.

And a heady arousal that stunned all of my senses.

Wyatt Durand wanted...me. And I could feel it with every touch.

I didn't think.

I was beyond reason as I wrapped my arms around his neck, savoring his masculine, sexy scent as I fell deeper into the earthshattering embrace.

God, yes, I'd thought about what it would be like to be the center of Wyatt's lustful attention.

I'd imagined what it would be like to be this close to him.

But even my imagination hadn't been crazy enough to conjure up something like *this*.

He stood, pulling me up with him until I was plastered against his muscular form.

My body started to shiver with desire as his tongue hotly demanded entrance and I opened to him like it was the most natural thing on Earth to do.

I'd never been held like this, kissed like this, like having me close to him was necessary to his very existence, and the carnal lust it fired in my body was almost overwhelming.

Heat flooded between my thighs, and my nipples were so hard that it was erotically painful as my breasts abraded against his very solid chest.

He felt good.

So. Damn. Good.

And he smelled and tasted like a sinful, arousing fantasy.

He wrapped his arms more tightly around me, his big hand stroking down my back until it finally landed on my jean clad ass so he could nudge my hips close enough to feel just how much he wanted me.

The man might be built like a tank, but there was nothing awkward about his sensual, persuasive assault on my senses.

He released my mouth and nibbled on my bottom lip, teasing me.

One of his hands released my hair from the clip that was restraining it behind my head, and his warm breath caressed my lips as he speared that hand into the fat, liberated curls.

I released a mesmerized sigh as I threaded my hands into his coarse, dark hair and yanked his mouth back to mine.

I needed to be fused with this enigmatic, gorgeous male, and if this was the only time I was ever going to experience something like this, I wanted it to last a little while longer.

I was panting when we finally came up for air, and I was clinging to Wyatt because my legs wouldn't quite hold me up.

"Fucking hell, woman," he said hoarsely as his mouth trailed from my sensitive earlobe to my neck. "You're killing me."

"Wyatt," I murmured, my voice merely a whisper as I tilted my head to give him access to anything he wanted.

"If you don't stop talking to me in that *fuck-me* voice," he warned ominously. "I'm not responsible for the consequences. Has it become crystal clear to you that you're exactly my type of woman?"

I smiled.

I couldn't help it.

He had no idea what it felt like to know that he wanted to get me naked so badly that his patience was razor thin because of that desire.

The feel of his lips on my skin making me half crazy, I muttered, "I think I'm starting to believe that, even though it seems incredible to me."

As insane as the idea was to me, I couldn't deny the fact that Wyatt Durand *was* just as attracted to me as I was to him.

"Christ!" he suddenly exploded as he moved away from me and ran a hand through his hair. "This has to stop. I can't have you close to me without wanting you naked."

I pushed my unruly hair from my face and sat back down in my chair, every nerve ending in my body protesting over the loss of Wyatt's powerful body moving beyond touching distance.

I let out a shaky breath before I answered, "I would have let you get me naked, and I haven't been with anyone in years. I'm not into casual sex."

It was the truth.

It had been a long time for me.

I'd been married, but my sexual relationship with Justin had never felt like this, and I could count the number of guys I'd slept with on the fingers of one hand.

I'd never wanted to be so close to any of them that I could happily climb inside them and never come out again.

There was something about Wyatt that drew me to him.

For me, this wasn't a simple physical attraction.

I glanced at him, and he looked just as confused as I was right now.

God, he was one big, frustrated, beautiful male, and I wanted nothing more than to go back to where we'd left off a moment ago.

"Do you think I don't already know that you're not into casual sex?" he asked tersely. "If I wasn't aware of that, we'd be upstairs in my bed and not discussing this right now."

I reached down, grabbed the clip for my hair from the floor, and started to confine it at the back of my neck again.

Wyatt stepped forward and took the clip from my hand and put it into his pocket.

He lifted his whiskey, tossed back what remained in the glass, and then put the tumbler back on the counter before he picked me up from the chair.

"Wyatt!" I squealed in surprise, wrapping my arms around his neck to keep myself steady in his arms. "What are you doing. You can't carry me. I'm too heavy."

But apparently, he could and did carry me very easily until we reached the living room.

He shot me a grin that made my heart stutter as he sat on the couch with me in his lap. "You didn't feel heavy to me," he said in a husky baritone. "Relax. I know this can't go any further, but I want your gorgeous body plastered against me for a little while longer. Evidently, I like to torture myself. Stop squirming around and tell me why you haven't been with anyone for years."

He wrapped a strong arm around my waist and started to toy with my hair like he was fascinated by my red curls.

I stilled and just savored the delicious feeling of Wyatt's ripped body beneath me.

My weight on top of him didn't seem to faze him, so I stopped thinking about the fact that I wasn't exactly a dainty female.

Truthfully, I wasn't quite ready to be separated from him right now, either.

I shrugged and wrapped my arms loosely around his neck. "Sex takes a certain amount of trust for me, and after what happened in Montana, it was really hard for me to trust anyone again. I've been focused on my blog, my catering gigs, and putting together my comfort food cookbook. I've stayed busy without dating. I wasn't ready. What about you? I don't see you dating anyone."

"No woman would have me," he answered gruffly. "I'm a surly guy with no sense of humor. I work a ridiculous amount of hours, and I think it's already been established that I'm not boyfriend or husband material. I don't have a heart to give to anyone."

I whacked him on the shoulder. "None of that is true, and you know it. You love your family. And you've had a relationship before. I'm assuming you were faithful, even if she wasn't."

Wyatt certainly wasn't heartless, and he was far from cold.

"Cheating on a woman I was committed to never even crossed my mind," he said nonchalantly. "I don't think the Durands are made that way. My father loved my mother until the day he died. He was never interested in another woman. And you've seen how ridiculous Tori is over Cooper and how Chase is with Savannah. I think we're either all-in or we don't commit. I'm the latter. Simone made me realize that I wasn't cut out for committed relationships. I prefer peace and solitude to that kind of craziness."

Okay, that kind of sounds like a warning.

It was also bullshit, and I knew it.

Maybe Wyatt didn't feel like sticking his neck out again, but he was the type of guy who would make an amazing, incredibly devoted partner. He couldn't see that in himself, but it was perfectly clear to me.

He'd just picked the wrong partner to trust, and that was something I *definitely* understood.

Something told me that he'd convinced himself that he wasn't equipped to handle a romantic relationship because he'd been let down by someone he'd cared about enough to marry.

I could relate to that better than most people.

It was also possible that he'd never really gotten over Simone and just wasn't able to love someone else.

The more that I thought about that, it made sense.

Hadn't he said that he didn't have a heart to give away?

Maybe that's what he's trying to warn me about without really saying it.

It made my heart ache that he was still pining over a woman who had never deserved him in the first place.

"I think I should probably go to bed," I said as I slid off his lap.

For some reason, it really bothered me to feel this attracted to a guy who was still hung up on someone else.

Wyatt might be physically attracted to me, but it was obvious that he'd left his heart with the woman who had ripped it from his body years ago.

We could be friends.

I already considered him a friend.

How could I not after everything he'd done for me?

But it couldn't and never would be anything more.

If I had sex with him, I'd definitely get emotionally attached, and it would hurt. A guy like him would wreck me, and I was wiser than I had been a few years ago.

"Shelby?" he rumbled as he reluctantly released me so I could stand up. "What in the hell just happened?"

"Nothing. I-I just don't think this is a good idea," I stammered nervously. "I consider you a friend, and I'd rather not lose that friendship over a temporary attraction to each other. Goodnight, Wyatt."

I felt emotionally drained and confused.

I had to get out of this room and away from him so I could think straight again.

"Wait," he demanded before I could flee. "You said you had a hard time trusting anyone. You let your guard down tonight, at least for a little while. Does that mean that you trust me?"

I couldn't lie to him, so I simply answered, "I do. I wouldn't have let you touch me if I didn't."

With that, I turned my back to him and slowly walked away so it didn't look like I was running scared, even though that was exactly what I was doing.

I might trust Wyatt, but I wasn't so sure I trusted myself when I was with him.

Chapter 15

Wyatt

"I heard that Shelby is spending the day with Tori tomorrow to get ready for the charity gala," Chase mentioned casually after we'd finished up some work in my office. "Why didn't you mention that she was coming with you?"

I shot my brother a warning look from my chair behind my desk, even though I already knew that he wasn't getting his ass up from his chair to leave my office until he had satisfied his curiosity.

Chase was my brother.

He knew inviting anyone to come with me to this charity gala was unusual for me.

Hell, I even recognized that tone of voice he was using.

He was digging for information while trying to keep his approach nonchalant, hoping that I might spill my guts to him if he was subtle about it.

Chase had tried this ploy many times over the years. I wasn't fooled by his laid back attitude. He was trying to figure out my real motivation for asking Shelby to come with me.

"I just asked her yesterday," I informed him. "And since she's doing me a favor by coming with me so I don't have to put up with a bunch of superficial chit-chat, I gave Tori my credit card to take care of anything Shelby needs."

"That's kind of short notice for her," Chase observed.

"Not deliberately," I explained reluctantly. "I wasn't sure that I should even ask her."

My brother sent me a probing look. "Why?"

Frustrated, I raked a hand through my hair as I confessed, "Because I was a dumbass several days ago. I kissed her. She kissed me back, and then suddenly started acting like she regretted it. Things have been a little tense between the two of us. It took two fucking days for her not to look at me like she was terrified I'd kiss her again."

Chase grinned, and I desperately wanted to deck him to wipe the smile off his face.

"I don't think Shelby's the type to be scared off that easily," he observed. "So...you're attracted to her."

"I am," I agreed grudgingly. "I thought that attraction went both ways, but I'm not so sure about that anymore. I don't know what in the hell I was thinking. That asshole of an ex-husband of hers not only put her through hell emotionally, but he hit her, Chase. Maybe she just got scared."

Chase, Cooper, Jax, Hudson, and Marshall all knew about Shelby's history now because we were all working on solving the mystery of who broke into her home.

My brother shook his head slowly. "I think you're on the wrong track with the assumption that she regrets it. She certainly doesn't seem like she's intimidated or afraid of any guy. What did you say after you kissed her?"

"Nothing. We were just talking before she decided she needed to get out of the room like her gorgeous ass was on fire. Taking off on me with no real explanation seems to be a habit for when she's with me. I think I'd just told her that after what happened with Simone all those years ago, I wasn't cut out for romantic relationships and that I usually preferred my solitude."

Chase rolled his eyes and shot me a you-did-not-really-say-that-to-her look. "You said that after you'd just kissed her?"

I wanted to end this conversation like it had never happened, but I asked, "Why wouldn't I say that? It's true. Before Shelby came to stay with me, I did prefer my solitude."

"Did you bother to mention that you feel a little differently since she's been there?" he questioned.

"Probably not," I admitted. "But obviously it was implied. I wouldn't encourage her to stay if I didn't want her there."

"Take it from me," Chase said drily. "It's a really good idea to never assume that a woman knows what you're thinking. That could very easily be misinterpreted. Like…*yeah, I just kissed you, but it meant absolutely nothing to me because I'd rather be alone.*"

I scowled at him. "That's not what I meant, and I'm not as intuitive as you are when I'm talking to a female."

"If you kiss a woman you really like, I'd strongly advise that you don't immediately tell her that you'd rather have your solitude," Chase said in philosophical tone. "Especially a woman like Shelby. I don't think she's the type to sleep with a man without her emotions getting involved."

"She said she wasn't ready for another relationship," I said defensively.

"Was that past tense or present?"

"Fuck!" I cursed irritably. "I don't know. It's not like I'm used to discussing anything emotional with anyone. I took it literally. It sounded like she was warning me that she wasn't about to get involved with another guy after what happened to her. I can't say that I blame her. I'd seriously like to hurt the bastard who treated her like shit. What idiot could be married to a woman like Shelby and not appreciate the fact that she was his?"

Chase shrugged. "I don't know. I'll never understand that myself. I can't help you there. But I understand why you're drawn to her. I like Shelby. I have since the first time I talked to her about my wedding. You care about her. Admit it. She's the first woman who's gotten your attention since Simone."

"She's nothing like Simone," I said, my voice guttural. "Shelby is different from any woman I've ever known. She's been through a lot of shit, but it hasn't made her bitter. In fact, she's made it her mission to help everyone she can, even though she's gotten burned. She lost her restaurant, which was always her dream, but she's managed to turn it into something positive by doing something else she loves. Christ! She turns almost everything into something positive. And she actually likes me. There's something seriously wrong with that. There's nobody who wants to be my friend, especially not a female."

"You're screwed," Chase said morosely. "Never give a woman you want a reason to put you in the friend zone. I'm assuming you are attracted to her."

"Probably way more than I should be," I told him, seeing no reason not to be honest now that I was already spilling my guts to him. "But I never should have touched her. She's Kaleb's cousin, and I'm not like you, Chase. I've never been a charming type of guy. Shelby deserves someone who can tell her everything she ought to hear, the stuff she never heard from the prick she was married to. Someone who can say all of the right things. I'm not that guy. You know that. I'm a cynical asshole."

He shook his head. "No, you're not. Not with the people you care about. Not when it's really important. And you've done a lot of nice things for Shelby, even if you can't always find the words you think she wants to hear. Actions really do speak louder than words sometimes, Wyatt. Shelby is intelligent. She sees that."

I sent Chase a skeptical look. "You're not going to slam me for being attracted to Shelby after I gave you so much shit about Savannah?"

He grinned. "Not now. I think you need my help. But maybe later. Honestly, you kicked me in the ass when I needed it, so I probably shouldn't give you a hard time at all. Right now, I think we need to figure out exactly how to set Shelby straight about what you really want from her. I don't think you want to be stuck in her friend zone. What do you want from her?"

"I have no fucking idea," I confessed huskily. "I'm attracted to her physically. Always have been. But I think there's more to it than that."

Chase shrugged. "Let her know you're interested, and make it very clear that she's the only woman who matters to you right now. I haven't seen you give two shits about a woman in a long time. I think Shelby would be good for you, Wyatt. She couldn't care less about your money, your power, or the luxury product and fashion industry. If she likes you, she actually likes *you*."

I lifted a brow. "I find that a little frightening, don't you? I'm not exactly a likable guy."

Chase chuckled. "Shelby is a smart woman. She can see who you really are beneath your bullshit. I think you're just out of practice when it comes to dealing with a female who isn't interested in your money."

Out of practice?

The truth was, I had no idea how to deal with a woman who didn't make my money their first priority.

"Maybe you think that I'm better at charming women than you are," Chase mused. "But do I really need to remind you that I had the woman I wanted right in front of me, a woman who really cared about me, and I almost fucked it up?"

"That was different. It was obvious that Savannah wanted the same thing you did. It was also obvious that everything would work out once you pulled your head out of your ass. I'm not sure I can say the same thing about this situation. Hell, I don't even know what I want, but it's definitely not to be stuck in her friend zone forever."

"You're crazy about her," Chase stated confidently. "And you've never been a guy who gives up on anything you really want."

"I didn't say I was giving up," I told him. "I'm just not sure what my strategy is going to be going forward."

"No strategy," Chase insisted. "For once in your life, lead with your damn emotions. This isn't a business transaction or a rescue operation. You need to talk her into giving this a chance. You kissed her. She kissed you back. There's obviously an attraction there on both sides. I'm not exactly sure what made her run away from it, but you're perfectly capable of making her see that she has the wrong impression. She's your date for the charity gala tomorrow night. I know Shelby well enough to know that she wouldn't have agreed to go with you if she didn't want to be there with you."

"Like I said," I answered. "She's doing it to help me out. You know I suck at small talk. It would be easier to have a date."

"Maybe you should convince her that's not the only reason you want her there with you."

It wasn't.

It never had been.

I'd only used that excuse to get her to attend with me.

I'd suffered through some of these types of events on my own when I absolutely had to attend.

"You're not a man who is willing to waste an opportunity, Wyatt," Chase said in a thoughtful tone.

Maybe not, but like Chase had said, this wasn't about business.

It was personal, and I didn't do anything personal well most of the time.

Shelby had called this thing between us a temporary attraction, but it sure as hell didn't feel like something temporary to me.

In the beginning, maybe I had thought I'd get over that attraction, but I hadn't.

My preoccupation with her was rapidly turning into an obsession for me, and it wasn't something I could just ignore or compartmentalize anymore.

Nor did I think it was going to go away anytime soon.

I was going to have to put my nuts on the chopping block to figure out what Shelby was really thinking, and I was a guy who had always been highly in favor of keeping his balls exactly where they belonged.

Chapter 16

Shelby

"You look absolutely beautiful, Shelby, but Wyatt is going to be ticked off because you didn't let me pay for anything today," Tori said with a sigh.

I surveyed myself in the mirror of Tori's master bedroom, feeling more attractive than I had in a very long time.

I'd completely blown my budget, but maybe it was worth it to feel like I looked nice for a change.

My confidence had been shot down in every way possible after being married to a man like Justin.

He'd built me up until I really believed that he loved me.

And then, once we were married, he'd done everything in his power to make me feel like I was nothing so I didn't question what he was doing behind my back.

Little by little, I was regaining my assurance in some areas.

I was no longer convinced that I was nothing.

But he'd dug so hard to undermine my confidence in my personal appearance and sexuality that it was hard to shake off those uncertainties.

Tori and I had gone shopping, gotten our hair, nails, and makeup done a little earlier, and both of us were ready to head out for the charity gala.

With Tori's encouragement, I'd finally selected a stunning, navy blue, formal dress. I wasn't exactly sure about the plunging neckline or the slit that went up my thigh on the side, but I loved the flowy material that swooshed when I walked and hit right above the top of my foot.

My heels weren't something I'd use again anytime soon since I didn't cook in strappy sandals, but they went with the dress perfectly.

The hair stylist had suggested leaving my hair down and flowing down my back, but she'd done a very elegant style to sweep it off my face with beautiful clips that matched the dress. She'd left just a few wispy, curly locks of hair that framed my face.

My makeup was a lot more dramatic than my usual, but all of the colors were blended perfectly so it didn't look completely overdone.

"You look gorgeous yourself, and I couldn't let Wyatt pay for my clothing and everything else we did today," I finally answered. "He asked for a favor, and after everything he's done for me, I was happy to do it. Although I have no idea what it's like to mingle at a gala. Do you have any tips for me before we go?"

I turned away from the mirror and smiled nervously at Tori, who was breathtaking in a deep red, formal gown.

Cooper and Wyatt were waiting patiently in the living room having a drink until Tori and I were ready to go.

I hadn't seen Wyatt yet, but I knew that he'd gotten ready at home before coming to Tori's to pick me up.

"Just be yourself," she insisted. "This isn't a business event, although there will be some rich people there. It's about the only event that Wyatt makes an appearance at because it's a fundraiser that my father started after my mother died. We all try to attend every year to carry on the tradition. We always went with my dad before he passed away, and this fundraiser was important to him because my mother died of ovarian cancer. It raises a lot of money for research. You don't have to be anyone except who you are. You're good at talking to everyone. Just have a good time. You're about to knock Wyatt's socks off right now, which I'm going to enjoy watching."

"We're just going as…friends," I protested.

Tori snorted as she fussed with her hair in the mirror. "I hate to break this to you, but I don't think Wyatt thinks you're just a friend. He's attracted to you, and I think the feeling is mutual, right?"

I wasn't sure how Tori knew that, but she was so perceptive that it was scary sometimes.

She and Cooper had dropped over to Wyatt's house several times, as had Chase and Vanna. But it wasn't like she'd had tons of time to observe the way Wyatt and I interacted.

"Was I that obvious?" I asked softly. "It's really not difficult to be attracted to your brother. He's been really good to me, he's crazy intelligent, and he's ridiculously gorgeous. But you know my history, Tori. It's really difficult for me to believe that a guy like Wyatt is genuinely attracted to me."

"I think he probably feels the same way. Let me tell you something about Wyatt that might help. He doesn't think he's gorgeous," she informed me matter-of-factly. "He's never thought that. He was always a tall guy, even when he was younger, and he was self-conscious when he was a teenager. He towered over other guys in high school and it took a while for his body to fill out and catch up to his height. He's also never been a smooth talker, which some women probably expect from a guy with that much money."

I gave her an astonished look. "That's crazy. He's probably the hottest guy I've ever seen, and I'd rather talk to someone who's brutally honest than some guy who feeds me bullshit."

In my mind, Wyatt was the epitome of tall, dark, and ridiculously handsome.

He was tall, brawny, and gruff, but I certainly didn't see any of those things as a negative.

It was hard to believe any single female wouldn't find him droolworthy.

Tori shrugged. "I feel the same way. I think he's handsome, but he thinks I'm biased because I'm his baby sister. I'm glad someone appreciates him and all the good qualities he has. Didn't I tell you when you first met him in person that he'd grow on you?"

"You were right," I said wistfully. "He did. I misjudged him."

"Not your fault. He usually doesn't make a very good first impression," she quipped. "He can come off as pretty grumpy and abrasive, and you had your reasons for not liking him at first. He isn't a guy with pretty words, but he makes up for it with his actions. I'm glad you understand him. Very few people do. So what are you going to do about that attraction if you don't mind me asking?"

"Nothing," I rushed to assure her. "I'm not Wyatt's type. We're better off just being friends. Anything else could get…complicated."

I really didn't want to tell Tori about the kiss or that I suspected that Wyatt might still harbor feelings for a woman who had never deserved him.

It was his secret to tell, not mine.

If he hadn't shared his feelings about Simone with his sister or brother, I wasn't about to let the cat out of the bag.

"I think you *are* Wyatt's type," Tori said with a smile as she turned toward me. "He probably hasn't let you know that, but he's been even more reserved and careful since he got out of the military. He saw some…pretty bad things there."

She'd chosen her words carefully, and I already knew why. Wyatt was her brother, and he'd told me that he didn't share his military background with anyone except his family.

I nodded. "I know that he was special forces. I don't think anyone could function as an operative like that without having it change them. He told me about what happened with Simone, too."

Tori's expression was shocked as she asked, "He actually told you about Simone and that he was in special forces?"

"No specifics," I assured her. "But he did share that he was special forces in the military, and the basics about what happened with his ex-girlfriend."

"Then he likes you even more than I thought. I still don't know much about what happened with Simone, except for the fact that she slept with someone else. They were together for a long time, but we only met a few times. I didn't like her. I thought she was using Wyatt, but I didn't know her well enough to tell my brother what I thought. I feel bad sometimes that I was relieved when they broke up. And he never told anyone but family about his involvement in special forces while he was active. I'm not sure Simone even knew why he was deployed so often, but I doubt she cared as long as she had access to his funds. He still avoids sharing that information unless he has to for some reason."

Apparently, no one had mentioned to Tori that Kaleb had been informed that all of my friends' spouses had been in special forces or that I knew, too. Apparently, that subject hadn't come up yet. I hesitated about mentioning it, but it would be awkward if she found out and I'd never told her that I knew.

I quickly explained what had happened, and why Wyatt had told us the truth.

"I understand," she said after I'd told her. "It makes perfect sense why Wyatt would tell you and Kaleb about it. My brother wouldn't have said anything if he hadn't already cleared it with Hudson, Jax, Cooper, and Chase. Cooper didn't tell me you knew, but I'm glad you do. Wyatt trusts you, Shelby, and he isn't a guy who trusts easily," Tori mused.

"That makes two of us," I said drily. "I wasn't sure I could ever trust anyone again after what happened to me in Montana, especially a guy."

Tori knew my entire history now, as did the rest of my friends.

Her expression was gentle and sympathetic as she asked, "But you trust Wyatt?"

I nodded slowly, a big lump in my throat. Although I didn't want to tell her what I suspected about Simone, there were other reasons why I couldn't get too attached to Wyatt. "I do trust him. He's never been anything but honest with me, but I'm still not his type, Tori. I don't dress up like this every day. I'm a chef who wears jeans and a T-shirt almost all of the time because I get dirty in a kitchen every single day. And I usually smell like whatever food I cooked by the end of a long day. My ass is too big because I love to eat, and it will be a very long time before my makeup and hair looks this decent again. Wyatt and I come from two different worlds, and whether he likes it or not, he does have a public image."

Tori chuckled. "Considering how much my brother likes to eat, you smelling like gourmet food is probably an aphrodisiac to him. Don't underestimate Wyatt. He doesn't give a damn what other people think, and the media eats that indifference up like it's candy on the rare occasions that he exposes himself to public scrutiny. Besides, you're gorgeous, and any man would be lucky to be dating you, but it would take more than that to get his attention. You're real, Shelby, and I doubt any woman has spoken to him like a person and not the CEO of Durand in a long time. It's not surprising that he's drawn to a woman like you."

I picked up my clutch purse as I said firmly. "We're just friends. I'm doing Wyatt a favor tonight, but we aren't dating."

I had to end this conversation because it was killing me.

Any kind of relationship with Wyatt, other than what we had right now, just wasn't possible.

Things had been tense between the two of us after he'd kissed me, but we'd eventually fell back into our old routine, and I didn't want to make a fool of myself.

I was attracted to him in a way I'd never experienced before, even though I'd been married before.

But I couldn't let myself hope for anything more.

I'd been an idiot once, but I wasn't as naïve as I used to be, and I didn't want to get my heart broken.

Sadly, considering the way I already felt about Wyatt, I knew he'd have the power to shatter me if I let myself believe we could be anything more than friends.

I was an optimist, but in this case, I had no choice but to be realistic.

Tori smiled as she picked up her bag. "I'm ready. I think I look as good as a woman with freaky amber eyes is going to look."

Her eyes were beautiful and unique, but I knew they made her self-conscious. "You look amazing, Tori. Your husband will be ogling you all night, just like he does every single day." I hesitated before I added, "Thank you for today. I had an incredible time."

It had been a long time since I'd had a friend like Tori, and I was more grateful for our friendship than she'd ever know or realize.

I'd isolated myself for a long time after Justin's arrest. I'd wrapped myself up in a cocoon so I could make it through that horrible period of time it had taken to prosecute my former husband. I'd been so incredibly lonely that it made me really appreciate the fact that I now had a friend who I could trust here in California. And this friendship had led to several others that I now valued, too.

She reached out and hugged me without hesitation because that was just the kind of warm, genuine person she was, and it made my eyes well up with tears.

How long had it been since anyone had cared about me outside of a family who was over a thousand miles away?

I blinked those tears back, knowing that I'd screw up my makeup if I didn't.

When she finally let me go, she said, "I had a great time, too. But Wyatt is still going to be pissed off that you wouldn't let me pay for anything. He was pretty adamant that he'd cover all of the expenses for this charity gala."

"I'll talk to him about it," I promised her. "He can't just demand something and expect to get it every time he does."

"He usually gets exactly what he wants," Tori said drily. "Most people fear him."

"I don't," I informed her. "I can handle your brother."

"Thank God," she said jokingly. "Other than myself, you might be the only woman who can."

Chapter 17

Wyatt

"I think she's danced with every man under the age of ninety at this event except for me," I griped to Chase as we waited for our drinks at the bar, my eyes locked on Shelby as she danced with yet another man at the charity gala.

Christ! She was beautiful, and it wasn't like I could fault any man for asking her to dance, but every single time it happened, it annoyed the hell out of me.

Shelby had knocked me on my ass from the moment I'd seen her at Tori's earlier.

Granted, she always made my cock stand at attention, but there was something about the way she looked tonight that stunned me.

It wasn't just that damn dick hardening, sexy dress, either, or the way those silky, endless curls fell loosely down her upper back.

It was the sensuality that she was throwing off tonight.

Hell, I loved it, but it pissed me off that I wasn't the only guy who noticed it.

I'd barely had a chance to speak a few words with her since we'd arrived at the gala. I'd made the mistake of going to get some drinks soon after we'd gotten here, and some bastard had swooped in for her first dance.

I'd lost track of how many men had caught her near the dance floor after that for another dance, but I was damn sick of watching her with other men.

Yeah, I'd told her to enjoy herself when we'd had dinner before the event, but I could sense that she really wasn't enjoying every dance.

Knowing Shelby, she felt obligated to accept any male who asked because she didn't want to offend anyone I knew or anyone who donated generously to this charity event.

She was currently in the arms of Jonas Meredith, a very wealthy, older entrepreneur that I'd always gotten along well with…until tonight.

"It might help if you'd ask her to dance yourself," Chase suggested as he handed me a whiskey. "She's been so busy that I'm not sure that anyone even knows that she came with you."

"I can't dance," I reminded him irritably.

Chase smirked before he took a sip of his wine. "You can dance as well as I can," he corrected after he'd swallowed. "You just don't most of the time, and you're out of practice. It's not like Dad didn't teach all of us to dance. There's no way you've forgotten how, Wyatt. Dancing was ingrained in us at childhood."

My chest was tight as I watched Shelby laugh, and then inconspicuously move a little to loosen Jonas's hold on her.

Bastard!

The older man wasn't the least bit subtle about his efforts to move his hand down until he could touch Shelby's ass.

"That asshole is married with several grandchildren," I growled. "And he's trying to feel Shelby up."

"He's probably had a little too much to drink," Chase said with a shrug. "He gets a little grabby after he's had a few. That's why Tori always makes some excuse not to dance with him at this event. Obviously, she didn't have a chance to warn Shelby about Meredith's wandering hands before she accepted."

I tossed back my whiskey and slammed the empty glass on the bar. "Then I guess I'm dancing tonight," I said hoarsely.

I might not be a great dancer, but Shelby needed rescuing right now. She was smiling and laughing, but I knew her well enough to recognize that her smile was fake as hell.

She couldn't wait to get away from Meredith, and I was going to make the end of this dance come a hell of a lot faster.

I ignored Chase's low, amused laugh as I strode toward the dance floor to rescue Shelby.

I'd avoided dancing because it was what I usually did.

But this time, things were different.

I'd brought Shelby here.

I hated seeing her dance with other men.

Therefore, she'd only dance…with me.

"Your dance is over, Meredith," I rumbled as I bodily moved him away from Shelby and took her into my arms. "Get lost, and don't come back."

The older man sputtered indignantly, but he didn't argue as he made his way off the dance floor.

"Are you okay?" I asked Shelby as she relaxed in my arms.

"I'm fine," she murmured close to my ear. "I just wasn't sure how to end the dance without making a scene. He made it pretty clear that he's a big donor. I'm sure he's a sweet man, but I think he's had a little too much to drink."

"If anybody ever touches you like that again, make a damn scene," I told her resolutely as my senses were bombarded by something other than her usual scent of strawberries and vanilla.

She was wearing the most cock stiffening scent that I'd ever inhaled. There was a touch of vanilla, but she also smelled like tropical, exotic flowers, and her fragrance had been driving me crazy all night long.

It was vibrant and bold, just like her behavior this evening.

I was barely able to keep a leash on my desire to haul her away like a caveman to a quieter area.

The only thing stopping me was my protectiveness toward Shelby. The media that was present at this event would make anything I did turn into salacious gossip.

That was the reason I'd been gritting my teeth all night, every time some lecherous asshole took her to the dance floor.

I'd never been reluctant to dance with *her*, even if I was out of practice.

I'd been hesitant to get this close to her because it was difficult to keep my hands off her.

But I'd rather take that chance than to watch another man lay hands on Shelby's curvaceous body.

"Every other dance you dance tonight will be with me," I informed her in a graveled voice as I tightened my arm around her waist possessively. "No more assholes trying to cop a feel. I don't give a rat's ass how big of a donor they are to this event. I should have asked for the first damn dance and made it clear that you were here with me."

Her body plastered perfectly against mine, she tilted her head back and smiled at me, that damn perfect dimple back on her cheek. "Jonas is the only man who got a little overenthusiastic," she said cheerfully.

"Doesn't matter," I said with a grunt. "You're here with me."

She shot me an exasperated look. "You're being bossy again. It's not like men are falling all over me. Most of them asked out of politeness, and the majority of them were married and old enough to be my father."

"Every one of them looked at you like they wanted to get you naked. I should know. I was watching every single one of them, and they were looking at you like I look at you."

"Then why didn't you just ask me to dance yourself?" she asked with a frown. "You're an incredible dancer."

I ignored her question since it wasn't one that I wanted to answer right now. "Have I told you how beautiful you look tonight?"

She nodded slowly, the gorgeous smile on those incredible, full lips growing wider and more sensual. "Many times, starting at Tori's house and spilling over into that amazing dinner we all had before we came here. It's been a major confidence booster since I know you aren't the kind of guy to bullshit me. Did I thank you for that dinner? The food was incredible."

It was a good dinner at one of San Diego's best restaurants. Tori, Chase, and their spouses had been with us, but all I'd been able to focus on was Shelby. I could have been eating at a fast food place. I'd barely registered the quality of the food earlier because all of my attention had been on her.

Not that Shelby wasn't always beautiful, but tonight, I could tell that she felt beautiful, and that confidence looked especially good on her.

"You did thank me for dinner," I confirmed as we moved around the floor, Shelby following me like we'd been dancing in sync like this forever. "But you still haven't explained why you didn't let Tori use my credit card. I told you that I wanted to pay for everything for this event since you're doing me a favor by being here with me."

Her body matched mine perfectly, and by now, she'd probably realized that every sway of her hips drove me closer to insanity.

My cock was harder than granite. I had absolutely no control over my dick when Shelby was in the same room with me.

Strangely, I really didn't give a shit about my personal discomfort right now. It felt too damn good to claim her and make sure every bastard in the room knew that she was with me.

"Do people always obey your every command?" she teased.

"Almost always," I answered honestly. "Everyone except you and my family, who basically ignore everything I say."

"I've never been especially good at taking orders," she said in a breathless tone that made my cock twitch. "I could afford to pay for those things thanks to your help on my blog. I don't need your money, Wyatt. I wanted to be here. And I'm having a good time, especially now that I'm dancing with the hottest guy at this gala. I guarantee that every woman here wants to be me right now, and I've never been that woman who gets the attention of Prince Charming. It's nice, even if it's only a fairy tale."

I scowled down at her. "I'm no Prince Charming."

She moved her arms around my neck as the music slowed, and shot me a mischievous look. "Oh no, you don't. If you're not Prince Charming, then I can't be Cinderella, and I'm enjoying this fantasy at the moment."

"Is that how you feel?" I asked skeptically.

Hell, if she was happy, then I'd gladly pretend to be anyone she wanted.

"Yes," she said with a small giggle. "I'm full of good food and champagne, and I'm extremely happy with my gorgeous rescuer right now. Don't pop my bubble, mister. Just keep dancing with me."

Hell, she was tipsy. Even though she'd been on the dance floor almost constantly, she'd managed to quickly toss back glasses of champagne that the staff had been passing around in abundance between dances. Anything stronger had to be grabbed at the bar, but she hadn't seemed to mind the champagne. In fact, she'd tossed a few back as soon as we entered the event, which made me wonder if she'd actually been a little nervous. I probably shouldn't take advantage of her somewhat intoxicated state, but I was a guy who always used every advantage I could get, and I saw no reason to stop that inclination right now. I pulled her tightly against me as the lights grew dimmer and the beat of the music slowed.

I'd stay right here, holding her as long as she wanted, doing whatever the hell I could to keep her smiling and laughing.

Shelby Remington hadn't experienced much joy in her own life over the last several years, yet she went out of her way to make other people happy.

"I'm not the hottest man in the room," I told her as my hand slid up her back to toy with her silken curls.

Christ!

Her damn scent.

Her damn seductive voice.

Her damn dress.

Her warm, willing, voluptuous body plastered against me.

Every single thing about her made me crazy, and it fucking tested my control.

But I was starting to actually enjoy this kind of madness.

I closed my eyes as she snuggled closer, her head resting on my shoulder as I savored how right it felt to be here like this with her.

One of the best parts about it was the fact that she was initiating that contact.

She wanted it as much as I did.

I still wasn't sure why she'd run away from this intense chemistry between the two of us, but I was certain it wasn't because she didn't want to be with me.

Okay, maybe she *was* a little touched by the alcohol at the moment, but she wasn't totally hammered, and I wasn't imagining the way her body responded to me.

"I didn't ask you to come with me tonight just to help me out." I'd had to force those words out of my mouth, but I'd already decided that figuring out what was in Shelby's head was worth putting my nuts on a chopping block. "I asked you to come because I wanted you to be my date. I want a hell of a lot more than to just be your friend, Shelby. I haven't been with anyone in a long time, but if you're willing to be more than a friend, I'll bust my ass to be that guy that you trust enough to give me a shot."

I felt her body tense up a little as she said cautiously, "I know we have this weird attraction between us, but—"

"It's not a brief attraction," I interrupted. "There's a lot more than that between the two of us. And yes, I'd like to find out exactly what it is."

Okay, I'd thrown the idea out there, and I really hated how much I wanted to hear her answer.

She pulled her head back to look at me, her expression confused as she asked softly, "Why?"

"Why does any single guy want a single woman?" I rasped. "There's something here. There's something about you that won't let me let go of the idea unless you're not interested. Jesus! Do you have any idea how uncomfortable this conversation is for me? Put me out of my misery here, woman. You said that you trust me?"

A plethora of emotions danced in her eyes as she looked back at me, and I wanted to pick her up, carry her out of here, and make her decision for her.

But I didn't.

This was an answer I was going to have to work for this time, and it was important enough for me to wait.

She started to shake her head slowly as she said, "We're from two different worlds, Wyatt. I'm a chef from a working class background. I'm not a gorgeous model, a celebrity, or anyone remotely special, and you're…Wyatt Durand."

"Bullshit!" I said harshly. "We're two single people who are attracted to each other. You're a beautiful, intelligent, hardworking woman who cares about other people and about your profession and what you do. There's no fucking reason that we *can't*."

"You don't date, and neither do I," she reminded me.

"Maybe I haven't in a long time, but you changed my mind, which rarely happens," I admitted. "Is that the only reason you're hesitating?"

She started to shake her head again. "No."

"Then tell me what the problem is, and I'll tell you that's bullshit, too."

She closed her eyes for a moment, and when she opened them again, I could see the same fear in her eyes that I'd seen in the days following that extraordinary kiss. "I haven't dated in a long time, either, Wyatt, and I'm not convinced that's really what you want."

"Why?" I questioned, genuinely confused.

"I think you're attracted to me, but I don't think you really want *me*. If I thought you really did, I'd do this. I'd take my chances and beg you to take me to bed, even though I'm not into casual sex. I want to be with you. I want to see what it would be like to be with a guy who's genuinely attracted to me."

Christ!

I couldn't have this fucking discussion with her here.

Frustrated with our environment, I growled next to her ear, "Get your purse. We're getting out of here, Cinderella."

She sighed. "Did the carriage just turn into a pumpkin?"

She sounded so forlorn that I had a hard time staying in a highly frustrated state of mind.

"No," I said gruffly as I grabbed her hand. "But I think it's time for me to convince you that if the goddamn slipper fits anyone, that woman is you."

I didn't say another word as we said our goodbyes to my family, and I hustled her out of the ball.

Chapter 18

Shelby

Wyatt had been unusually quiet on the way home from the gala. In fact, the tension between the two of us had been so heavy that I hadn't even tried to question him before I got my own thoughts straightened out.

I'd stayed silent on the ride home, trying to figure out why in the hell he was so determined to convince me that he wanted to date me.

If he was finally determined to try to forget the woman he cared about, why me?

It wasn't like Wyatt couldn't attract a woman from his own circle. Probably a gazillion of them if he'd just drop that standoffish attitude of his.

I lifted Xena onto the couch and rubbed her belly absently as the silence between the two of us started to get so uncomfortable that I had to force myself not to squirm.

The pleasant buzz I'd gotten from too much champagne was wearing off, and I didn't feel quite as bold as I had at the gala.

Neither one of us had gone upstairs to get out of our formal clothing, and I couldn't help watching Wyatt's every move.

I'd never seen a guy wear a tux as casually or as well as he did, and as I continued to ogle his massive, incredibly fit body, it was almost impossible for me to believe that he'd been completely sincere about wanting something other than friendship.

Yeah, we had this bizarre attraction to each other, but dating? Being his girlfriend? Some kind of intimate partner?

What I'd said to him earlier was true though.

If I thought there was a chance we could be something more, I'd probably throw caution to the wind and hop into his bed, even though the thought scared the hell out of me.

I was thirty-five years old, and I'd never experienced this kind of attraction.

But...

There was still the Simone thing.

He couldn't just will those emotions away by finding himself a girlfriend.

I took a sip of the wine he'd given me when we'd gotten into the house and watched as he poured himself a drink.

He threw back half of his drink as he strolled to the other end of sofa and finally perched on the wide arm of the couch like he was too antsy to sit down.

Troubled by his obvious edginess, I started to speak, "Wyatt, I—"

He held up a hand to stop me. "Don't, Shelby. The first thing I need you to explain to me is exactly why you think that I don't want you when I thought I'd made it pretty damn clear that I do. Do you still have feelings for your ex?"

I wanted to laugh because I wanted to ask him the very same question.

"No," I confessed softly. "I made a mistake, and I paid dearly for falling for that con. It wouldn't even be possible for me to still have feelings for a person I never even knew. It's part of my past. I learned from it, and I'm trying to move on with my life. I thought you preferred your solitude to having a woman around."

Well, any woman who *wasn't* his ex-girlfriend anyway.

"I wasn't interested in a romantic relationship and haven't been for a long time. Now, I'm interested, but the ironic part of this whole thing is that I finally found a woman I trust, and I'm not sure if she wants to give me a shot."

My breath caught as I saw the disappointment in his eyes.

I knew exactly what it was like to completely give up on relationships because you were disillusioned.

I'd have to be fool not to understand that Wyatt wasn't a guy who opened up like this to just anyone.

Obviously, he was sincere.

Maybe he was trying to get over his past and move on with a woman he...liked.

"I'm sorry," I said, my heart aching because I wanted nothing more than to throw myself in his arms and tell him I wanted him, which I did. "I just didn't understand that you were truly interested in me."

He shrugged. "What man wouldn't be, Shelby? There's not a damn thing about you that hasn't gotten my attention from the very beginning. You're different from any woman I've ever known."

My heart squeezed inside my chest at his words.

Truthfully, I'd never meet a man like Wyatt Durand, either, and I still wasn't quite sure what to do with this Wyatt who was, for him, spilling his guts to me.

I was honestly still stunned that he wanted to date me.

I guess the question was, could I start something with Wyatt while I still believed he was trying to shake off his feelings for an old lover?

Hell, maybe a new, honest relationship with someone who really cared was what he needed to get over her.

I stood, trying to find a way to feel less vulnerable. "A big part of me wants to give it a try, but I'm not going to lie to you and tell you that I'm completely ready for it." I took a deep breath, knowing I was going to have to bear my soul to Wyatt so he'd understand. "Justin cheated on me. Over and over again. I didn't know about all of the other women until it all came out during his prosecution. It completely killed any confidence I had left that I'd ever be enough for any man. I went through counseling in Montana, but those feelings have never quite gone away."

Wyatt reached out, took my hand, and entwined his fingers with mine. "I understand," he said huskily. "And I'm perfectly willing to convince you that you're more than enough."

Honestly, I believed him. He understood what it was like to be rejected for the man he was and be sought out only for his money.

I nodded and swallowed hard. "The last thing you need is a woman who doesn't completely have her shit together emotionally."

God, I really wanted to fall into bed with Wyatt, and take whatever he wanted to give me, but my insecurities when it came to romantic relationships were hard to shake.

Honestly, this entire discussion was surreal.

It wasn't that I didn't believe him when he said he was attracted to me, but there was still a part of me that didn't believe it was real.

His dark gaze locked with mine as he asked in a low, rumbly baritone. "I'm not going to push you for anything more right now, but for once in my life, I'm going to be an optimist. You didn't say you'd never be ready, and I have all the time in the world to prove that you're more than enough for *this* guy."

He wrapped an arm around my waist and pulled me between his legs.

I went willingly and slipped my arms around his neck as our gazes locked. "You've never had sex with me. My ex used to tell me that screwing me was like having sex with an ice cube."

"Bastard!" Wyatt cursed. "You have to know that wasn't true, right? I've kissed you, Shelby. You're probably the most responsive woman I've ever been with in my life. The guy was a sociopath."

I sighed. "Rationally, I know what he was trying to do, what his motivations were, but I don't have a lot of other relationships to compare it to. I had a long-term relationship with another chef in Chicago, but he cheated on me, too, eventually. So maybe I was an easy target for Justin because I wanted to believe that someone could see me as the only woman in the world who mattered to him. And I've never been as attracted to a man as I am to you, Wyatt. That's why this whole thing is terrifying."

He tugged me until my ass rested on his powerful thigh, and wrapped both arms around me so firmly that it almost felt…protective. "Okay, so you've had more than one idiot in your life," he said huskily. "I'm not one of those idiots, Shelby."

My heart tripped, and I tried to remind myself that my life and Wyatt's life were polar opposites.

How much could we really have in common other than this crazy physical chemistry?

And how long would that last when his heart still belonged to someone else?

But what else did we need if the chemistry and attraction was mutual?

Two single people having sex didn't have to involve a total commitment if they were both willing.

He wanted to be with me, and God knew that I wanted to know what it was like to be with a man who actually found me sensual and desirable.

Maybe I'd never had sex without some kind of commitment, but Wyatt made me tempted to try it out.

Honestly, my other committed relationships in my life had been a complete façade. The words had been spoken, but they'd never meant anything.

No amount of reasoning could change the profound feeling of rightness I experienced in Wyatt's arms.

Being rational also didn't work when it came to the way I felt about Wyatt.

Every cell in my body craved him, even though he was probably a perilous addiction.

He wasn't a normal guy, and I was a very mundane female with a boring job and a fulfilling but predictable life.

"No pressure, but if you decide that you're ready for more, I'm available, and fuck knows I'm willing. Unfortunately, I've never been a patient man, and I'll probably try to do anything possible to make the decision go my way," he said hoarsely as he put a hand behind my neck and tugged my mouth persuasively closer to his. "If you want me to back off, you'll have to tell me, because I'm a stubborn asshole."

I could feel his warm breath on my lips, and I wanted him to kiss me more than I wanted to take another breath.

I also wanted to strip off that very attractive tux from his body and beg him to fuck me, and put me out of my misery.

I'd never had great sex, and I really wanted to know what it would feel like to be with a guy who really wanted me like this.

Wyatt did.

I could feel it in every nerve ending in my body.

The chemistry between us was off the charts hot.

And the pent up desire to be that close to him was getting agonizingly painful.

He was waiting, frozen in place until I made the decision of whether or not I wanted him to touch me.

I could sense it.

"Kiss me, Wyatt. Please."

"Fuck!" he cursed. "I should be trying like hell to keep my hands off you, but that's not going to work for me. I can keep my dick in my pants for now, but I'm definitely going to have to touch you."

I wanted to sob with relief when his warm, insistent lips covered mine.

It felt like it had been a year since he'd kissed me, since I'd felt like this, rather than a few days.

The way that Wyatt kissed me like he couldn't wait another second to touch me set my entire body on fire.

I closed my eyes and savored the feeling of being desired by a man like Wyatt Durand.

He wasn't gentle.

He didn't work us slowly into a passion that built over time.

He was overwhelming from the moment he touched me, but I wasn't complaining. I wanted him with the same intensity, the same greediness.

I plastered my body against his, relishing the feel of his powerful body this close to mine.

Except I wanted…more.

I wanted to touch his bare skin, explore his powerful body, do insanely bold things that I'd never been able to do with a man before.

I had a feeling that almost nothing would be off-limits with Wyatt, and that he was a man who liked to satisfy a woman in every way possible.

"Wyatt," I panted as he released my mouth. "I want…"

"Don't say it, Shelby," he said in a gruff, warning voice. "Or I'll have you upstairs, out of this sexy damn dress, and in my bed naked before you can say another fucking word."

My core clenched hard in reaction to his words.

Dammit! I needed to put some space between myself and temptation personified.

But knowing what I should do didn't make it any easier to stand up again and put some distance between the two of us.

"You're right," I said shakily as I smoothed my dress down. "I probably need to think about this when I'm rational."

Wyatt caught my hand before I could go very far. "I already know what I want, Shelby. I'm not a man known for my patience, but I'll try to give you a chance to make your own decision. Now get your gorgeous ass upstairs before I change my mind. I'm used to getting whatever I want whenever I want it."

I squeezed his hand before I let it go. The old Wyatt was back on the surface, but I wasn't fooled. "You're not all that demanding," I teased.

"Don't let this patient demeanor fool you," he grunted. "When I finally lose my patience, I'll probably be the most demanding asshole you've ever seen."

Chapter 19

Wyatt

I stepped out of the shower later that evening still just as edgy as I'd been when I'd stepped in, even though I'd just gotten myself off for the second time in the same damn day.

"Fuck!" I cursed out loud as I grabbed a towel and started drying my nude body, my frustration of my earlier conversation with Shelby still eating at me.

Nothing had been decided.

I didn't have a fucking plan.

And I wasn't a guy who went into anything without some kind of strategy.

Chase had suggested that I listen to my emotions, but in my mind, that was the kind of shit that could get you killed.

Yeah, I wasn't in Delta anymore, but since my approach of being completely analytic and skeptical of anyone or anything had worked to keep my ass alive, I'd stuck with it. It hadn't hurt to be the same way with my business, either.

I'd let my guard down once with Simone, and look how that had turned out.

I knew right after that relationship ended that I dodged a bullet, that I'd really never known her, but her parting words had hurt enough that I'd been content with never trying that relationship shit again.

Until I'd met Shelby Remington, and she turned my very controlled world upside down. I was tired of trying to convince myself that my life hadn't changed since I'd met her.

Maybe my balls were blue, which I definitely didn't enjoy, but I liked coming home every night knowing I was going to see her.

Knowing my house would be filled with life.

Knowing I'd see her gorgeous smile and her beautiful face.

Knowing she'd ask me how my day went and expected more than a cursory response.

Maybe I wasn't used to a woman who really cared about me as a person, but it was fucking addicting.

However, for some damn reason I didn't understand, I wanted more than just a friendly face at the end of the day from her.

Even though I might end up sucking at it, I actually wanted to try the relationship thing again.

I wanted Shelby in my bed. Whatever head trip her ex had done on her to make her think she wasn't the most desirable female on the planet was bullshit, but part of her obviously still believed that.

I also wanted Shelby permanently living in my home. Solitude wasn't really all that appealing to me anymore, and the thought of coming home to dead silence was actually a little depressing.

Hell, I'd even told Tori and Cooper to stop looking for a home for Cujo because I was keeping her. Shelby adored the mutt, and I was used to having the canine diva around now. The dog was better off with me.

I understood Shelby's hesitance to commit to anything because of her past, and I'd meant it when I'd said that I'd wait until she was ready.

But that didn't mean that I wouldn't do everything in my power to make sure that she ended up with me. Maybe I didn't have a romantic bone in my body, but I'd treat her a hell of a lot better than either of those former idiots.

I tossed my towel in the hamper and entered the master bedroom naked, which was normally the way I slept.

I was ready to hop into bed, already thinking about how I could convince Shelby to see things my way, when I heard a noise downstairs.

My eyes flew to the bedside clock.

It was after one in the morning.

Shelby had said goodnight almost an hour ago and was headed toward her room.

I grabbed a pair of sweatpants and pulled them on before I slowly opened the bedroom door.

I'd set all of the alarms before I'd gotten into the shower.

There was no possible way anyone could have entered the house without me knowing about it.

It had to be Shelby, but what in the hell was she doing?

It wasn't until I'd gotten down the stairs that I heard her muttering to herself in the kitchen.

Even as I stood at the entryway to the kitchen, I couldn't understand what she was saying, but I couldn't help but stare at her gorgeous body as she moved around the room.

Xena was conked out in the corner, obviously exhausted from watching one of her humans work.

Shelby's sultry red curls were loose around her shoulders, which was unusual, especially when she was in the kitchen.

She was obviously wearing what she slept in. Her cotton shorts barely covered her ass cheeks, and the thin tank top did very little to confine her stunning breasts.

Not Shelby's normal cooking attire.

And she definitely was…cooking.

Or was she…baking?

Now that I'd arrived at the kitchen, I caught the scent of something that smelled suspiciously like freshly baked cookies.

I watched curiously as she opened the oven and shoved a baking sheet in before closing it again.

She always moved around the kitchen like she was happier here than any other room in the house, but I'd never seen her in this room as scantily clad as she was at the moment.

And it was a sight that I couldn't stop watching, even though I probably should.

I folded my arms across my chest and leaned my shoulder against the entrance to the kitchen, unable to stop myself from staring.

My cock was rock-hard from imagining those long, bare legs wrapped around my waist as I buried myself to my balls inside her.

Christ! I had no idea how much longer I could hold out before I seriously tried to seduce her into my bed, but I seemed to be enjoying the agony. I couldn't move away and go back to bed if I wanted to right now.

And I didn't want to.

I wanted to know what the hell she was doing baking cookies at this time of the night.

She'd gotten up early to go out with Torie, and she'd consumed more alcohol than usual earlier.

Shelby shouldn't be flitting around the kitchen in a baking frenzy like a beautiful, half-naked fairy, but she was.

"I can't do it," she muttered as she attacked more cookie dough in the bowl, her words finally somewhat understandable. "I really, really, really want to, but I just…shouldn't."

I raised a brow. Okay, now I was more interested in her words than I was at the back view of her body and her lush ass.

What exactly is it that she shouldn't do?

Oh, hell no, she *should* and she *would*.

If she was thinking about our earlier conversation, there was no way in hell I was going to let her talk herself out of giving this relationship a shot.

"What in the hell are you doing?" I questioned, no longer able to stay silent.

She startled and swung around quickly, her adorably startled face smudged with flour. "Oh, God, you scared me. I'm so sorry. Did I wake you up? I know I probably shouldn't be making noise down here at this hour."

I shook my head as I straightened up and walked into the kitchen. "I wasn't asleep. And you live here, Shelby. You can go anywhere you want in this house. But it is a little different for you to be in the kitchen this late. Why are you down here?"

I hated the fact that she obviously felt more like a guest here who didn't want to disturb a host.

"I'm baking," she said sheepishly. "When I'm frustrated or trying to work out a problem, I bake cookies like I used to do with my Aunt Millie. I'm not a pastry chef, but the smell of cookies and the familiar actions of making them are relaxing."

I moved closer and looked at all of the cookie sheets filled with fresh baked cookies as I drawled, "I'm assuming you have something pretty heavy on your mind. It looks like you're making enough cookies for the entire neighborhood."

She shrugged. "I got a little carried away. I decided to do chocolate chip."

Shelby looked so adorably embarrassed that I wanted to ease her nervousness somehow, but I knew if I touched her right now, I was screwed. I wouldn't be able to walk away.

I picked up a warm cookie from one of the sheets and popped half of it into my mouth.

I closed my eyes and savored the explosion of chocolate and sweetness as I chewed.

When I opened my eyes again and swallowed, Shelby was reaching into the fridge for the milk.

"I got it," I insisted as I took the carton from her hands and reached for two glasses. "This isn't a kitchen where you have to serve anyone. So do you want to tell me what's on your mind?"

I put her milk beside her, but she made no move to drink it or to grab herself a cookie.

Instead, her focus seemed to be glued to the bare skin of my chest and torso as if she really liked what she was seeing.

It was probably the same lust-filled look I'd been giving her earlier, but damned if it didn't feel good to know she felt the same way.

Her eyes flew to mine, her expression guilty as hell, like she'd just realized she was gawking at me.

She suddenly turned her attention to the last of her cookie dough and started to drop it onto a cookie sheet as she said unhappily, "I think you already know what I was thinking about."

I popped the rest of the cookie in my mouth and swallowed it before I answered, "You said you were frustrated. I was just wondering if I could help."

She didn't look at me as she continued to drop cookies on the sheet. "I think you just noticed the way I was looking at you. Do you really think it helps my sexual frustration to be in the same room with you right now."

I almost choked on my milk.

Alright, *now* we were getting somewhere. She was suffering the same way I was at the moment.

Oddly, there was no satisfaction in that knowledge.

There was just a primitive need to end that discomfort for her.

She continued, "After what happened with my ex, I had no desire to have sex with anyone. I didn't think about it. I didn't want it. I was perfectly happy with staying busy and burying any sexual desire that I had. Until I met you. Now it's almost impossible for me not to think about having sex with you about a million times a day, and I don't like it. It makes me uptight and crazy, and getting myself off doesn't help. At all."

I started to grin as I watched her take the cookies out of the oven and slam the oven door with more force than necessary after she put the last batch in.

Really, it wasn't funny. I knew what that edginess was like, but Shelby was so damn cute when she was irritated that I couldn't stop myself from being a little amused. "Do you honestly think that I don't feel the same way?" I asked her. "That I haven't jacked off thinking about you, too? Say the word, Shelby, and I'll put both of us out of our misery."

There was crazy sexual chemistry between the two of us.

If nothing else, I could fix that issue, at least for a while.

She turned to me and crossed her arms over her mouthwatering breasts. "If you really want to know, that's what I was thinking about, Wyatt. I was trying to decide if I could hop into bed with a guy who still has feelings for another woman. It would be an idiotic thing to do, but I'm still tempted. I'm thirty-five years old, and I have absolutely no clue what sex would be like with a man who is really physically attracted to me. And I know you are attracted to me."

"And exactly who do you think I still have feelings for?" I asked as I searched her face to try to figure out what the hell she was thinking.

"Your ex," she said emphatically. "You said you didn't have a heart to give away. I think part of it still belongs to her. I'm not asking for you to be crazy about me or anything, but it might be uncomfortable to sleep with you if you still care about her."

Simone?

Oh, hell no.

But as I looked into Shelby's hesitant gaze, I knew that was truly what she thought.

"Do you really think I'm that much of an idiot?" I grumbled, offended that she thought I'd be hanging onto any feelings for a woman who had never given a shit about me in the first place.

She shook her head slowly. "No. You're probably the most intelligent person I know, but sometimes feelings last—"

"Mine didn't," I growled as I moved closer to her and slapped a hand on each side of the counter, essentially penning her in until I had a chance to explain *exactly* how I felt. "She burned me, Shelby. I'll admit that the relationship made me wary, but I'd have to be a total idiot to still be pining for a female who probably didn't care whether or not I ever came back from a deployment alive. Justin was your one big mistake. She was mine. End of story. The only female I even think about right now is you, and I *am* crazy about you, whether you want that or not. Do you understand that?"

I waited long enough to see her nod that she understood, and then I forced myself to turn away and started to walk back toward the stairs.

If I didn't leave, I knew I'd probably do something she *definitely* wasn't ready for right now.

Chapter 20

Shelby

I stood there for several minutes after Wyatt's departure, my heart hammering against my chest wall because of his firm denial about having any feelings left for Simone.

He doesn't love her. He doesn't feel anything for her anymore.

Not only had he made it clear that he didn't have feelings for Simone, but he'd let me know that he *was* crazy about…me.

I finally moved to take the cookies out of the oven and to finish cleaning up.

I hadn't realized until those words had left Wyatt's lips that he'd said exactly what I wanted to hear. What I'd *needed* to hear because I felt exactly the same way, and feeling that damn vulnerable alone was terrifying.

I started the dishwasher after I'd cleaned the kitchen, wondering if he was angry or if I'd hurt him by assuming that he still had feelings for a woman who didn't deserve them.

I smiled a little as I heard Xena snoring comfortably on her bed in the corner of the living room. At some point, she'd obviously gotten bored watching me bake cookies.

I climbed the stairs, my heart aching because I'd jumped to a conclusion due to my damn insecurities.

Wyatt had never been anything but honest with me, and I'd screwed up by thinking he still cared about another woman.

Wyatt was attracted to me.

He liked me, and we were friends.

He felt the same crazy chemistry I did.

Did I really want to toss the opportunity away to explore this relationship because I was still a little insecure after my nightmare marriage to a jerk?

I'd told him we came from different worlds, but that had really never mattered, either.

It was just another excuse to avoid getting hurt in the future.

I stopped at Wyatt's bedroom door, but I couldn't hear anything but silence.

He's probably asleep.

It was after two in the morning.

My heart heavy, I went to my bedroom, sat on my bed, and picked up my phone.

Maybe I should text him so he'll see it first thing in the morning when he wakes up.

If I didn't let him know how I was feeling somehow, I'd probably never sleep. The last thing in the world I wanted was to inadvertently hurt the one man who had been really good to me.

Me: *I'm so sorry, Wyatt. I made an assumption I shouldn't have made. I think I was insecure, and I assumed it wasn't possible for this to be anything more than a passing attraction because I'm not really the type of woman a hot billionaire would notice. I should have just asked you for the truth like you asked me about my feelings for Justin. I hope I didn't mess this up, because I know what I want now. And just FYI…I'm crazy about you, too.*

I pressed the button to send the text before I could change my mind.

Whatever happened tomorrow, I was going to be honest with Wyatt and not let my stupid, leftover self-doubt from my trauma with Justin get in the way of my future relationships.

I'd isolated myself long enough.

If a man as self-contained as Wyatt could speak his mind, I could find the courage to do the same thing.

If I didn't explore this inexplicable attraction Wyatt and I had, I knew I'd regret it for the rest of my life.

I'd never felt like this before, and I might never experience this kind of a connection with a guy again.

Regardless of what my ex-husband had said, I was apparently enough for Wyatt at the moment, and I needed to start believing exactly what he said.

He wasn't a charmer and he didn't spew bullshit, which was one of the many reasons I found him so attractive.

My phone still in my hand, I startled as my phone pinged from an incoming text.

Wyatt: *Do you really expect me to sleep after a text like that?*

I frowned as my thumbs flew to text him back.

Me: *I thought you were already asleep. I couldn't sleep until I apologized. Are you angry?*

Wyatt: *No. Not if you really meant what you just typed. I'm assuming that I'm the hot billionaire you were referring to in that text.*

I smiled, wondering how he could doubt his ridiculous hotness. Seeing that massive expanse of bare skin over his muscular torso and chest in the kitchen had almost sent me into a lust-filled meltdown. Wyatt was ripped, and I'd been salivating to trace those six-pack abs with my tongue.

Me: *You're the only really hot billionaire I'm attracted to. Is it really weird that we're texting each other when we live in the same house?*

Wyatt: *Nope. If I come over there, we won't be talking. It's safer. Now that I'm fully aware of your insecurities, I think I'd rather make sure that they're banished before anything else happens. You matter to me, Shelby, and not just because I want to fuck you.*

Tears welled up in my eyes, and when I blinked, they started to track down my face like a river.

At my age, it probably shouldn't be the first time I'd heard that from a guy, but it was, and those words meant more to me than any fake compliments ever could.

Me: *I care about you, too, Wyatt.*

Wyatt: *Do we want to discuss the terms of this new relationship?*

Me: *No rules and no terms. This isn't a business deal. Let's just be honest with each other.*

Wyatt: *Agreed. I'm officially asking you out on our first date tomorrow. Fair warning…I'll probably suck at the whole dating thing, but I'll give it my best shot.*

My heart skittered.

Although it was hard for me to comprehend, Wyatt really wasn't confident about his appeal to women. Tori had made that clear to me.

He had no idea that women would be falling all over him if he didn't scare them away with his grumpy, cynical hardheadedness.

Me: *It really doesn't matter if you suck at it or not. I already like you, and you don't have to worry about whether I'm attracted to you or not.*

Wyatt: *Any idea of what you'd like to do?*

I thought about that for a moment.

Me: *Honestly, I'd just like to do something for fun. I've been here for a year, and I've been to almost none of the fun things or San Diego attractions like Balboa Park and the zoo. Or Sea World. Those things would probably be ridiculously boring for you though since you grew up here. I've also never done escape rooms. Maybe it's a little silly, but I think it would be fun. I'm open to whatever. You're the one who knows California. I'm a recent transplant.*

Until recently, I'd had no friends in San Diego, and I'd been entirely focused on making a living.

I hadn't sought out anything to do for fun for years.

Wyatt: *I'm not exactly an expert on fun things to do, either. You know me, Shelby. Do I seem like the kind of guy who looks for fun things to do? I haven't been to any of the attractions since I was kid.*

I sighed.

He probably hadn't since he was a workaholic who had no idea how to have fun.

Wyatt was way too solemn. He took the world and himself much too seriously.

He'd had a happy childhood, but after that, his life had been about duty, family, and sacrifice for the good of Durand Industries.

It was probably beyond time that Wyatt started thinking about doing things for his own enjoyment.

Me: *Then I think we should see what fun feels like together.*

Wyatt: *I'd like to see what a lot of things feel like when we're together.*

A soft laughed escaped my lips because I could almost hear his voice grumbling that comment.

It was flirtatious in a Wyatt sort of way.

Me: *It wasn't my idea to wait. I know what I want.*

Wyatt: *You sure about that?*

Me: *Yes. How long will it take me to convince you that I am now?*

Now that he'd told me that he didn't have feelings for another woman and that he was crazy about me, I didn't have any reservations anymore.

Wyatt: *One more late night baking session in the kitchen in those skimpy pajamas will probably kill me off.*

Me: *They aren't exactly sexy?*

I wore those shorts and a tank for comfort.

They weren't an outfit that would seduce any guy.

Wyatt: *On you, they're definitely sexy.*

I sat there for a minute, trying to figure out if he was serious.

I finally decided that he was because Wyatt never said anything he didn't mean.

I had a few body issues from my previous relationship, but I was starting to realize that Wyatt didn't seem to see anything about me that wasn't attractive to him.

I wasn't quite sure how to handle that, but I could definitely get used to being with someone who didn't point out every fault I had.

Me: *Thank you.*

Wyatt: *For what?*

Me: *For making me feel like I'm attractive again. I haven't felt that way in a long time.*

Wyatt: *You're beautiful. I even thought so when you thought I was an asshole. Now take your gorgeous ass to bed before I come over there so I can convince you in person.*

My body shivered in anticipation, and I wanted to beg him to come over here, but I didn't.

I felt closer to Wyatt than I ever had before, and for now, that was enough.

Chapter 21

Wyatt

"That was so much fun," Shelby said with a happy laugh as we lingered over our drinks after a good Italian dinner the next evening. "But it was hardly fair that you had our puzzles and clues figured out before I ever got close. How did you do it? How did you work out the puzzles without even asking for hints?"

The escape room afternoon had been highly entertaining. It was something I'd excelled at because I'd developed a lot of critical thinking and problem-solving abilities with time limits in the military.

"How do you know I had it all figured out? Maybe I didn't. Maybe I was waiting for you to solve everything because I couldn't do it," I told her before I downed the last of my drink.

She shot me an exasperated look. "Maybe because you moved on the second I said I had one figured out. I didn't even tell you what the solution was before you were working on the next item. You were just going through the motions to help me get there both times."

"You were quick," I protested. "From what I understand, there are a lot of people who don't solve them the first time."

She was brilliant, and I'd been thoroughly impressed by how quickly her mind worked to resolve a puzzle. Not that I'd ever doubted her skills. She was a problem solver who could roll with whatever was happening and make it look easy. I'd never once suspected that she was working with a short staff at Chase's reception, and I had a feeling that wasn't the first time she'd had to figure things out quickly.

She'd dealt with a high pressure career for years in a field where failure wasn't an option if she wanted to keep her job.

"How did you discover this restaurant?" she asked curiously before she took another sip of wine.

I shrugged. "Chase says it's some of the best Italian food he could find outside of Italy. He brought Savannah here recently. I have to admit that he was right."

It wasn't a fancy place, but I wasn't going to impress Shelby with a fancy restaurant unless the food was really exceptional, so I'd opted for the good food.

She sighed. "I've never been to Italy, but this was delicious, and the service was excellent. I like that we got patio seating. It's so nice outside tonight."

My gut was satisfied with the food, and Shelby was happy, so I'd done what I'd set out to do today.

I hadn't expected to have that much fun at the escape room, but I had.

Watching Shelby, being with her when she was happy and laughing until that adorable dimple showed often was probably the most satisfying thing I'd done in a long time.

There probably weren't many women in my circle who would have found an escape room to be that entertaining, but I liked that Shelby could find happiness in such a small thing.

Hell, I'd been willing to fly her anywhere for this date, but she'd insisted that she'd rather do something fun here in San Diego.

She wasn't impressed with my money.

All she wanted was to be in my company doing something fun, and it didn't really matter to her that it was a very cheap date for me.

It was humbling that she actually just wanted to be with me, and that she didn't give a shit what we were doing.

"Tell me more about Chase and Savannah," Shelby requested. "How did they meet? I've gotten to know her pretty well, but I don't know much about their relationship history. Were they together long before they got married?"

Hell, it was an innocent enough question, and I knew Shelby was asking because she was genuinely curious. But since she didn't know about Last Hope yet, I had to be careful. She probably knew that Savannah had been kidnapped, but she didn't know the details about how Chase and I were involved in her rescue. "Chase and I have known Savannah for most of our lives. She's been Tori's best friend since childhood. Did she tell you that she was kidnapped near the Darien Gap in Panama when she was on assignment there doing a story?"

Shelby nodded. "She did. It's so crazy that all of my female friends have gone through similar experiences. Vanna told me about getting attacked by one of Chase's corporate enemies, too."

Not so weird, really, since all of them had been Last Hope rescues or had gotten involved with the organization in some way, but since Shelby was in the dark about Last Hope, it was impossible for her to connect the dots.

"Chase stepped up to take care of her once she came back to the States after the kidnapping in Panama. I guess it took them that long to realize that they were meant to be together. My brother flipped out after that second attack on Savannah by someone who saw us as the enemy. They almost separated because he was being an idiot about putting her in danger by being with him. Once he got his head on straight, he couldn't wait to marry her. That wedding got planned in record time, as you probably already know." I hesitated before I added, "Chase and I both have enemies, Shelby. You can't be a major player in our business without pissing people off. You should probably know that once the public realizes that you're an important person in my life, it could put you at risk. I don't put myself out there as much as Chase does, and my face is probably less recognizable. He's always been the spokesperson for Durand because he's a lot more personable when he's speaking to the media. But I'm still the co-CEO for the company, and I've made a lot of decisions that made me enemies."

She shook her head slowly. "Do you really think I'm going to let something that's unlikely to happen decide whether or not I'm with you, Wyatt? I was probably the most despised woman in Montana for a while after what Justin did."

"You were a victim, too," I growled.

She shrugged. "Not everyone saw it that way. It was guilt by association. Some people had a hard time believing I was innocent and ignorant because we were married and living in the same home. I stayed with Kaleb because I didn't want to put Aunt Millie in danger. I didn't leave the house. I couldn't go anywhere except to testify. Justin may have been the one who went to prison, but I felt like I was living in my own prison there. That's why I had to move. I had to go someplace where people didn't recognize my face everywhere I went. It took a while, but I finally realized that I didn't have to live in isolation anymore here."

Fuck! I'd known things were bad for her in Montana, but I'd never realized quite how bad they were because it had been a regional story. It must have been pure hell for her to put up with the public abuse while she was still trying to get over that bastard's betrayal.

"Are you sure you're ready to go back there again?" I asked with a frown.

"No," she answered with a weak smile. "I'll probably never feel ready, but my family wouldn't be encouraging me to do it if the story hadn't died down completely. It's the last thing in my past that I have to resolve. My entire family lives there, and most of the people who know me in Crystal Fork aren't going to judge."

My gut was telling me that Montana was a bad idea for her right now, but I'd chalked that up to the fact that I was protective when it came to Shelby.

Kaleb would make sure that Shelby was safe and that she didn't face any criticism there. He knew the environment better than I did. Marshall had also done a lot of digging into her past looking for anyone who still held a grudge against Shelby, and he'd come up empty-handed. Still, there could be some psycho we didn't know about who hated her there enough to come here and break into her home.

Maybe that was something we needed to look at more closely.

If going back to Montana was something that Shelby really needed to do to feel like that chapter in her life was closed, I wanted her to do what she needed to do. However, before she went, I had to make sure we'd exhausted any possibility that she'd expose herself to any risks while she was there.

"What happened?" Shelby said softly. "You look so serious. Are you thinking about the fact that someone could dig up my past someday because I'm involved with a very rich and very powerful man. It could happen, Wyatt. My past could expose you to public scrutiny at some point. I've never thought about that, but you're a very private man. It wouldn't be pleasant."

The hesitation in her beautiful eyes made my chest ache. Shelby had been through so much in the last few years, and she was obviously still blaming herself for one fucking mistake. "Do you really think I give a flying fuck what anyone else thinks? I'd destroy anyone who says anything about your past without a single hesitation, not because it bothers me, but because it would hurt you. Chase and I have faced plenty of public scrutiny about things that aren't even true. If the press can't find a story, they make one up. I've learned to ignore the shit that isn't true and squash anything or anyone that would hurt my family."

"I don't care about myself," she replied matter-of-factly as she reached out and gripped my hand tightly. "I just don't want anything from my past to ever hurt you, Wyatt."

I couldn't remember a time when anyone had ever worried about how I felt. Most people assumed I didn't have any emotions. "It won't," I rumbled as I gripped her hand, not wanting her to pull away from me over something that meant nothing to me. "It's unlikely that anyone will ever dig up your past, and other than the fact that it might hurt you, I don't give a shit. For the most part, the press leaves me alone because I'm boring."

"No. It's probably because they're terrified of you," she said with a small laugh.

She wasn't wrong. I'd gone after more than one news agency that had tried to dramatize Tori's first kidnapping, and the news had died down before it had ever really started.

I raised a brow. "I think you're the only person who isn't afraid of me. I'm no Prince Charming to anyone except you, Cinderella."

She smiled until that adorable dimple was denting her cheek. "Because no one else looks very hard. Beneath that cynical, grumpy exterior, I see who you are, Wyatt. It's almost hard to believe that other people can't, but I'm not complaining. As hot as you are, it would suck having to peel other women off your incredible body every day."

"What if I'm not really the princely guy you see?" I asked hoarsely. "I'm not a nice man most of the time, Cinderella, and that's a hard title for a guy like me to live up to."

She let go of my hand and smacked me playfully on the forearm. "You don't have to live up to it. You're already the hottest and the most thoughtful guy I've ever dated, and if you deny it again, you're going to piss me off."

I grinned at her, resigned to letting her think what she wanted for now. "I guarantee there will be plenty of instances when I'll piss you off in the future."

She shrugged. "Same. I can be stubborn sometimes. I still have some leftover baggage from my past, and I have some odd habits, like my cookie baking in the middle of the night when I'm upset or frustrated. Maybe you should take some of those cookies to your office tomorrow to get rid of them."

Although I never wanted to see her upset or frustrated again, I wasn't going to complain about a houseful of cookies. I'd already devoured several of them with my coffee earlier this morning.

"Not happening," I informed her. "Those cookies are mine, and since I don't plan on upsetting you in the near future, I'm keeping them."

Adding another mile or two to my morning run would be worth it if I could keep those cookies to myself.

Her completely delighted laugh reached places inside of me that I never knew existed before. Places that could probably use a little warmth after an extremely long ice age.

"You're impossible when it comes to my food," she accused.

"Guilty," I replied without an ounce of remorse.

Truthfully, I was probably impossible about *anything* that involved her, her safety, or her happiness, but I really needed to keep a lid on that shit right now.

Shelby Remington needed to trust me completely after what she'd been through, and I'd be damned if I was going to lose my shit like my brother and my friends did with their women.

I could handle the blue balls and the frustration of waiting if it got me exactly what I wanted in the future.

Chapter 22

Shelby

I sighed as Wyatt and I sat and watched the sunset on the water from his patio.

We'd spent a lazy Saturday at Tori's house swimming in her pool and eating burgers on the grill in the late afternoon.

Everyone had been there, which had given me a chance to catch up with Taylor and Harlow in person, too.

The last few weeks since I'd started officially dating Wyatt had probably been the happiest of my entire life.

The shift in my relationship with Wyatt wasn't exactly subtle, but it wasn't blatantly demanding, either.

It was…seductive.

And I'd had a very hard time not caving in and just telling him that I wanted him to take me to bed.

I was beyond ready.

We were two consenting adults who cared about each other, but I got the feeling that Wyatt was trying to make sure I trusted him.

He didn't try to convince me with words.

He simply acted like a devoted partner, and that was even harder to resist than words.

I was thirty-five years old, and I'd never had a guy who treated me like Wyatt did on a daily basis.

He rarely stayed late at work unless he had to anymore, and he'd even taken a few extra days off to surprise me with something new. He also made it a point to take me out to dinner often to try new restaurants, even if I had done a food video that day and had plenty of things prepared for dinner.

Wyatt made sure that we hit every tourist attraction in San Diego, and he'd even seemed to enjoy them, even if he probably secretly thought they were a tourist trap.

Once we'd finished covering those attractions, we'd started to go outside of the city.

Wyatt included Xena whenever possible, but since the weather was hot and the little Frenchie and hot weather didn't mix well, he got a dog sitter if we were going out for the day.

I'd probably seen more of California in the last few weeks than I had since I'd moved here.

I'd discovered that my concerns about the two of us having nothing in common were totally unfounded. Wyatt and I enjoyed a lot of the same things.

We loved checking out new restaurants together, getting outdoors whenever possible and spending time with his family and friends, who were now my friends, too.

More often than not, he gave me the option of where we were going when we had time off together.

Wyatt had taken the day off yesterday. We'd driven to Idyllwild to check out the San Jacinto Mountains simply because I happened to mention that I missed the peacefulness of the summers in Montana sometimes.

We'd done an easy hike, chilled out, and then had dinner at a cute café before we headed back to San Diego in the evening.

Okay, so Idyllwild wasn't exactly Montana. You could find peaceful places in California, but there were generally a lot of other people who wanted a piece of the serenity, too. The population in Southern California made it difficult to ever truly be alone in the great outdoors. But the trip had been heartbreakingly sweet because all Wyatt had wanted to do was make me happy, and he'd accomplished his mission. I'd enjoyed every moment that we'd spent soaking in the scenery together.

Wyatt thoroughly spoiled me. I had his full attention whenever we were together, and he seemed more relaxed and happier than I'd ever seen him.

He cared about me. He was attracted to me, and he made sure I knew it every single day, which had gone a long way in squashing my previous insecurities.

We'd gotten to know each other better, but he still occasionally surprised me.

Earlier today at Tori's house, I'd discovered that Wyatt had a wide range of adrenaline inducing skills including skydiving, rock climbing, scuba diving, and flying. I wasn't sure how many of his crazy skills had been acquired in the military, but he had mentioned that he'd been scuba diving and flying since he was young. They were activities he'd done with his dad, so those skills had been honed well before his career in the military had even started.

"Is there anything dangerous that you don't do as a hobby?" I asked him jokingly once the sun had disappeared from the horizon.

He grinned at me from the lounge chair next to mine. "I haven't done any of those things recently, but I have to admit that I've never seen the point in base jumping or bungee jumping. I also don't ride horses or I would have taken you to ride already since you enjoy it."

My lips curved up, but I tried not to laugh since he was obviously serious about not riding horses. "I completely get the other two, but I don't understand your aversion to horses. I could ride a horse almost from the time I could walk. If you know what you're doing, they're not dangerous."

"I was five when my parents decided I needed a pony ride," he drawled. "I fell and split my head open. It was so traumatic at the time that I still remember it, and I've never gotten on a horse since. Luckily, there are other modes of transportation that are a lot more comfortable than a horse."

I smiled back at him. "You have no idea what you're missing. There's nothing more relaxing than riding. Especially in a place with beautiful scenery."

"You obviously miss it," Wyatt observed.

I nodded as I took a sip of my water and swallowed it. "I do. But it's not exactly practical to own a horse in the city. One of the things I loved about moving back to Montana from Chicago was the fact that I got to ride a lot more. But I'm starting to love San Diego, too. It's nice not having to deal with the brutal winter weather, and being near the water is incredibly relaxing. There's also a much bigger variety of things to do here."

Wyatt shrugged. "It's not like we can't visit other places, Shelby. I can take you anywhere you want to go without much effort. If you want to see your family more often, we could just hop on my jet and go. They're a fairly short plane ride away."

He'd do it.

I knew that.

It wasn't the first time he'd offered to jet me off somewhere on a moment's notice.

God, that was one of the really seductive things about Wyatt.

He wanted to make me happy, and he was willing to do almost anything to make it happen.

I couldn't remember a time when a guy had given a shit about my well-being, and now that I had one, I realized what had been missing in my previous relationships.

"I'm already totally spoiled, thank you very much," I retorted. "And the picnic is next weekend. I'm a little nervous, but I'll be happy to see my family and people in town who want to see me."

Wyatt immediately reached out, took my hand in his, and entwined our fingers. "Enjoy seeing the people you want to see, and ignore the rest of them. They're not worth your anxiety about it. Everything will be fine, Shelby. Honestly, I am a little worried myself, but not about the town gossip. I don't like you going there without my security."

I'd heard him express those concerns several times over the last few weeks. Even though nothing had happened, Wyatt still had his security on my ass everywhere I went when he wasn't with me.

He had a concealed carry permit, which was difficult to get in California, but it didn't surprise me since a guy like Wyatt probably needed personal protection. He rarely used his own security personnel for himself or when we were together, but he was always armed with a Glock when the two of us went out anywhere.

According to Tori, Wyatt was an expert marksman, and I had no reason to doubt that claim considering his background in special forces.

However, I was starting to wonder if, after so much time had passed, we could back off on my security.

I'd insisted on not taking his security with me to Montana because I wanted some alone time with my family. His team was good at blending in when they were in the city, but they'd stick out like a sore thumb in Crystal Fork, Montana.

The police had gotten nowhere, and I was now willing to accept that the break-in was just a random incident.

Unfortunately, Wyatt *wasn't* willing to accept that yet, and because I didn't want him to worry, I hadn't protested about his security tailing me all the time. I'd actually gotten so used to it that it really didn't bother me that much anymore.

"I'll be on Kaleb's jet on the way there, and you're coming to pick me up," I reminded him. "I'm staying with Kaleb, and he's not going to let me go anywhere alone. Nothing is going to happen to me, Wyatt. It's been a long time, and nothing else has happened. I think we have to assume that it was a one-time incident."

"Assuming anything is dangerous, Shelby," Wyatt answered, his tone deadly serious now. "It really hasn't been that long, and this wasn't a typical burglary."

"The police are at a standstill with the case," I said softly. "No one can find anything, and nothing has happened. It makes sense to assume that it was done by someone with a really bad sense of humor."

"It wasn't amusing," Wyatt growled. "We're still working on it, and we'll eventually figure it out. I'm not going to be comfortable with you going anywhere alone until we do. My gut is telling me it's not safe."

While there was a part of me that loved the protective, alpha male part of Wyatt, I also didn't want him to worry about my safety.

There was probably nowhere safer than Crystal Fork.

If someone really wanted to hurt me, they probably would have tried something already, security or no security.

"I'll be fine, Wyatt. Are you going to worry the entire week that I'm alone in Montana?" I queried gently.

"Probably," he said gruffly as he reached out a powerful arm, wrapped it around my waist, and bodily pulled me into his chair until I was on top of him.

I squealed, and then I laughed as I landed in his chair instead of my own.

It was a big lounger, something suitable for a guy his size, but I still ended sprawled on top of him, and his powerful grip wasn't going to allow me to go anywhere.

Our eyes locked, and his tone was grim as he stated, "There will never be a time when I won't be concerned about your safety, even if we do resolve the break-in. There's a lot of crazy people out there, Shelby, and just being with me could put you in harm's way. Maybe that's something you should still consider while you're trying to make up your mind about whether or not you want to take me on for something permanent."

His beautiful gray eyes were tumultuous as he stared back at me, and his arm tightened even more possessively around my waist.

I understood his concern because of what had happened with Savannah, but it still pissed me off just a little that he thought I'd run away from him because of that kind of threat.

And I'd already made up my mind a long time ago on the more permanent relationship.

I lifted my hand and palmed his stubbled jaw. "Do you really think I'd give you up for something that has almost no chance of happening, Wyatt? I know that fear is very real for you, but I'd never give up a man like you for something like that. I wouldn't give up my happiness for something like that. Was Savannah willing to give up Chase, even after what happened to her? No, she wasn't. Be cautious if it makes you feel better. I can handle that. But don't ever assume that I'd toss away a guy who makes me this happy over something like that. It pisses me off. I know I've made some dumb choices in the past that I regret, but I'm not an idiot."

He lifted a brow. "No, you're definitely not an idiot. Are you happy, Shelby?"

"I was until you gave me that stupid warning," I snipped back.

He smirked, his gray eyes lighter and warmer than they were a moment ago. "How long are you planning on being angry?"

"I'm not sure," I said stubbornly, but I made no effort to get up and leave the delicious heat of his massive body. "I'll let you know when I decide that I'm not pissed off about it anymore."

Wyatt moved quickly for a guy his size, and before I knew it, I was flat on my back beneath him, staring up at his handsome face.

His gaze was heated, but his gorgeous lips were tilted up into a teasing smile. "What can I do to convince you to get over it faster?" he asked in that low, sexy baritone that made me want to rip his clothes off.

Um…Fuck me?

That would probably work.

After a few weeks of agonizing, sensual torture from being this close to Wyatt, that was exactly what I needed.

I just wasn't exactly sure how to tell him that I didn't have a single hesitation about being his girlfriend anymore.

Hell, I actually wanted every female on the planet to know he was mine.

Wyatt had systematically broken down every one of my defenses and fears.

We'd talked about it.

He'd shown me in every way possible that he wanted me, that he cared about me, and I believed him.

I was convinced.

I wanted Wyatt so damn much that I didn't care about any lingering insecurities that I might have anymore.

What I had with Wyatt was nothing like my previous relationships.

"Take me to bed?" I suggested.

The intensity in his gaze made me shiver with anticipation as he growled, "My patience is wearing pretty thin, sweetheart. Make sure you know what you're asking for right now. You better be certain you're willing to take my ornery ass on permanently because you'll be mine."

I sighed happily. "I'm already yours, but I'd be more than happy if you'd seal that deal."

Wyatt moved so fast to get us out of the lounge chair that it made my head spin.

He picked me up and headed for the stairs before I could even protest that I was perfectly capable of walking upstairs on my own.

Chapter 23

Wyatt

I'd never been a foolish man, and I wasn't about to give Shelby another chance to change her mind.

I took her face in my hands and kissed her, my dick already hard and ready to get inside her gorgeous body.

Christ! I'd never wanted a woman this badly, and there was no way in hell I could give her the sweet seduction she deserved this time.

I'd waited too damn long, and the uncertainty of the last few weeks had nearly killed me.

Getting myself off on a daily basis had stopped helping a long time ago.

Our lips still locked together, Shelby tugged my shirt up impatiently. *Good!*

She was just as damn eager for me as I was for her.

I fucking loved the way she was going after what she wanted, and I felt like the luckiest asshole on Earth because I was the guy she so desperately needed right now.

Hell, I needed her, too, and I'd never wanted to be a man who needed anyone.

I took a deep breath when I had to release her lips to pull the shirt over my head.

Calm the fuck down, Durand. She's not about to change her mind.

In fact, Shelby was shedding her own clothes faster than I was, so I raced to get my jeans and my boxer briefs off.

When I was done getting my clothes off, I simply watched as Shelby shed the rest of her clothing.

Little by little, she revealed the gorgeous body and creamy skin I'd fantasized about for so long.

The woman was a goddess, her breasts firm and exactly the right size.

Full hips.

Lush ass.

Thighs a guy my size would want to cradle his hips when he was hammering into her beautiful body.

And long, long legs that I hoped to hell she'd wrap around me because she wanted more.

My breath left my body in awe when she pulled the tie from her hair and those fiery curls spilled over her bare shoulders.

When her emerald green eyes met mine, I could see the slight hesitancy there, and it nearly killed me.

Did she really think I wouldn't think her body was exquisite?

My woman had been incredibly bold up until this moment, and she had no reason to doubt that she was anything other than perfect.

I stepped forward and wrapped my arms around her waist as I said huskily, "You're the most beautiful woman I've ever seen, Shelby. Don't get shy on me now."

She sent me a broad smile and wrapped her arms around my neck. "I should have known you'd say that, but it's not easy being with a guy for the first time who has the hottest body I've ever seen."

I savored the feel of her soft, warm, bare skin against mine as I buried my hands in her glorious mass of silky curls.

I didn't have a hot male body. I was almost forty. I was fit because I worked at staying in shape, but I was battered from years of minor injuries that I'd acquired on various ops in the past.

I had my share of scars, but Shelby didn't even seem to notice them.

"The only thing I want to do with this body right now is make you come until you're screaming my name," I informed her, my voice rough with desire.

I yanked the top sheet and the comforter down, picked her up and tossed her on the bed.

"Caveman," she accused in an amused tone as she looked up at me with a yearning glance that made me feel like a damn neanderthal.

The primitive urge to satisfy her yearning was probably something I'd never be able to reason out, but it didn't matter. I was way beyond the point where I needed to rationalize how I felt about Shelby Remington.

If she wanted…

If she needed…

It was my fucking job to make sure that her needs and wants were appeased.

I hesitated for a brief moment at the side of the bed, my primal urges satisfied just a little by seeing her naked in my bed.

This was exactly what I'd wanted to see for a very long time. Probably from the first moment I'd seen her in my kitchen after Chase's reception.

Maybe I hadn't admitted that to myself back then, but Shelby Remington had definitely grabbed me by the balls from that day forward.

She sent me a sultry smile, and my dick twitched as she looked at me like she wanted to devour me as she murmured, "God, you're big everywhere, Wyatt."

Not gonna lie, it was hot as hell that she was staring at my cock with an awed expression. It was also a very large stroke to my male ego.

I grinned at her as I got on the bed, crawled to her like a damn stalker and pinned her beneath me.

"Is that a complaint?" I asked as she wrapped her arms around me and ran her hands up and down my back like she wanted to touch every inch of my naked body.

She smiled cheekily back at me. "Nope. Just an observation."

I dipped my head and kissed her, and the heat that was constantly simmering between the two of us exploded.

The moment she moaned against my mouth, her hips lifting to meet mine, I almost lost it.

I wanted to bury my cock into her welcoming body so damn bad that I had to force myself to slow down.

I was a big guy, and I needed to use some damn finesse to satisfy her first because I wasn't going to last very long this time.

I forced myself to slow down, and savored the sensitive skin of her neck, exploring every inch of her bare skin that I could find.

This was about Shelby.

And my goal was to make her crazy before I finally sank into her incredible body.

I was *definitely* going to orgasm soon after that happened.

I wanted to make damn sure she was satisfied and ready to take me.

My dick twitched in protest as I slid down her body to her breasts, but I ignored it as I took one of her hard, pink nipples into my mouth and teased it.

I moved from one to the other, biting and licking, and getting off on the pants and moans that left her lips.

"Wyatt," she whimpered as her hands speared into my hair. "I need…"

Fuck! I knew what she needed, and I was going to give it to her… eventually.

A fundamental need like I'd never experienced before ate at my gut. I wanted to push her over the edge while she thought about nothing but me while she climaxed harder than she ever had in her life.

I leashed that fucking urge, knowing she'd enjoy it even more if I made her insane before that happened.

She yanked at my hair like a wild woman as I moved lower, my mouth trailing over her stomach, getting to know her body like I knew my own.

When I finally got my head between her thighs, I breathed in the heady scent of her arousal, and pushed her legs open wider.

"Wyatt," she murmured in a needy tone. "You don't have to. Nobody has ever made me come that way."

Bullshit! It wasn't like she *couldn't* get off like this. Obviously, those other idiots she'd been with had just never tried hard enough or long enough.

Any guy who knew where a women's clit was could get her off with oral sex.

I was going to thoroughly enjoy being the first to eat her pussy until she shattered, and it wouldn't be a problem for me if it took her a long time to get there.

I could easily bury my head between her legs for hours.

I put a hand on her belly as I stroked the other up and down her thighs. Her whole body was tight. "Relax, sweetheart, and enjoy the ride."

I played with the short, red curls that were neatly trimmed.

Her hands fisted my hair as she panted. "Wyatt, I don't think I can…"

She *could* and she *would.*

Her words trailed off as I stroked a finger between her slick folds. *Jesus!* She was wet, hot, and ready.

The erotic scent of her arousal was making me crazy. I lowered my head, desperate to taste that molten heat.

Her lusty, full-throated moan as my mouth connected with her pussy was like a siren's song to me, and I stopped teasing and licked her from bottom to top before I found her engorged clit.

"Oh, God, yes," Shelby groaned, her hands gripping my hair until her short nails dug into my scalp.

I shoved my hands under her until I could grip her ass tightly, keeping her exactly where I wanted her as my tongue stroked over and over her clit roughly.

Every tremor…

Every fucking erotic sound that left her lips…

Every time she bucked her hips…

It spurred me on.

The only thing that was going to move my mouth away from where it was right now was a dire emergency, and I wasn't sure that even that occurrence could tear me away from Shelby.

My woman was going to come hard.

And I was going to be here to taste it.

"Jesus, Wyatt!" she shrieked, her legs starting to tremble. "I think I'm going to…"

Oh, hell yes, she was going to come.

Maybe it had been a long time, but I knew a woman's body.

I bit down lightly on her clit, and moved my tongue faster, giving her the stimulation she needed.

Yanking one hand from her ass, I buried two fingers into her tight, hot channel, laser-focused on giving her as much pleasure as I possibly could.

Shelby was desperate for release, and my gut was clawing at me to give it to her.

The moment my fingers found her g-spot, she imploded.

"Oh, my God, Wyatt," she screamed as her orgasm rolled over her.

Her inner muscles clenched down hard on my fingers, and I tried not to think about how damn good that was going to feel with my cock inside her.

Fuck! I really wanted to watch her come, but I kept my face planted between her thighs, drawing out her pleasure as long as possible and indulging in the taste of her climax.

Just feeling her come apart and knowing it was the first time it had happened for her was enough for me right now.

I slipped my fingers out of her once the spasms calmed, but I lazily lapped at her clit until she was purring with satisfaction before I crawled up her body.

Damned if I didn't feel like the caveman she'd accused me of being. I got a very primordial gratification from meeting the needs of my woman when I looked at the satiated expression in her beautiful eyes.

She shook her head slowly like she was stunned as she murmured, "I didn't know it could be like that. Before you…"

I swept my fingers over my chin and my jaw to dry my face without losing the taste of Shelby as I grumbled, "Before me, you were with fucking amateurs."

She wrapped her arms around my neck as she let out a captivating laugh. "Obviously, I've finally found a real stud."

Chapter 24

Shelby

My body was quivering, and I was still in shock that I could come that hard from oral sex, but I wasn't completely satisfied.

My body was clamoring for Wyatt, to get him inside me, to feel that connection.

"Fuck me, Wyatt. I need you," I whispered before I nipped at his earlobe.

"Condom," he said roughly.

"I have an IUD, and I've been tested. I haven't been with anyone since those tests."

"I haven't either. I'm clean," he rasped as his intense gray eyes met mine. "You sure?"

Mesmerized by the possessive heat in his gaze, I simply nodded.

"Then I'm probably screwed because this won't last very long."

He kissed me, his mouth claiming mine, the taste of myself on his lips.

It wasn't a gentle kiss.

It was rough and demanding.

Erotic and carnal.

And I reveled in the knowledge that Wyatt wanted me like this.

He released my mouth and nipped at the sensitive skin of my neck as he rumbled, "You want my cock now, beautiful?"

It was obvious that he needed to be in control right now, needed to hear how much I wanted him, and his raw dominance was hotter than hell.

"God, yes," I hissed, my hips lifting from the need to get this man inside me. "Please."

"The second I take you, you're mine, Shelby," he growled.

God, I really, really wanted to be taken by this man. "And you'll be mine," I whimpered.

"Already am, sweetheart," he answered in a rough baritone filled with heat.

I gasped as Wyatt buried himself to his balls with one powerful surge of his hips.

It wasn't painful. It was just startling, to suddenly have a guy this large inside me.

I sighed in relief, ignoring the discomfort as my body stretched to accommodate his size.

"Fuck, Shelby!" Wyatt cursed, his tone tense, like he was trying to hold onto his control. "You're tight, but you feel so damn good. You okay?"

"I'm fine," I assured him softly. "I need you, Wyatt. Fuck me."

I'd wanted this man for what seemed like forever, and I wasn't going to be completely sated until he put out the fire that had been raging between the two of us for weeks now.

I moaned as he pulled back and buried himself again.

I wrapped my legs around him, matching the insanely hot pace that he was starting.

My head rolled back on the pillow. I was completely lost to the fierceness of the passion that flowed between us like molten lava, and I didn't care if I never found myself again.

There was just Wyatt…

The intense heat that was incinerating me…

And the pulse of my connection to him.

My hips rose for each forceful thrust, our bodies colliding over and over, doing a crazy dance that only the two of us understood.

This was what I'd needed for so long.

"Harder," I pleaded. "Don't hold back."

I wanted everything he had.

I needed to see him lose that iron control of his for once and let go.

He moved one of his hands beneath my ass and yanked my hips up with every stroke, making our bodies connect harder than I could ever manage by doing it myself.

"You're coming with me," he demanded, shifting his body and grinding down on my clit with every deep penetration until I thought I was going to lose my mind.

My hands moved down to his upper back. I held on, reaching for anything that would ground me, my short nails digging into his back.

I closed my eyes, my body shaking as my climax started to roll over me like a freight train at max speed.

"Open your eyes, Shelby. Look at me. I want to watch you come this time," Wyatt ordered.

I'd give him anything he wanted right now, so I opened my eyes, and they instantly clashed with his.

This man could play my body like an instrument, but I could tell by the wild look in his eyes that he was just as affected.

"Wyatt!" I called out with abandon, not caring if the distant neighbors could hear me.

I let go and rolled with my powerful orgasm, trusting Wyatt to catch me when I finally came down.

My inner muscles spasmed and clenched hard, and I knew I'd milked Wyatt to his own release when he threw his head back with a loud, almost tormented groan.

"Holy shit! Holy shit! Holy shit!" I chanted, unable to get any different words to leave my lips.

I felt completely destroyed as I panted for breath, my heart ready to pound right out of my chest.

How had I ever gotten to the age of thirty-five without knowing that sex could be this good?

Honestly, I probably knew the answer to that question.

There was something between Wyatt and me that I'd never experienced in a relationship before. It was a connection that I couldn't explain if I tried.

Wyatt rolled on his back, taking me with him until I was sprawled on top of his body like a limp noodle.

His arms tightened around me, like he was afraid I was actually going to go somewhere.

We stayed just like that for several minutes, and I basked in the unfamiliar post-coital bliss.

Wyatt had just rocked my world, and I probably wouldn't move if the house fell down around the two of us.

"That was definitely worth waiting for," Wyatt said after he'd recovered, his teasing tone amused.

I lifted my head to look at him. "Was it?"

The experience had been earthshattering for me, but Wyatt had made it that way because he was a damn stud.

His brows lifted. "Surely you don't even have to ask that question. I'm laying here butt naked and unable to move because you almost killed me. You're a fucking goddess, sweetheart, and I'm the lucky asshole who has you in my bed."

Relief flooded over me as I surveyed his earnest expression. I knew he was telling me exactly what he thought.

He continued, "Certainly you don't believe that ice cube bullshit anymore. You're hotter than hell in bed. I'm pretty sure that I have the marks on my back to prove it."

I smiled at him, my heart aching because I'd found the one man who made me feel like a sexual goddess.

Not only had I found that guy, but he was Wyatt Durand, the most amazing man I'd ever met.

I stroked a gentle hand over his hair as I said, "You make me so happy that it's scary sometimes."

"I feel the same way," he replied. "There aren't a lot of women who would put up with my cranky ass."

I shook my head. "Your cranky ass is only one small part of who you are, Wyatt, and I happen to like it."

Wyatt was a fascinating mix of characteristics that were often conflicting, but he was an irresistible puzzle that I could never resist trying to figure out.

He could be grumpy to someone who didn't know him, but there was so much more to Wyatt Durand than what most people saw on the exterior.

He was supportive of anything I wanted to do in my career.

He was highly protective of the people who were important to him.

He had an innate kindness inside of him that he didn't really want anyone to see.

He was brilliant and driven to keep Durand Industries a company that would make his father proud.

Yeah, he could be sarcastic and abrasive, but his life experiences had made him throw up those defenses.

I couldn't fault him for wanting to protect himself. I'd done the same thing myself after what had happened in Montana.

If he didn't protect himself, there would be people in his world who wouldn't hesitate to destroy him.

"I think you're the only person who's ever said that they actually like me the way I am," Wyatt mused.

"I adore you exactly the way you are," I corrected, and then leaned down to kiss him.

"That's convenient," he answered when I'd pulled back from the kiss. "Because you're stuck with me now."

I sighed. "I could think of worse fates to have."

"I think I probably stink," he said as he slapped my ass lightly. "We need a shower."

"Are you trying to say that I smell ripe, too?" I teased.

"Nope. I'm just trying to convince you to come with me," he said in a wicked baritone as he disentangled our bodies and rolled out of bed.

I rolled onto my back as I retorted in a playful voice, "I'll think about it. You go ahead. I'm thoroughly exhausted."

"Then I'll help you get there," he warned before he picked me up off the bed.

His brute strength was so ridiculous that he made carrying a not-so-dainty woman look easy.

"Wyatt!" I squeaked. "I'll walk. Put me down."

Like I wasn't going to eventually find my way to the shower if Wyatt's hot body was in there naked?

He completely ignored my protests and carried me into the master bathroom.

"You don't have to do a thing. I'll be more than happy to make sure every inch of your body gets clean," he informed me.

Images of Wyatt stroking soap over my entire body with those talented hands of his made every nerve in my body tingle.

He opened the massive shower and turned on the water.

"Only if I get to do your body first," I told him in a sultry tone. "You've gotten to know my body much better than I've gotten to know yours."

I ached to explore Wyatt's nude body, and I was going to get my opportunity right now.

"I thought you were exhausted," he reminded me gruffly.

"I think I'm getting my second wind," I informed him as I stroked my hand down the small marks I'd inadvertently made on his back.

"Then I'm completely screwed," he answered in a tone that was far from unhappy about my sudden recovery.

I snorted with laughter as he enthusiastically carried me into the shower.

Chapter 25

Wyatt

"I told you not to wait up," I said to Shelby as I walked into the kitchen.

It was close to midnight on Monday evening.

I'd been in a foul mood when I'd walked through the door moments ago.

Urgent meetings on a product situation had kept me in the office all damn night.

Normally, I wouldn't care how long it took to iron out an urgent problem, but with Shelby leaving for Montana early Wednesday morning, I'd really wanted to spend the evening with her.

It didn't matter that we'd spent the entire day in bed together yesterday, barely finding time to get up to eat a meal.

I was still pissed off that I hadn't been able to take her out to dinner tonight as planned.

I'd expected to come home to a dark house, with Shelby already in bed. She was a morning person. We usually had coffee together after I went for a run, and then she went straight to work on whatever tasks she had planned that day for her blog or her cookbook.

Instead, she was in the kitchen, fully clothed in a pair of ass hugging jeans and a lightweight summer shirt.

"You said that you didn't have time to eat when I talked to you earlier," she said cheerfully. "I know you. You probably didn't make time for food after that, either."

I hadn't.

My meetings had gone back-to-back all evening until the issue was resolved.

I was starving, and whatever she was making smelled incredible.

I shrugged my jacket off and dropped it on a chair at the kitchen island. I walked into the kitchen and snagged her around the waist as she started to sprint to the oven to do something.

"Didn't we talk about the fact that you're not here to serve me? You work hard all day, Shelby. You should be in bed."

She turned, wrapped her arms around my neck, and then shot me a dazzling smile that made my dick instantly hard and changed my mood entirely.

Shit! It was pretty damn difficult for a guy to be in a bad mood when he got to come home to a woman like Shelby.

I kissed her, which was my first priority. I'd been thinking about her all day, which was probably pathetic considering how much time we'd spent together over the weekend.

"I'm not serving you," she informed me once I'd let her come up for air. "I'm taking care of you because you had to work a really long day. Isn't that what two people who care about each other do? You've taken care of me many times by helping me out with business things in the evenings, taking me out for dinner so I didn't have to cook, and supporting me in everything I do. Do you have a problem with me staying up a little late to make sure you're okay? It's not like I'm usually in bed by nine or ten. I usually don't sleep until midnight anyway."

The stubborn look on her face warned me not to argue with her, and I didn't. It wasn't the first thoughtful thing Shelby had done for me since I'd known her. I replied honestly, "Your habit of doing nice things for me all the time takes some getting used to. I'm happy to see your beautiful face after a shitty day, but I didn't expect it."

She shrugged and gave me a soft kiss before she answered, "Get used to it. You work too hard, and I know you don't eat when you're involved with issues at Durand. Sit down," she instructed as she slipped out of my arms. "The food isn't a big deal. It's just a pasta casserole with mushrooms and cheese and some bruschetta bread. You can devour a few more cookies for dessert."

I smirked as I rolled up my sleeves and sat down. What was no big deal for Shelby would probably take hours of prep in the kitchen for someone else.

I also knew this wasn't a meal that she'd done for a video earlier. Her whole day had been slotted to work on her cookbook.

She dropped a plate piled with pasta in front of me, and then put a plate of small, toasted French bread slices with tomatoes and parmesan cheese beside it.

I picked up my fork, my stomach rumbling from the smell of the food. "You're not eating?"

She shook her head as she leaned her ass against the counter with a bottle of water. "I ate some of the casserole and bruschetta earlier. I have a hard time working all day and not eating for sixteen hours. I think you're superhuman. Did everything work out okay?"

I started to shovel my food down while telling Shelby about the incident at work.

As usual, the food was exceptional, and I felt like a very fortunate asshole to have a woman who cared enough to wait up for me and make sure I ate something substantial.

I probably would have looked for something to make a sandwich and downed a plate of cookies if she'd been asleep.

It felt almost normal to sit here in the evening with Shelby, eating and talking about our days now, but this was something I never wanted to take for granted.

Maybe it was mundane for some people, but I'd spent far too many years alone not to appreciate a woman who cared as much as Shelby did.

It was fucking addicting.

And I was going to hate every night that she was gone until I could go pick her up in Montana.

Thank fuck she'd finally agreed to stop her apartment search and stay here with me now that we were committed to this relationship.

I wouldn't have to go through the hell of wondering if I was going to be able to get her to stay after her visit to Montana.

Once I'd wolfed down the food, I dropped my fork on my empty plate. "That was incredible, babe."

The food that had been no big deal to her had tasted like it came from the finest restaurant.

"Cookie?" she teased as she held out the container she'd stored cookies in.

I held up my hand in surrender. "Can't. Maybe for breakfast." I reached for my suit jacket and pulled a box and an envelope from the pocket. "I got you a little something."

I slid the velvet box across the counter first.

She sent me an admonishing look. "Wyatt Durand, you have to stop buying me things. I'm spoiled rotten, and every time I mention anything that I plan on buying for myself, you beat me to it."

I shrugged. "I like buying you things, and I haven't really gotten you much."

She snorted. "I've gotten more gifts from you than most women probably get from their significant other in years."

Okay, so I had updated her cell phone, her laptop, and added some kitchen gadgets that might be useful to her. I'd gifted her a few of the limited edition products from Durand. I'd found out from Tori that the perfume Shelby had been wearing the night of the charity ball had been a tiny sample size bottle because of the price. So yeah, I'd gotten her a few of the largest bottles I could find. But for a guy with my money, they *were* little things.

Hell, it wasn't like I'd bought her a new vehicle. She'd nixed that idea immediately because she said she had a perfectly good car with plenty of miles left in it.

She wasn't spoiled rotten. She'd crushed too many of my gift ideas to be spoiled rotten.

I nodded toward the box. "This one is a little more personal. You can't refuse a personal gift from the man in your life."

This relationship was still new. Eventually, she'd get used to the fact that anything I gave her wouldn't even make a tiny dent in my net worth.

I watched her face as she opened the box.

Her jaw dropped as she eyed the contents.

"Oh, Wyatt," she said, her tone awed and surprised as she gingerly touched the earrings.

The diamond and emerald drop earrings were small on the gaudiness scale, but large enough that she'd probably think they were an elaborate gift.

They were delicate and classy though, smaller than some of the dangle earrings I'd seen her wear. "The emeralds match your eyes, and I thought you'd like the leaf motif since we both love the outdoors."

The leaves of diamonds and emeralds alternated as they dropped, with a larger emerald leaf at the bottom and top.

"They're breathtaking," she said as she lifted one from the velvet bed. "I don't think anyone has ever given me such a thoughtful gift."

I frowned as tears filled her eyes and the droplets starting rolling down her cheeks.

Since Shelby wasn't the type of woman who broke into tears for no reason, it was alarming.

I immediately got off my ass and went around the counter.

"Hey," I said as I wrapped my arms around her waist. "The earrings were supposed to make you happy, not make you cry. I thought you could wear them in Montana since they aren't formal jewelry. What's wrong?"

I swiped her tears away with my thumbs.

She looked up at me, her expression honest and open as she said, "I've never gotten a piece of jewelry from a man because he thought the stones matched my eyes or because it meant something significant. Honestly, the only thing I've ever gotten was a plain wedding band that I picked out myself. These are…special. They mean something. You were thinking about me and about us when you got them."

Christ! Of course I was thinking about her and us. The earrings were personal, and I'd had them designed specifically for her. Wasn't it normal to think about your girlfriend when you bought her jewelry? "What else would a guy be thinking about when he's buying his woman jewelry? Don't cry, sweetheart. I fucking hate it when you cry."

She gently put the earring she was holding back in the box, and wrapped her arms around my neck. "I'm not upset. I'm touched, Wyatt. Thank you. It's the sweetest gift anyone has ever given to me, and I love them. I know they were probably wildly expensive, and I'll probably be terrified of losing one, but I'll think about you and how lucky I am to have you every time I put them on."

Okay, I could live with that. I wanted to give her a ton of gifts that would make her think about me when I wasn't around.

Fuck! Shelby was grateful for the smallest of things, and sometimes I didn't feel like I deserved her.

Of course, that didn't mean I was going to let her go for her own good like my brother tried to do with Savannah.

Maybe I didn't deserve her, but she was better off with me than some of the other assholes she'd been with in the past.

I didn't have an altruistic bone in my body, and I wasn't about to sacrifice the best thing that had ever happened to me.

Shelby was mine, and I was keeping her.

I'd just have to keep trying to be a better man.

"You waited up for me and made me dinner because you knew I wouldn't stop to eat," I grumbled. "I think that's more thoughtful than simply getting you some earrings. Don't start thinking I'm an amazing guy. You know I'm a dick most of the time."

"No, I do not know that," she said adamantly. "I think you're the hottest, handsomest, most thoughtful stud in the world, and I adore you. *You're* going to have to get used to *that*. Now, take me to bed. You're probably exhausted."

I grinned as I saw the stubborn expression on her face. "Not *that* exhausted, babe."

I had something else to give her, but I had a feeling she wouldn't be all that excited about that one.

I'd talk to her about that…later.

Her lips curved up into a seductive smile that made my already hard cock just a little harder as she accused, "You're insatiable."

"Guilty," I said huskily. "But if you're too tired or too sore from our marathon weekend, I'd happily just go to sleep as long as you're with me in my bed."

She started to slowly unbutton my dress shirt. "Not a chance, mister. I'm about to be deprived of my stud for almost a week. I'm going to miss you, Wyatt."

I picked her up and headed for the stairs with a lump in my throat.

It felt damn good to hear her say that because I was going to fucking miss her, too.

Chapter 26

Shelby

I woke up suddenly in the middle of the night the following evening. A quick glance at the clock told me it was after three in the morning. Wyatt and I had gone out for dinner, and then relaxed at home because I was leaving for Montana in the morning. We'd wanted to spend as much time as possible together.

We'd gone to bed early, but we hadn't slept until around midnight. Wyatt had been determined to show me how much he was going to miss me, and I certainly hadn't complained about making it an early night. I didn't think I could ever get enough of Wyatt Durand, and he acted like he felt the same way.

I reached out my hand reflexively so I could get closer to his warm, welcoming body. I usually fell asleep in his arms, and we woke up tangled together, but all I felt when I reached for him was cool sheets.

"Wyatt?" I called sleepily, wondering what he was doing up this late.

I rolled onto my back, concerned that something might be wrong. The room was dark except for a very dim strip of light that was coming from under the closed bathroom door.

I was startled when Wyatt suddenly came barreling through the bathroom door fully dressed.

What in the hell is he doing?

He didn't look like he was headed to his office for some kind of emergency. He was wearing jeans and an older T-shirt.

I sat up in bed, totally awake now. "What's wrong?"

Something wasn't right.

His expression was grim, and he was all business as he replied. "I have to go out. I'm not sure how long I'll be. I planned on driving you to the airport in the morning, but I'm not sure I'll be back in time."

I lifted a hand to push the hair out of my face as I replied, "That's fine. I can get there on my own. Are you okay? Where are you going? Is something going on at work?"

I was seriously concerned now. Wyatt hadn't been this abrupt with me in a long time, even when he was upset with work issues.

Usually, he talked to me about almost anything that was on his mind.

At least, I thought he did.

He came to the side of the bed and looked down at me. "Not exactly," he said evasively as he raked a hand through his hair. "Fuck! There's something I should have told you about, but I can't do it right now. We'll talk when you get to Montana and I'll explain everything."

Wyatt's demeanor was so out of character that it worried me even more. "You can't even tell me where you're going?"

He shook his head. "Not without telling you everything, and I don't have that kind of time right now. Trust me?"

"I do. But this doesn't make sense, Wyatt. It's after three and you can't give me a clue about where you're going? Is something wrong with your family or our friends?"

He leaned down and gave me a brief kiss. "They're all fine. I'm sorry. I hate like hell to do this, but I have to get going. I promise that I'll tell you everything as soon as we see each other again. It's not something I really want to discuss on the phone."

Okay, what in the world is going on with him?

This was not the Wyatt I'd gotten to know and adore.

As he strode toward the door, I said, "Please tell me this has nothing to do with another woman."

The words had come out of my mouth before I could think about them.

Maybe they were a knee-jerk reaction to all of the secrecy that I couldn't even begin to understand.

Maybe they were a product of my past and being cheated on in both of my only other committed relationships.

Maybe they had slipped out because I suddenly remembered the night of the break-in, when Wyatt had been mysteriously out late at night for no apparent reason with Xena.

What possible reason could he have for leaving in the middle of the night to go somewhere that he couldn't tell me about?

Wyatt turned as he reached the door. "If you need me to tell you that, then you really don't trust me."

The tone of his voice had been cool and stoic, and he didn't say another word as he walked out the bedroom door.

I supposed that I could go after him and apologize, but I had no idea what to think right now.

In the end, he hadn't given me the assurance that I'd wanted, which only made me more confused.

It wasn't his family or friends.

It wasn't work.

He didn't exactly deny that he was leaving to go to someone else.

It was after three in the morning, and he had to leave for an urgent situation?

If his weird behavior didn't have *another woman* written all over it, what did?

Tears began to trickle down my face, and my heart felt completely crushed by his words.

Because...

"Dammit!" I said out loud to the empty room.

I was in love with Wyatt Durand.

I'd known that for a while now, but it had seemed too soon to say those words out loud, and I had no idea whether Wyatt felt the same way.

I knew he cared about me, and I knew that he was definitely attracted to me, but love?

I wasn't even sure that Wyatt believed in love.

He was a guy who wasn't even sure he had a heart.

Our relationship had progressed so easily, so naturally, so damn perfectly that I hadn't wanted to spoil it by jumping the gun.

Now, I was kind of glad that I hadn't said it out loud because I'd feel even more rejected and vulnerable than I did right now.

There is absolutely no proof that Wyatt is with another woman!

Shit! I wanted to believe that wasn't the reason he'd run out of here in the middle of the night, but it *was* the most reasonable explanation.

He wants me to trust him.

Well, I had trusted him until he pulled this disappearing act.

It was a bit much to ask a woman to blindly trust him when he was leaving the house after three in the morning without giving her a single explanation.

Something brief would have been fine.

He could have explained more later.

I released a tremulous sigh and swiped the tears from my face.

I probably shouldn't have implied that I thought he was going to see another woman.

It was an old insecurity that didn't belong in my current relationship. Wyatt had never given me any other reason not to trust him, and he was usually the most thoughtful man I'd ever met.

We'd talk about this incident like adults.

I trusted that he cared about me enough not to hurt me intentionally, but I was going to struggle with this issue until he gave me a reasonable explanation.

I definitely wasn't the kind of woman who could put up with mysterious disappearances all the time from a guy I cared about and was committed to in a monogamous relationship.

There's nothing I can do about it right now. He's obviously not coming back, and I won't see him for almost a week.

I was about to get up to turn off the bedroom light and try to get a few more hours of sleep when Xena came into the bedroom whining like she'd lost her favorite toy.

Poor girl.

I scooped her up and brought her onto the bed with me.

She snuffled, licked my face, and then settled down beside me.

Xena usually preferred to sleep downstairs with her comfy bed and her favorite blanket. She liked having space to switch rooms or positions when she felt like it at night.

She rarely came upstairs, even though she was a younger Frenchie and could easily navigate her way up the stairs if she wanted.

I laid down beside her and snuggled the dog close to me.

Obviously, she was just as unhappy as I was about Wyatt leaving in a rush.

When he went downstairs, Wyatt always made time to give Xena her dose of affection.

It had probably confused the poor canine when he'd left so abruptly.

"I know exactly how you feel, sweetie," I muttered as I petted Xena. "Maybe we'll forgive him later, okay? He could have a perfectly good explanation for being a jerk."

God, I really, really hoped he had a good explanation.

Or…maybe he wouldn't.

But for now, I had to give him the benefit of the doubt, even if things looked incredibly suspect at the moment.

The dog licked my face one more time, grunted her agreement, and then settled down to sleep.

"Please don't hurt me, Wyatt," I murmured to myself as I closed my eyes and tried to relax. "I'm not sure I can handle it."

It wasn't like I hadn't known my share of heartbreak in the past, but I was afraid that I might never recover from this one if it happened.

Chapter 27

Wyatt

"I'm glad that shitty op is over," Cooper said as he wolfed down his breakfast.

It was mid-morning, and Tori, Cooper, Chase, and I were having a late breakfast at a family diner before we went home to hit our beds for a while.

Cooper was right. Everything that could go wrong did go wrong on this particular mission, but my former teammates had pulled it off anyway.

It had been fraught with issues from the start, which is why I'd been more concerned than usual from the moment Marshall had notified us that the mission was going down soon.

As usual, none of the Michigan team had hesitated because of the difficulty of the op, but *I'd* been sweating the outcome.

"Did Shelby leave for Montana?" Tori asked as she reached for a glass of water.

I nodded, my heart heavy as hell. "I assume so. Her planned departure time was early. She said she'd get to the airport on her own. She woke up as I was leaving the house."

"Is she cool with your involvement in Last Hope?" Chase asked.

"She doesn't know about it yet," I confessed. "I have to tell her. I can't keep leaving at weird hours without her knowing where I'm going or what I'm doing. We went for weeks without a mission. And then this one suddenly popped up."

"That's usually the way it happens," Cooper said drily. "How in the hell did you explain where you were going in the middle of the night if you haven't told her yet."

I shrugged. "I didn't. I told her to trust me and that I'd explain when I saw her again. She was worried that something was wrong with my family or our friends, so I did tell her that it was nothing like that. I told her it wasn't work-related, either. I didn't want her to worry."

Tori's jaw dropped as she looked at me. "And she had no problem with that?"

"She asked me to tell her that I wasn't going to see another woman?" I said in a graveled voice.

"And?" Chase prompted.

"And I told her if she needed me to tell her that, then she didn't trust me," I grumbled. "Shelby and I have been tight. She's the only woman in my life. Why in the hell would she need me to tell her that?"

Tori dropped her utensils onto her empty plate with more force than necessary. "Oh, for God's sake, Wyatt. You really are a knucklehead sometimes. Of course that was her logical conclusion. Where in the hell else would you be going at three in the morning if it's not work, family, or friend related? You should have told her before this even came up. She probably does trust you, but that's way too big of a stretch, and trust is built over time. Shelby has been cheated on in both of her prior relationships. Obviously, her mind is going to go there when you pull an idiot stunt like that. If Cooper did something like that, I'd be pissed and wonder what he was doing that he couldn't tell me about. Put yourself in her place. How would you feel if she did that to you?"

My little sister was furious, and if looks could kill, I'd probably be dead on the floor of this diner right now.

I looked at Cooper and Chase for support, but they both shrugged.

"I gotta agree, man," Cooper commented. "I'd never do that to Tori."

"Vanna would never stand for it," Chase seconded.

"Do you have any idea how much you probably hurt her," Tori said tersely. "At the very least, you could have assured her that there wasn't another woman in your life. This relationship is fairly new, and Shelby was completely destroyed by an idiot she trusted enough to marry."

"It was a knee-jerk reaction to her not trusting me," I admitted. "Fuck! I'm crazy about her. I've never felt this way about a woman before. Give me a damn break."

"Unless you're willing to give this relationship up, I suggest you tell her the truth as soon as possible," Tori advised with a sigh. "Shelby has grown a lot since I've known her, and I think you're responsible for some of those changes, Wyatt. She talks more openly. She trusts easier. She's a lot more open with her emotions. You gave her a guy she can trust. Don't mess that up because your pride is wounded. You've changed, too, because she's a woman you can trust. Shelby is someone who doesn't give a crap about your money or the Durand name. She cares about you."

"Do you think I don't know that?" I rasped. "I made a mistake. I'll fix it."

Truthfully, I'd known my crappy comment wasn't the way to handle the situation almost as soon as I'd left the house in the middle of the night.

I'd been torturing myself about the fact that I might have hurt Shelby since I'd arrived at Last Hope headquarters for the op.

Everything Tori had said made sense.

It probably was the logical place for Shelby to go when she had no idea what was happening.

But fucking hell, it made me crazy that she'd ever think I'd do anything to hurt her.

I didn't see any woman but her, much less want to fuck someone else.

Then again, I wasn't sure how I'd react if she'd done the same thing to me. I probably would have lost my shit if she'd taken off in the middle of the night for no apparent reason. I would have wanted to go with her wherever she was going and help her solve whatever problem she had.

Is that what she'd wanted to do by asking so many questions? Had she wanted to help?

I'd seen the legitimate concern on her face for my well-being, and then I'd turned around and rebuffed that concern by being a jackass.

"It might help to give her a call," Chase mused. "Even if you really can't tell this story on the phone."

I shook my head. "It's something that needs to be explained face-to-face, and it's going to take time. She's with her family right now. And I did try to call her. She's not picking up."

"She's probably still flying," Tori suggested in a much gentler voice. "Go home, Wyatt. Get some sleep. You're allowed a mistake or two. If you tell Shelby as soon as possible, she'll understand."

Chase and I were starting a slew of international meetings tomorrow that would last for days, so we were taking the day off to catch up on our sleep.

"I'd feel better if I was there with her," I said tersely. "She wouldn't take my security with her, and I'm not comfortable with that."

"You don't think Kaleb will make sure she's safe?" Chase asked.

"It's not that I doubt that his intentions are good, and I've warned him to keep an eye on her, but no one seems to think she could be in danger because it's a small town. He thinks she's safe there," I said tightly.

"And you don't?" Cooper questioned.

I shook my head as I pushed my empty plate away. "There's a lot of people in Montana who could hold a grudge against her because of what her ex-husband did. I have a bad feeling about Shelby being caught out alone anywhere. She's been constantly guarded or with me physically since the break-in. There hasn't been an opportunity for anyone to make a move, and I'd prefer they didn't have one now. My gut isn't feeling right on this one. I'm not sure if it's true gut instinct or if I'm too personally involved to tell the difference between concern and gut instinct."

Gut instinct had kept me and my team alive more than once, and I tried to never discard that feeling that something wasn't right.

However, I'd never had to listen to my gut when a target was someone I cared about as much as Shelby.

"Marshall mentioned earlier that he has a small lead," Cooper said. "Yeah, it's one of many, and the others haven't panned out, but maybe he'll have something once he's investigated it."

I lifted a brow. "Yeah, but in the meantime, Shelby is in Montana without security in a town where everyone thinks nothing bad can happen there."

"I get it," Chase agreed. "We've all been around the block enough to know that bad things can happen anywhere. We don't know this possible stalker's motives. You're right. It could be someone who wants to get back at her in Montana. It makes sense. Maybe they know she's going to be there for that annual picnic, which is why nothing has happened again here. How secure is Kaleb's place and her aunt's ranch?"

I'd already checked into that, and they definitely weren't secure enough for me. "They have regular home security systems but that's about it. No security cameras, and no secure entry gates. The properties are too easily accessed for my peace of mind. The picnic is Saturday, and from what I understand, practically the whole damn town is there, but that also means that Kaleb, Tanner, and Devon will all be there to watch out for her."

"The last of the meetings is the Sunday morning breakfast meeting," Chase reminded me. "Take off early if it makes you feel better."

That wasn't a bad idea. I was going to give Shelby enough time with her family before I went to pick her up, but I didn't think Kaleb would mind if I dropped in on him at the last minute. "I might take you up on that," I answered. "I could be in Montana by Sunday afternoon instead of Tuesday."

It wasn't ideal, but it was better than worrying longer about Shelby's safety.

Cooper stood, "I'll take care of the bill on the way out. My wife looks like she's about to go face down in her empty plate."

I nodded, noting that Tori did look exhausted.

Hell, we were all wiped out from little sleep and the dangerous op we'd managed earlier.

Tori rose and walked directly over to me. "Everything will be okay, Wyatt," she said softly as she leaned down and hugged me. "Shelby has more common sense than most people I know."

I hugged my little sister back, even though she'd raked me over the coals only a few minutes ago.

I couldn't blame Tori for standing up for a friend, especially when I'd been an asshole.

She hugged Chase as well. "Both of you go home and rest," she insisted.

"On our way," Chase said as we both rose from our seats. "Vanna is a little worried because none of us slept much, but I really needed some food."

Chase and I said our goodbyes, and we both headed for our vehicles.

I'd sleep for a while, and then I'd try again to call Shelby.

Maybe she didn't want to talk to me, but I really needed to hear her voice.

Chapter 28

Shelby

It felt almost surreal to be eating a family dinner with Aunt Millie, Kaleb, Tanner, and Devon at the ranch in Montana on Friday night. I'd missed all of them so much, and seeing the four of them around the table brought back some very fond memories of my childhood.

There had been so many tears and hugs since I'd arrived on Wednesday. It felt good to be back in Montana, but I couldn't help but feel like I was more of a visitor now than a resident.

Life had moved on in Crystal Fork, but nothing had really changed much with the town or the people who lived here. However, I *had* changed. This would always be the town I grew up in and loved, but it didn't quite feel like home anymore to me.

Maybe because I left most of my heart in San Diego?

God, I missed Wyatt.

I hated the way we'd parted, and the uncertainty about our relationship.

I felt like part of my soul was missing, and I really needed to talk to him.

He'd called more than once and left messages, but those messages had been brief and to the point, only saying that he wanted to talk to me. I'd called him back and left similar messages, but things were so chaotic here with the annual picnic happening tomorrow that we hadn't connected. Every single time he'd called just happened to be during a moment when I didn't have my phone on me. Twice when I was in the shower, and another time when I was in the hot tub at Kaleb's home.

I knew that Wyatt had meetings scheduled day and night because of the barrage of international associates that had flown in to discuss big issues at Durand. I wasn't surprised that I couldn't reach him, but I was disappointed.

I needed to hear his voice, even if he didn't want to discuss the disappearing act the night before I'd left for Montana.

Now that I'd had time to think rationally, I was fairly certain there was nobody else. It might be the most rational explanation, but my heart wasn't buying it.

Maybe I had been burned hard before, but Wyatt wasn't one of those other guys, and he wasn't a game player.

I found it hard to believe that he could treat me like I was that important to him and then turn around and screw another female.

Because we spent almost all of our free time together, it was also unlikely that he could have maintained any other relationship.

Wyatt and I were connected in a way that I'd never experienced with anyone else, and I couldn't feel that way if those feelings weren't reciprocated.

I'd jumped to a hasty conclusion because of my past experiences, and in the process, I was afraid that I'd hurt him.

However, the way he'd handled the situation wasn't exactly ideal.

As much as I'd tried, I still couldn't figure out a logical solution for his behavior, but I was more than willing to listen.

Wyatt was that guy I'd dreamed of finding when I'd married the wrong man because I wanted that dream so badly.

After Justin, I'd given up finding that kind of connection with a man.

I'd convinced myself that it didn't exist, and that I'd be okay with that reality.

Until I'd met Wyatt Durand.

My attraction to him had been a force I couldn't possibly fight, even though I'd tried in the beginning.

He'd become as necessary to me as breathing in a short period of time.

He was my confidante, my companion, and my heart's desire.

He knew me, and I knew the real Wyatt. The guy beneath that formidable exterior of his that very few people seemed to recognize.

I wanted to believe that he needed me as much as I needed him, even though we'd never really expressed those emotions to each other.

I had to be an optimist until I had proof that I was wrong.

It would rip out my soul if I was wrong, and I didn't want to face that until I knew what was really going on with Wyatt.

"Are you okay, honey?" my Aunt Millie asked as we finished our dinner. "You look like your thoughts are a million miles away."

Not a million, but maybe a little over twelve hundred miles away.

I pulled myself back into the present, and smiled at my aunt. "I'm good. I was just thinking about what else I can get done for the picnic tomorrow."

I was so lying my ass off, but I didn't really want to share what happened with Wyatt with my family right now.

My emotions were still too raw, and I wasn't sure what to tell them anyway.

The whole thing could be a misunderstanding.

They knew Wyatt and I were dating, and how much I cared about him. I preferred to leave it that way for now.

Aunt Millie shot me an admonishing look. "I think you've helped enough. You prepped almost all of the food today. Between you and my sons, you haven't left much for me to do tomorrow."

Kaleb and his brothers had arranged almost everything except the food. I'd asked him to leave that to me.

"And because I've been so helpful," Kaleb said jokingly from his seat next to me. "I think I get the first piece of this pie."

I slapped his hand as he reached for the beautiful huckleberry pie that was sitting in the middle of the table. "Oh, no, you don't," I warned as I cut a piece and put it on my plate. "I haven't had a piece of huckleberry pie in a long time. If you guys get to it first, I'll never get a piece."

I stood to go get the ice cream, keeping my eye on my piece of pie as I pulled it from the freezer.

I didn't trust any of my cousins with huckleberry pie, and my Aunt Millie made the best one in Montana. She had friends who brought her the best huckleberries in the state in exchange for a few pies and some of the jam she made.

I watched my cousins argue over the pie as I plopped a scoop of vanilla ice cream on mine with a smile.

It was hard to believe that three of the richest men in the world were squabbling over a pie, but my cousins' wealth hadn't really changed them much. Not to anyone who really knew them. While they might be sharks and were revered in the business world, they still acted like normal brothers when they were alone.

Everything about this family dinner felt familiar, including seeing my cousins argue about their portions of my Aunt Millie's pie.

"You're not nervous about tomorrow?" Kaleb asked as he put ice cream on his pie. "You've seen enough of the people in town to realize that nobody cares about what happened over a year ago, right?"

We'd gone to town several times, and other than curious glances from people I didn't know well, no one had acted weird. I'd been welcomed by old friends, and ignored by everyone else that either didn't remember me or know me.

I'd been uptight at first, wondering if people would be pointing fingers and gossiping, but it hadn't happened yet.

"I'm not nervous," I said with a sigh. Even if there was a little talk, I'd be gone soon, and it wouldn't affect me much. "It's nothing like it was over a year ago. You were right."

I also realized that I'd changed over the last year, and I wasn't nearly as vulnerable as I'd been before.

I'd gotten stronger, and I was much more capable of dealing with criticism about the incident because I didn't feel the same guilt as I had right after it had happened.

Wyatt had helped me with that. He'd made me realize that I was a victim, no matter what people said about me.

"Please don't tell me you're mooning over being separated from Wyatt," Tanner said drily. "It's only been a few days."

"And he'll be here on Tuesday," Devon said teasingly. "You can manage being separated for a week."

My aunt glared at her sons. "You boys stop teasing Shelby right now. I'm thrilled that she's with Wyatt now. He's such a nice boy."

Kaleb smirked, but as the oldest, he knew when to keep his mouth shut.

I nearly smiled myself because I wondered what a grumpy, cynical Wyatt had to say when Aunt Millie called him a *nice boy* to his face.

Honestly, I was pretty sure he was charming and dropped the bad attitude around my aunt. He was fond of her, and she probably got away with calling him anything she wanted.

"Wyatt's still concerned about your safety because the person responsible for your break-in hasn't been caught," Kaleb said in a more serious tone.

"You've been careful," Aunt Millie observed. "No one has let Shelby go anywhere alone. Do you think we should still be worried?"

I shook my head and sent Kaleb a warning look. The last thing I wanted was to upset my aunt. We had been careful, and despite my familiarity with the area, my cousins hadn't let me take a step outdoors alone. "You've all done your security duties well," I said as I smiled at my family. "I haven't had a single issue in San Diego since the break-in. I think we're going to have to assume that it was an isolated incident."

"Try convincing Wyatt of that," Kaleb replied grimly. "He isn't going to be happy until this person is caught. None of us are going to let you out of our sight tomorrow. While I agree it's very unlikely that anything will happen here, I'm glad that Wyatt is so bullheaded about it."

"Me, too," Devon agreed.

"I'd very much like to see this person caught," Tanner added. "Even if it was just a prank by some teenager or teenagers. At least we'd know who did it."

"We may never know," I warned all of them. "There was really nothing to investigate since they left no evidence behind. And Wyatt can't keep a security detail on me forever."

"You obviously haven't learned how stubborn Wyatt Durand can be," Kaleb said wryly.

I shot Kaleb an amused smile and reflexively fingered the object that Wyatt had insisted on giving me Tuesday night before I'd left. "I know exactly how hardheaded he can be, believe me. I had to put my foot down pretty hard on not having his security all over me here, but it would have been weird here in Crystal Fork. It would have drawn more attention to me, no matter how well they try to blend in. When has it been possible for that many strangers to come to Crystal Fork without raising some eyebrows? I wanted to come back to town with as little fanfare as possible, and I really just wanted time alone with all of you."

"It's been so nice having you home," Aunt Millie said tearfully. "I know I'm not your mother, but you've always felt like a daughter to me."

Tears welled up in my eyes as I reached across the table to take her hand. "And you've always been like a second mom to me. I'll get home more often now that everything has died down. I promise."

The four people sitting at this table were the only family I had. My aunt was like a mother to me, and my cousins were like brothers. Now that it wasn't painful to be here anymore, I'd try to make sure I saw them all as often as possible.

"I hope so," my aunt said as she squeezed my hand. "It's a short plane flight, and my sons can send one of their fancy jets to pick you up more often now that you're comfortable being here."

My heart ached over all the stress I'd put my family through because of my stupidity with Justin, but I knew none of them blamed me for what happened. And I no longer blamed myself for my one big mistake.

Thank God that horrible period of our lives was over now, and we could just be family again.

Chapter 29

Wyatt

"I'm here," I said to Marshall as I strode into his office at Last Hope headquarters a little before noon on Sunday. "What in the hell was so important that I had to delay my trip to Montana."

I was impatient as hell.

My endless meetings were finally over, and all I wanted was to get to the airport.

I still hadn't been able to connect with Shelby by phone, and I was cranky as hell because of it. I'd forced myself not to try to call her yesterday because I knew the annual picnic would take up most of her day. However, when I'd tried to call her on my way to see Marshall to let her know I was arriving early, my call had gone straight to voice mail.

Fuck! Was she pissed off or upset? Had she turned her phone off?

She hadn't sounded angry when she'd left her voicemails, but that didn't mean she wasn't hurt or still confused about what had happened Tuesday night.

My goal was to end this uncertainty as soon as possible in person, and I really couldn't get that accomplished when my ass wasn't on my jet headed for Montana.

I'd even tried to call Kaleb to let him know I was on my way, but he hadn't answered his damn phone, either.

Marshall stood up and slapped me on the shoulder on his way toward the door. "Let's go down to the meeting room. I sent out an emergency signal to everyone else. They should all be here by now. I have a theory about who might have broken into Shelby's apartment."

I'd done my last meeting this morning alone, but I had no doubt that Chase had hightailed it to the headquarters as soon as he'd gotten the emergency signal.

Marshall had my attention, and I followed him down the stairs.

For a man who had ended his special forces career because of a leg injury that had left him with a limp, Marshall moved quickly, and I had to hustle to keep up with him.

Everyone was present when we arrived in the meeting room.

Chase, Hudson, Jax, Harlow, Cooper, and Tori were already seated at the large table.

No doubt Taylor and Savannah would be present, too, if they were already members of Last Hope. They were planning on coming on board as advisors, but they hadn't made it official yet.

I took a seat next to Chase, and before anyone could start bombarding him with questions, Marshall held up a hand. "This isn't an emergency because of a mission we need to run. I have some news on the break-in at Shelby's apartment. Since I know you're all concerned, I thought an update was in order as soon as possible. Since I didn't want Wyatt to leave before I could get us all together, I decided it needed to happen right now."

Every set of eyes in the room were glued to Marshall, including mine.

"What did you find out?" Chase asked abruptly.

"This is just a theory," Marshall answered gruffly. "But it all makes sense when you put everything together. Because we had nothing, I started to investigate people Shelby might not suspect had a grudge against her, but who she made contact with fairly frequently, including anyone she interacted with at The Friendly

Kitchen. There was one person who stood out." He clicked the remote and a picture came up on the enormous screen in the meeting room. "This is a guy she speaks to fairly often according to the manager at the soup kitchen. His name is Theodore Lee Young."

"Ted?" I said as I eyed the large photo. "She talks about him. Shelby said he lost his wife and children in a car accident."

"That's true, but there were suspicions of abuse. Some people swore that his wife was probably trying to escape with her children from his abuse when the accident happened and that Ted was most likely chasing her down. He'd done it before. But they never had enough proof to arrest him for it."

"Fuck!" I cursed. "I guarantee that Shelby had no inkling of those suspicions. She felt sorry for him. Hell, she even told him about her own family and what happened. She also mentioned that he was ex-military."

"That much is true," Marshall confirmed. "But he was discharged for psychiatric issues."

I wasn't going to question exactly how Marshall had gotten that information. After years of working with him, I knew there was little to nothing that Marshall couldn't dig up with his worldwide sources and technical skills.

The older man continued as he switched the image on the screen to two women. "I just dug up the information that he's also a person of interest in the murder of two sex workers, but they don't have enough to arrest him yet. But I suspect that will happen soon."

I eyed the women's pictures for a moment, every muscle in my body tight because I noticed one big similarity. "They're both redheads," I noted tersely.

Marshall nodded and changed the image again. "And this is his deceased wife."

"Son of a bitch!" Chase spat out. "She's a redhead with long hair, too."

"I have a feeling it's no coincidence that the victims were chosen for their similarities to his late wife," Marshall concluded. "I can't say that Shelby is a doppelganger for Young's wife, but they both have the same curly, red hair and green eyes. Like I said, it's just a theory—"

"It's him," I said roughly. "It all makes sense, and I can feel it in my gut."

Everyone around the table was agreeing as my phone rang.

I pulled it from my jean pocket like a man possessed, hoping to God it was Shelby.

It wasn't.

But it was the next best thing.

"Kaleb," I answered sharply. "Where in the hell is Shelby?"

"That's why I'm calling," Kaleb replied. "I don't want you to panic, but I lost sight of her and I can't find her. She just went out to the barn a little bit ahead of me. We were planning on taking a ride. She was on my property, and I went to meet her out there minutes later, but she wasn't there. We're searching the property now, but I wanted you to know. We found her cell phone near the barn. I called the police already, but they aren't particularly concerned. They want to wait to see if she comes back on her own before they file a missing person's report since nobody saw anything. She's an adult, and she's only been missing for a short time. I've got every available person I've got out looking for her. We'll find her, Wyatt."

"Do the police know about the history of her break-in?" I asked angrily.

"Yeah. They don't think it's related since it happened in San Diego."

"Fuck! What kind of police force do you have there?" I grilled him.

"One that only deals with an occasional speeder or drunk in town," Kaleb said, his tone disgusted. "We're trying to get someone else higher up to listen. Someone who believes that someone can go missing, even in a small town."

"Good luck with that. She could be dead by then," I growled. "I'm on my way to Montana now. Let me know the second you see her if she's located."

"Got it," Kaleb agreed. "I'm on my way out the door to join the search."

I disconnected the call, trying not to lose my shit as I stared at the concerned faces around me.

"I think we all know what happened, even if no one else believes it," Hudson said in a grim voice. "The question is, how do we get her back before something happens to her. We have no idea where he's taking her or what his plans are. Montana is a big state with a lot of places to hide out."

"Or he could just keep driving into another state," Jax considered.

"If the police aren't on board, no one is even going to be looking for her yet except her family," Cooper added in a disgruntled voice.

"We have to do something," Tori said tearfully.

Marshall scowled. "I don't suppose there's a single one of you who would agree that this is happening on US soil, that it's not a government reject case, and we could get ourselves in trouble if we interfere." He looked around the room before he added unhappily, "Didn't think so."

"I'm not asking for Last Hope's involvement," I growled. "But I am going after her myself. I should have said fuck the international meetings and gone with her in the first place since she refused my security. I shouldn't have let her leave my damn sight. My gut was telling me that something wasn't right, and I didn't fucking listen."

"Screw it!" Marshall barked. "We're helping. What do you need? Did you give Shelby the tracker?"

"I did. She agreed to wear it, but I'm not sure how often she's had it on. Can you see if she's wearing it?" I asked, my voice hoarse with emotion.

Please, sweetheart. Even if you hate me right now, please be wearing that damn tracker.

I'd given Shelby a satellite GPS tracker Tuesday night that Marshall had designed for me. I knew the first thing that would go if she was ever abducted was her cell phone. Anything flashy would have drawn attention, so it was simply a leather cord to put around her neck with a tracker that was disguised as a small silver pendant with scrolls so it looked like some kind of simple, decorative jewelry.

She hadn't loved the idea, but I'd told her we could destroy it once she returned from Montana. I'd just wanted some kind of protection for her while she was in Montana because my gut had been screaming at me not to leave her vulnerable.

I understood that Kaleb believed there could still be danger for Shelby in Montana, but I wasn't completely convinced that someone would have eyes on her every moment while she was there.

In the end, to make me feel better, she'd agreed to wear it, saying it was better than having security on her tail.

I just wasn't sure how seriously she'd taken the possible risk, and whether she'd wear it all the time, especially considering she may still think that I'd been going to see someone else Tuesday night.

Christ! I hated myself for not just taking a few moments to at least tell her some of the truth.

Tori was right. Now that I'd had time to think about it, what else could she conclude? Plus, there was her history to consider. She'd been with some fucking idiots in the past who had taught her not to trust any guy when it came to fidelity.

It took time to get over shit like that, and I shouldn't have taken her statement about another woman so personally.

My heart was thundering like I'd just run a marathon as I watched Marshall connecting to the tracking program.

"Do we know what kind of vehicle he's driving?" Chase asked.

"No vehicle registered to him that I could find. He either borrows vehicles or steals them and dumps them," Marshall muttered, his fingers not pausing as they flew over his keyboard. "So it would be almost impossible to even ask for a police BOLO, even if we could successfully convince them that this is serious. As soon as I'm finished here, I'll get in touch with some contacts at the FBI. I could be wrong, but I doubt that Young's plan is just to kill her and dump her body somewhere immediately. That wasn't what he did with the two women he killed. They think he held them for a day or two. He's probably been waiting a long time for this opportunity to snatch Shelby. She looks a lot more like his deceased wife, which was probably why he targeted her in the first place. If he has transportation, he's taking her somewhere. Young hasn't been at the shelter for the last few days, and if he's capable of murdering two women in cold blood, he could easily steal some mode of transportation or carjack someone."

The rational part of my brain told me that Marshall was probably right about Young wanting to hold Shelby rather than killing her outright, but I didn't want that bastard touching Shelby in *any* way. Not a hair on her goddamn head.

"Got it," Marshall said as he used the remote to put the info on the large screen. "She's wearing the tracker and it's obviously not been identified. It looks like Young is still on the move."

The relief that coursed through my body almost made me lightheaded.

She was wearing that damn tracker, and we'd know exactly where she was located.

"I'm headed to the airport," I informed the room as I rose from my chair, so anxious to get to Shelby that I couldn't think about anything else.

"I'm right behind you with some gear," Chase told me as he got to his feet. "Marshall, we'll need a helicopter if this ends up being a remote area. He can't drive forever. He has to stop at some point."

"I'll have a few hours to cover everything while you guys are in flight, and I'll keep monitoring the tracker. Are you going to need backup?"

I shook my head. I was going to need Chase to fly, but I didn't want to get anyone else involved. "We can handle it. If you can get the police to listen, have them intercept. It would be faster."

"Do you really think they're going to buy that we have GPS tracking coordinates on her?" Hudson asked drily. "Nobody even believes that she's really missing."

"It's safer for us to covertly take her back," Cooper mused. "If anyone tries to intercept, she'll end up dead. This lunatic is a loose cannon."

"Wyatt!" Marshall called as I started to exit the meeting room.

"Yeah," I said impatiently, not bothering to turn around.

"Keep a straight head, and don't kill this asshole. I know you're going to want to take his head off, but it's not worth your future with Shelby. Get in, get your woman, and get the hell out. I'll have the feds there by the time you get her out to arrest this piece of shit."

"She's my entire fucking life now," I admitted in a graveled voice. "I'm going to do whatever I have to do to make sure she gets out of this alive."

"Understood," he replied. "But deadly force is a last resort. Shelby is your priority."

"Damn right she is," I growled as I headed for the door.

Chapter 30

Shelby

I woke up feeling dazed and confused.
What the hell...?
Pain exploded from what felt like every location on my body.

I was struggling for air, and it hurt just to take in a breath.

I forced myself to calm down, and breathe shorter and shallower.

The room was dark, and when I tried to move to a more comfortable position, I didn't get far.

I jerked at the bindings around my wrists and ankles that appeared to have me anchored to a bed.

Memories started to flash in my brain like brief clips of what had happened.

Kidnapped...
The off-grid cabin...
Ted...

Everything fell into place slowly until I could remember the whole ordeal.

I'd been in the barn with the horses at Kaleb's home when Ted had taken me by surprise from behind. He'd shoved something into my mouth so I couldn't scream. He'd then held a gun to my head, telling me if I tried anything stupid, he'd blow my head off.

His eyes had been wild and devoid of emotion, nothing like the man I'd known at The Friendly Kitchen, and I'd believed every threat he'd made.

The bastard had quickly bound my wrists and ankles when we got to the truck. He'd immediately dumped my cell phone. Hadn't Wyatt told me that would happen if I was abducted?

I held back a pain-induced groan, wishing I'd listened to Wyatt's instincts. They were obviously a lot better than mine.

Ted had pulled the gag from my mouth after twenty minutes or so of driving, but nothing I'd said to him had seemed to sink in.

Any hope I'd had of eventually reasoning with him had disappeared the first time he'd punched me in the truck for trying to make him listen to me.

So, I'd listened to him, and every word he'd uttered like a madman had made my skin crawl.

I wasn't his first kidnapping, and the other two women he'd captured were dead.

He'd also been responsible for the death of his wife and kids because he'd chased them down like a maniac until his wife had panicked and crashed her vehicle.

In his twisted mind, he wanted revenge because his wife had been trying to leave Ted's abuse, and because I looked like her, he'd focused his wrath on me.

Ted had been the one who had broken into my apartment, and he'd told me ad nauseum what he'd done with my underwear to get himself off until he could kidnap me.

He had followed me many times, and he'd bitched incessantly about his inability to catch me alone in San Diego once he'd decided to target me. Even though Wyatt's security was discreet, he'd known they were tailing me.

He'd tried to follow Wyatt and me the first time we'd gone out together, but he'd given up almost immediately. Ted had mentioned that Wyatt was much too aware of his surroundings, and he was afraid that he'd get caught.

God, had Ted gone off the deep end and started stalking and murdering women after the loss of his family? Obviously, he'd been abusive with his wife and probably his kids, too. He'd probably never been quite right in the head, but it was terrifying that he could appear to be a grieving man when it was necessary.

According to Ted, he'd killed those other two women because of his inability to get to me after the break-in. I'd supposedly been his real target, and I'd been inaccessible. Did I really believe that? Not really. He'd killed because he wanted to kill.

He'd been watching me on my trip to the airport.

Because Wyatt's security team had accompanied me until I passed through security at the airport, Ted had never had a chance to snatch me in San Diego. So the bastard had followed me to Montana, hoping I'd be more vulnerable here.

Unfortunately, he had good technical skills.

He'd stalked me online.

He knew where my family lived, and he'd even known where I was going because he knew about the annual picnic.

I shuddered as I thought about the way he'd targeted the takeover of this particular cabin because it was off-grid, and because there was a defenseless older man who lived here alone. A man who was now dead somewhere on this property. He'd killed the owner, stolen his truck so he could ditch the stolen vehicle he'd used to get here, and had staked out Kaleb's home, successfully concealing the truck until he saw an opportunity.

He'd gotten that opportunity when he'd spotted me leaving the house for the barn with a pair of high-powered binoculars that he'd also swiped from this small, one room cabin.

All of his acts for his so-called revenge were diabolical, vile, and more evil than any normal person could possibly comprehend.

My body froze as a loud snore sounded from right next to me on the other side of the bed.

Ted?

Oh, dear God, he was lying right next to me, probably so drunk that he had passed out.

He'd been drinking from a hard liquor bottle on his way here, and he'd consumed a lot more alcohol once we'd arrived.

In fact, he'd been so drunk that he'd been unable to get aroused enough to rape me, which had put him into a rage so out of control that he'd beaten me senseless until I'd lost consciousness.

My jeans were probably still unbuttoned, but I was completely dressed, just like I'd been before I'd passed out.

Now that I was fully awake and my brain was mildly functional, my heart was beating so hard and fast that I could barely hear the murderer snoring beside me.

Bile rose up in my throat, and my eyes watered from the nausea I was experiencing because I was literally lying right next to a serial killer.

What in the hell was I going to do?

Accessing this off-grid home had been miles of dirt road without another structure around. Even if I could get free, I had nowhere to go. I couldn't move without experiencing pain so intense that it was crippling.

God, maybe I should have fought Ted harder in the very beginning, but because I knew him, and because I didn't want my head blown off, I'd thought it would be wiser to comply until he calmed down.

Of course, that was before I knew he could rape and kill someone without a single ounce of remorse.

I had no doubt that Ted would kill me just like he'd killed the others before me. He might wake up with a raging hangover, but he'd be sober and capable of carrying through with his plans.

I *had* to find a way to get the hell out of here.

My adrenaline and fear were blocking some of the pain at the moment, but I wasn't sure exactly what injuries I'd suffered, and if I could physically manage to walk my way out.

Frustrated tears poured down my face in the darkness as I tested the strength of my bonds carefully.

The thick rope was so tight around my wrists and ankles that it was cutting off my circulation, and there was no give in the material.

Dammit!

Don't panic, Shelby! Think! Try to think of another way out of this nightmare!

I tried not to let my hopelessness overwhelm me, but realistically, I knew my chances of getting out of this situation were slim to none.

Now, I wished that I had told Wyatt how I felt about him, and I really wished I'd paid closer attention to his aptitude for sensing possible danger.

Wait!

Wyatt!

The GPS tracker!

I moved my head until I could feel the small device around my neck.

Ted hadn't noticed it at all.

Was it possible that Wyatt knew I was in trouble? That he could track me using that tracker and notify the police?

I tried not to get my hopes up. By now, Kaleb had definitely sounded the alarm that I was missing, but I wasn't sure that he'd even call Wyatt until he knew exactly what was happening.

No one had been around when Ted had kidnapped me. They were probably still searching Kaleb's property.

Wyatt probably had no idea anything was even wrong, and he wasn't the type of guy to stalk me with a GPS tracker unless he needed to know my location.

Remembering the tracker gave me a ray of hope, but it was a long shot. I had a limited amount of time.

I had no idea what time it was, but the cabin was so dark that all I could see was a faint light from the moon and stars filtering into the bare window across the room.

It was then that I noticed that the window was starting to open.

Inch by inch.

Little by little.

So slowly that I couldn't hear it even as I tried to listen through Ted's intermittent snoring.

Someone was going to enter the cabin, and I didn't know if I should scream or hope it was someone who would help me.

My vulnerable state really hit home as I realized that someone else who was wide awake would be in this room very soon, and I had no idea what their intentions were going to be.

It could be someone with nefarious goals, but what could be worse than waking up the serial killer who was snoring beside me?

Ted was most definitely going to rape me, torture me, and kill me.

I decided I'd rather take my chances with whoever was coming into the cabin.

My body trembling with terror, I watched as a very large, black-clad figure entered the cabin so stealthily that the person didn't make a sound.

I couldn't make out much. Just the outline of the individual.

Because the body appeared to be so large, I assumed it was a male, which scared the hell out of me.

The second he moved away from the small pool of light at the window, I had no idea where he went.

I laid there motionless, afraid to twitch a single muscle until I knew what this person wanted.

My brain rebelled, and my body recoiled as I felt a hand cover my mouth and warm breath from the stranger wafting across my cheek.

"Don't make a sound, Shelby," a low, urgent voice said in a harsh whisper next to my ear. "It's Wyatt, and I'm getting you the fuck out of here. Nod your head if you understand."

Complete understanding was slow to reach my muddled brain.

Wyatt?

My Wyatt?

What in the hell was he doing here?

Even though I didn't understand what was happening, I knew exactly who was keeping me silent.

Every cell in my body recognized him, even if my mind couldn't quite make sense of the situation.

I nodded, and he instantly released his hold on my mouth.

I winced as the bonds were apparently cut from my limbs, and some of the blood circulation started to return to my hands and feet.

I bit back a gasp of pain as Wyatt lifted me off the bed and cradled me in his arms.

He strode back to the window, and transferred me to another shadowy figure outside the window.

"My name is Brock Miller, Shelby. I'm Wyatt's backup," a second man whispered loud enough for me to hear him as he held me securely in his arms. "Hang tight. You're safe with me. He needs to get out the window."

My first weird and random thought was that the guy holding me was just as bulky and as sturdy as Wyatt.

My mind whirled, but my body relaxed, and I gripped Brock around the shoulders for balance as Wyatt left the cabin just as covertly as he'd entered.

I hurt.

Bad.

Every movement was agony. I couldn't take a breath without the pain, but my stress was overriding that agony right now.

A million questions flew through my mind, but I knew I couldn't ask them out loud.

Who was Brock, and what was he doing here?

Why was Wyatt here?

Where in the hell were the police?

My guess was that Wyatt had tracked my location from the satellite tracker I was still wearing. I'd hoped someone would come, but I sure as hell hadn't expected Wyatt to show up in person.

By himself.

With only another man to help him.

Shit! Did he have any idea how dangerous Ted was?

I also had questions about how they'd pulled this off.

Not only had they found me, but they'd obviously found a way to get to me quickly in an off-grid location that was hard to access.

Without a vehicle.

The cabin wasn't all that sturdy and the only window faced the long driveway. I would have heard the vehicle coming and seen the lights in the window.

Apparently, they'd had a way in, and they had a way to get out.

"What the fuck!" Ted's voice sounded angrily from inside the cabin. "Where the fuck is she?"

"Haul ass for the chopper, Brock," Wyatt demanded harshly. "I'll call in the feds and be on your six."

Without another word, the man holding me took off like a shot toward the woods, tightening his arm around shoulders and ribs to keep me tight against his body.

I heard a gunshot.

And then another.

Following by multiple shots ringing out eerily in the silence of the dead of night.

Pain like I'd never experienced before shot through my ribs from Brock's grip on me and the hard pounding of his pace as I was jostled around in his arms.

Wyatt!

Where is Wyatt?

The horror of knowing he was still behind us, and hoping to God he wasn't in the line of fire were the last things I remembered before everything went black.

Chapter 31

Wyatt

I stayed on Brock's ass after I'd let the feds know they could move in, returning fire as he sped into the woods with Shelby.

I knew I probably wouldn't hit the asshole who was shooting from the window. He wasn't popping his head out anymore, but I hoped that it would keep him from wildly firing his gun.

I was grateful now that one of my guys from the team in Michigan had met up with Chase and me at the airport.

My brother had needed to stay with our ride, and I'd needed the backup.

Brock had been nearby on a brief vacation, and when he'd heard about what had happened from Marshall, he'd hopped a plane to Billings. He'd actually arrived before Chase and I had gotten into Montana.

Maybe we weren't Delta anymore, but the camaraderie of working that closely together for so many years had never faded for any of us. We'd had each other's backs for so long that we'd probably never stop being a team.

I could see the lights from a plethora of vehicles coming up the rough, dirt road toward the cabin to apprehend the asshole we'd left alive in the cabin.

I'd struggled not to put my knife into the assholes heart myself after seeing what he'd done to Shelby, but Marshall was right. She came first. Not only would the action traumatize her more, but I'd probably end up in jail, and I needed to be there for Shelby.

I wasn't giving up my life and my future with her for a piece of shit.

I watched Brock as he made his way through the woods like he knew exactly where he was going without a compass or directions.

His talent for tracking and finding his way around in the woods was one of the big reasons why I'd relented on using him as backup.

He'd discreetly left almost imperceptible marks as we'd come through the woods the first time so we could hightail it out by following that marked trail. The guy's ability to follow just about any trail was one of his many talents.

We moved quietly through the trees until we were well away from any danger of being shot.

"Hold up," I bellowed to Brock. "I'll take her now."

Chase had needed to land far enough away to avoid the heavily wooded areas, and to keep the noise of the helicopter from alerting Shelby's kidnapper.

One look at Shelby told me that she was out cold. "What the hell happened?" I growled as Brock passed me her limp body.

"She's alive and breathing," Brock informed me. "I think she passed out from the pain. That asshole beat the hell out of her, and I'm not sure we know the half of all her injuries."

"Fuck!" I cursed, wishing I'd gone ahead and plunged my Ka-bar knife into the murderous bastard's heart when I'd had the chance.

Brock and I were both wearing night vision goggles. I'd been able to see that her face was battered, but I'd tried to close that off and focus on my objective.

She'd been alive and obviously coherent when I'd pulled her out of the cabin, and the only thing I'd been thinking about was getting her as far away from further danger as quickly as I could.

But it wasn't as easy as it used to be for me to compartmentalize on a mission, even though I'd tried like hell to close off my emotions.

Shelby wasn't just another rescue.

Like I'd told Marshall, she was my whole fucking life. It was hard to close that shit down, especially when I'd seen that she'd been beaten, and I had no idea what else had happened in the hours that had passed before we could pull her out.

Because we'd worked together for so many years, Brock took point and resumed his journey without a word from me. He already knew that was what I'd want him to do.

I'd been the team leader, but my team hadn't always needed to rely on my direction.

We pushed hard, knowing we had to get Shelby medical care as soon as possible.

I'd probably lose my shit once she was safe, but for now, I had to keep my personal feelings on lockdown.

We'd been on the move for a while when Shelby stirred in my arms.

"Wyatt?" she murmured, her voice sounding confused and strained.

"I've got you, sweetheart," I crooned as I kept my pace toward the helicopter.

"I don't understand what's happening," she said with a small moan as she wrapped her arms around my neck. "I hurt all over. It's worse than when I was in the cabin."

Hell, she'd probably been so full of adrenaline in the cabin that she hadn't noticed the pain as much as she did now. She was also getting bounced all over the place by my movements. "We're almost there. Hang in there a little longer. I know you're hurting, but we're getting you to a hospital as quickly as possible."

"I don't understand any of this," she said, sounding more alert, but breathless, like every inhalation was an effort. "What are you doing here, and how in the hell can you see where we're going without tripping over something. It's dark."

"I'll explain everything," I promised. "After you get medical treatment and I know that you're okay."

I couldn't think beyond her well-being, and we were in no position to have a long conversation about something important at the moment.

I hated myself for not telling her sooner about Last Hope because it was a meaningful part of my life, even if the rescues didn't happen that often sometimes.

"I'm still not sure that I'm not hallucinating or in the middle of a hopeful dream of some kind," she said weakly. "Are you really here? Am I really free? And if I am, is Ted chasing us?"

I hated the fear I heard in her voice, and I needed to remove those concerns immediately. "You're really free, and that asshole isn't going anywhere. He's dead, Shelby. Do you understand? He's never coming after you again."

I'd gotten that radio message a few minutes ago, along with the news that they found the owner's body outside, behind the cabin. Young had shot himself in the head after a short standoff. Once the FBI had arrived, he'd known there was no other way out.

"He killed the owner of the cabin, Wyatt. His body is somewhere on the property, but Ted didn't say where exactly," Shelby told me in a tearful voice.

Because it upset Shelby, it wasn't a subject I wanted to discuss right now, but I'd sworn to myself that once I'd gotten her back that I'd never have another secret that she didn't know. I wasn't going to hide anything from her anymore. "They found his body. The feds came in right after we got you out. After a brief encounter with them, the bastard decided to kill himself."

She was silent for a moment before she murmured, "Thank God. He raped and killed two other women, too, Wyatt."

Fuck! Obviously, Young had bragged to Shelby about all of his crimes, which had probably terrified the hell out of her. "I know. Marshall dug up that information about the same time that you were kidnapped. The timing sucked."

"I honestly thought I was going to die," Shelby answered softly near my ear. "I don't understand why you're here, or how it's even possible, but I have to be the luckiest woman in the world because you came for me."

Christ! There was that gratitude…again. She would have been a lot more fortunate if the son of a bitch had never laid his hands on her in the first place.

"I'm always going to come for you, babe," I said honestly. "You owe your supposed luck to the fact that you trusted me enough to keep that GPS tracker on."

She sighed. "I didn't do it because I thought I was in serious danger. I did it because you asked me to do it, and I trust you. I didn't want you to worry about me. You saved my life, Wyatt. His plan was to kill me, and I don't think I had much time."

I had to force the next question out of my mouth. "Did he rape you?"

"No," she said as her body shuddered. "He was so drunk that he wasn't physically capable of it, which is why he beat the hell out of me. I lost consciousness for a while, and when I came to, he was out cold. Not long after that, I saw you coming through the window. I decided to keep my mouth shut and take my chances since the alternative was screaming, which would have woken up my kidnapper. God, how did any of this happen? I've spoken to Ted many times, and I've always felt sorry for him because he lost his family. I had no idea that he actually caused that accident. I never saw this side of him."

Okay, so the bastard really had bragged about *all* of his victims. "It's not your fault that you didn't know, Shelby. Sociopaths are good at manipulating people. I couldn't prove that you were in danger. Nothing suspicious has happened since the break-in. It was gut instinct for me."

"I wish I had your instincts," she replied woefully. "He was stalking me, Wyatt. He just made sure it wasn't obvious when he was doing it in person instead of on the internet. I think he read every blog and social media post I did and followed every video hoping I'd give out personal clues."

I'd already figured that out. I wasn't sure how often he'd been watching her in person, but I wished to hell I'd listened harder to my instincts instead of writing them off as overreactions because it was personal for me.

She continued weakly, "I'm not sure when he decided to target me. I'm assuming it started with the break-in. He hated redheads or any woman who reminded him of his wife, and I apparently looked like her in his mind. He was pure evil, Wyatt. I'm not going to lie and pretend that I'm not glad he's dead. I am glad that he can't hurt anyone else." She paused before she moaned, "Oh, God, why do I hurt so much?"

"Because some asshole kicked the crap out of you," I said furiously, wishing again that I'd been the one to kill the bastard who had touched her. "We're here, sweetheart. The painful part will be over soon."

I'd never been so damn glad to hear the thrum of helicopter blades as I was right now.

Brock hopped into the aircraft and reached for Shelby.

I handed her over reluctantly and followed them inside.

As soon as Brock and I pulled our helmets and goggles off, Chase hit the internal lights.

It was the first time I'd really seen the true injuries to Shelby's face, and it made me fucking livid.

Her entire face was swollen, and there wasn't an inch of it that wasn't purple with bruises.

She was dripping with sweat that was probably mixed with tears of pain, and I could see the real toll the trip to the helicopter had taken on her, but she'd obviously been trying not to complain.

"Fuck!" I cursed before I could stop myself for Shelby's sake.

Once Brock had gently put her down, I noticed that she was guarding her ribs, and I pulled up her shirt only to see that her entire side was covered with more bruises.

It was a miracle she was even coherent and that she could speak.

"I know it looks bad, Wyatt," Brock said carefully as he opened his medical pack. "But she's breathing and she's conscious."

She was also in a hell of a lot of pain.

I let Brock handle Shelby's emergency medical treatment because I wasn't equipped to do it at the moment. I took her hand and stayed glued to my spot beside her.

"I don't see a source for all the blood on her shirt," Brock said shortly.

Chase turned around from the pilot's seat. "Holy fuck! It's not coming from Shelby. It's Wyatt. He took a hit, Brock, and he's bleeding pretty badly."

"Oh, God, Wyatt. You were shot!" Shelby whimpered in an alarmed voice.

"Hospital, Chase!" I ordered. "I know that I took a hit, but I'm sure it's just a flesh wound. I'm worried about Shelby. Let's get moving."

My injury was insignificant.

I'd felt the sting of the bullet, but I'd ignored it.

I wasn't dying from it, and nobody was touching me until Shelby was treated, out of pain, and safe.

Chapter 32

Wyatt

"Do I even want to ask how in the hell you ended up with a bullet wound or how you probably saved Shelby's life?" Kaleb asked wryly the following afternoon in the lobby of a Billings hospital.

Despite the way she looked right now, Shelby's injuries weren't life-threatening, and she was being discharged. She wanted to go home, and since I'd be there to watch her, I wasn't about to argue. She'd be more comfortable there. They'd kept her overnight because she'd lost consciousness. They'd also done extensive X-rays. The worst of her injuries were her bruised ribs. She had internal contusions that were going to hurt like hell until they healed.

They'd treated the gunshot wound to my arm. Like I'd assumed, it was a simple flesh wound that had bled profusely.

I'd told Brock and Chase to head out as soon as we knew that Shelby was going to be okay. I'd stayed in her room the night before because I had a hard time letting her out of my sight. It didn't matter that her kidnapper was dead. I had to convince *myself* that she was going to be okay.

Kaleb and I had moved his vehicle to the front of the hospital, and we were waiting for the nurse to bring Shelby down in a wheelchair.

Since Kaleb had asked me to come with him to the lobby to wait, I'd known I was going to get some questions that I didn't want to answer the moment we'd sat down.

I hadn't explained to Shelby yet exactly what had happened. Her medical condition took priority, and I'd simply asked her to tell her family that the FBI had come to the rescue until I could explain.

She'd trusted me enough to do that, and everyone had bought it. Nobody had asked a lot of questions because they thought it might upset Shelby.

Well, everyone had bought that explanation *except* Kaleb.

He'd been shooting me skeptical glances since he'd first arrived at the hospital.

Chase had called him, and he'd been there in the emergency room soon after the helicopter had landed. He'd left to shower and sleep, but he hadn't been gone long.

My old friend had practically dragged me to a gurney to get my wound treated, so he knew that I'd been shot.

Somehow, I needed to contain that information. The hospital had been satisfied because the FBI had shown up to talk to me. They'd simply done their job in the busy ER and let the authorities deal with the criminal part.

I wasn't sure how Marshall did it, but he'd assured me that this incident wasn't going to expose Last Hope's operations.

The guy had some powerful friends that neither I—nor anyone in Last Hope—knew about if he could cover up the fact that we'd gone in and rescued Shelby before the rest of the calvary had moved in.

"Look," Kaleb said when I remained silent. "I trust you, which is why I haven't said a word to my family about my suspicions or that bullet wound. I'm just damn grateful that Shelby is going to be okay. But you can't blame me for asking questions about exactly how that happened. I love her, Wyatt. She's like a sister to me, and I don't buy the story about the FBI saving her?"

I let out a long breath. I didn't want to lie to one of my oldest friends. "I'd appreciate it if you kept the bullet wound to yourself," I said gruffly. "I got it after I pulled Shelby out of that cabin. I had help. You met Brock briefly, and you know that Chase was here. I sent them away before the rest of your family got here to avoid the questions about why they were here in the first place. I can't tell you all of it, but it's not because I don't trust you. It's just better if you don't know everything, and it's complicated."

"Does this complicated situation have anything to do with how you apparently knew exactly where Shelby was and who took her when nobody else knew?" Kaleb questioned stoically.

I nodded as I looked around to make sure no one had entered the empty space we were taking up in the lobby. "Yes. We have access to some intel that most law enforcements agencies don't."

"When you say *we*, I'm assuming that includes Chase and your other special forces friends, too?" he questioned.

"Yes," I admitted quietly.

"Government work?" he grilled me.

"Not exactly," I said evasively. "Let's just say that we use the skills we acquired to help people who are in bad situations. And in order to keep helping people, we have to keep our involvement a secret or we're done. We don't usually get involved with anything on US soil or anything that's being handled by US authorities. Shelby's case was different. If we hadn't gotten involved, she would have been dead by now because nobody local was taking her disappearance seriously. It was also safer for us to take her out covertly before the feds came in. You saw what happened when the FBI moved in. This asshole was insane, and I have no doubt he would have killed Shelby before he killed himself. He wouldn't have let her live, Kaleb."

Kaleb and his family now knew the basics about who the perpetrator was and why he'd done it. They also knew that Young was dead and that he'd never threaten Shelby again.

"Everything you've just told me will always stay just between the two of us," Kaleb replied. "I don't need to know everything else because I don't want to jeopardize whatever you're doing. The rest of my family will never know. I don't doubt that you're saving other people's lives. I know you, Wyatt. You might act like a hard-ass, but doing something good for people in secret is right up your alley. I'm just not exactly sure how to thank you for what you did, especially since I was the asshole who caused it to happen in the first place. I should have trusted your instincts and not let her out of my sight, even if it was just for a few minutes. Now that we know that Shelby's going to be okay, my brothers and I are going to find a way to get our small police department better equipped to handle something like this. I thought she was safer here, but I was wrong."

I shook my head. "It wasn't your fault. Hell, I don't think anyone could have foreseen just how crazy this asshole was, Kaleb. I am obsessed about Shelby's safety, and I'm not sure that obsession is going to get any better after this."

I'd come way too close to losing her, and even though Young was dead, I couldn't forget how vulnerable she'd been to a fucking serial killer.

"She's stubborn," Kaleb warned.

"I'm well aware of that," I said drily.

"Take care of her, Wyatt," Kaleb advised grimly. "She may not always show it because of her past, but her heart can still get broken, and she cares about you."

I shot him an irritated glance. "Did it ever occur to you that she could dump me?"

"Nope," Kaleb quipped. "I know Shelby. She wouldn't still be at your place if she didn't want to be there and if she wasn't serious about your relationship. She's crazy about you, Wyatt. It's obvious. At least it's obvious to the people who love her."

Yeah, well, Kaleb obviously didn't know about what had happened before she left for Montana, and I certainly wasn't going to be the one to tell him. "I feel the same way about her," I confessed. "And the last thing I plan on doing is breaking her heart. I'm more afraid that she'll get sick of my ornery ass and leave."

"She won't," Kaleb said confidently. "She has a lot of practice dealing with obstinate jerks, and she still loves all three of us."

"Yeah, but she doesn't have to live with you three," I pointed out.

"Why does it sound like you have no intention of letting her move out even though she's not in danger anymore?" Kaleb said.

"I don't," I confirmed.

I saw no reason to bullshit Kaleb, even if he was a protective male figure in Shelby's life.

"Friendship or no friendship, if you don't treat her right, I'll knock you senseless," Kaleb warned.

I smirked. "I don't think you'll ever have a reason to deck me."

"I believe you," he said reluctantly. "I just want you to know that her family is always going to be there for her if you aren't."

I reached out and slapped him on the back. "You won't have to be. From now on, you can just love her like you always have. Let me take care of everything else. I'm going to work from home until she's recovered, and she has a lot of worried friends that will be there for her, too."

There was so much more I wanted to say to Kaleb, like there wasn't a chance in hell that I was going to let anything bad happen to Shelby again. And that I was going to do my best to make sure she never had a reason to shed a tear again because it killed me to see her cry.

I wanted to tell him that she was mine, and that she was my everything.

However, I needed a chance to convince Shelby about all those things first.

"They're here," Kaleb said as he stood. "Are you sure you two can't stay longer?"

I shook my head. "I think she'll recover better in San Diego. I don't think she needs to see the place where she was abducted over and over right now."

Shelby was brave as hell, and she'd put this behind her. She'd decided on her own last night that she'd feel better while she was recovering if she could see Montana in her rearview mirror for just a little while.

It would also help if she had support to get over her kidnapping, and her friends in San Diego could be there for her and understand exactly what she was going through.

If she needed to see a special therapist, I could more easily provide that, too.

Selfishly, I also wanted her with me at home. I might live in the city, but my security was a whole lot better than it was here.

I clenched my fists and tried not to lose my mind when I saw her being wheeled toward the door by the nurse with all the rest of her family trailing behind.

Every time I saw her swollen and bruised face, I remembered how much she'd been through, and just how much I wished I could make Young pay for what he'd done to Shelby.

It also made me recall that I'd fucked up.

I should have been here in Montana with her.

I should have done a better job at keeping her safe.

I should have listened to my instincts, even though everything had pointed toward her being in the clear.

I'd failed at keeping her from going through this kind of pain, and I hated myself for that.

Unfortunately, all I could do was make damn sure it never happened again.

Chapter 33

Shelby

"If I didn't know that you were telling me the truth," I said to Wyatt on the plane ride home. "I'd say that this whole story was downright unbelievable."

He'd spent the last hour and a half explaining the existence of Last Hope, and answering questions.

He'd started from the time he'd joined Marshall's efforts in Last Hope and ended with exactly how he'd rescued me.

One of the things that had surprised me the most was that Hudson and Jax had personally rescued Taylor instead of sending an active team, and that all of my friends had somehow been a Last Hope interest at some point or another.

Even Tori's second kidnapping had ended with her being rescued by Cooper with Last Hope's assistance.

The other thing that had shocked me was that Tori and Harlow were actually volunteer members who lent their skills to the volunteer rescue organization. Savannah and Taylor weren't official members yet, but they planned on volunteering as advisors in the near future. Maybe I shouldn't be surprised that all of them wanted to be involved with helping people who had gone through the same thing they did, but the sheer scope of Last Hope's members was mind boggling.

"Do you understand why I didn't try to explain all of this in a couple of minutes now?" Wyatt asked drily as he lounged next to me on the bed, his back against the headboard.

Really, he wouldn't be explaining it *now* if I hadn't insisted on knowing immediately, but I let that slide.

He'd wanted me to rest on the ride home, but I'd reached my limit. I'd basically lied to my family to cover up the fact that Wyatt had come and rescued me himself.

I trusted him, but I'd wanted answers.

And…I'd gotten them.

We'd been talking about this for over an hour, and I still had questions.

"Does Kaleb know?" I questioned.

"No. I was forced to give him some brief information earlier today because he knew I'd gotten shot, and he suspected the fed rescue was bullshit. But that explanation was very basic, and I asked him to keep it quiet. All he knows is that some of the previous special forces members help people out of bad situations, and I admitted that I pulled you out myself. It's not that I wouldn't trust him completely with the information, but the less people who know, the better. We're filling a need that needs to be filled. There's a reason Marshall named the organization Last Hope."

They were saving the lives of hostages and kidnapping victims that would probably otherwise be dead without help, so the moniker definitely fit.

"I understand," I murmured. "I think it's an amazing thing you all do, but give me time to digest the fact that a group like this even exists. Why didn't you tell me before that night you pulled the disappearing act?"

Wyatt shrugged. "I trusted you enough to tell you, but I just hadn't gotten the opportunity. We were still getting to know each other, sweetheart. It wasn't something I wanted to spring on you out of the blue. Sometimes we don't do an op for months on end. It was a busy period for Last Hope. That was the third mission we'd run in a matter of weeks. Things don't usually happen that way. I thought I'd have time."

"Were you out at headquarters with Xena monitoring an operation the night of the break-in?"

"Yes," he answered simply. "Tori and Cooper were still there with me, too. We were just finishing up at headquarters. That's how I knew what happened to you."

It made sense now. That's why Wyatt was out with Xena, and why Tori was awake so late.

"Will I get to see this high-tech headquarters someday?" I queried.

I had to admit that I was curious to see where these secret operations were monitored and run.

Wyatt turned his head and grinned at me. "I'd show you, but then I'd have to kill you. It's a top secret place that's designed to look very mundane."

I snorted. "I think I'll risk it. I suppose that tour will have to wait. Right now, you can't even stand to look at my bruises."

His smile disappeared. "You're right. It kills me that I wasn't there to keep this from happening."

I reached out and took his hand. "You can't be with me every moment of the day, Wyatt. It was my fault. I was the one who went out to the barn by myself. I didn't want to wait a few minutes for Kaleb. I probably made the wrong decision when it happened, too. I probably should have fought Ted harder."

"He had a goddamn gun to your head," Wyatt reminded me. "You might have died, too. Don't second-guess the decisions you made, Shelby. It will make you crazy, and you're alive. You did everything right."

"Isn't that what you're doing?" I challenged.

"That's different," he grumbled.

"No, it's not," I insisted. "And it was your instincts that saved my life, Wyatt. If I hadn't been wearing the GPS tracker, I'd be dead right now. No one would have been able to find me before he killed me. And I'm still pissed off that you ended up shot. You could have died, too."

The emotional stress and the fact that he could have died doing that rescue overwhelmed me.

Tears started to flow down my cheeks unchecked.

"There is never going to be a time that I wouldn't take a bullet for you, Shelby," Wyatt rumbled as he turned and started to swipe the tears from my face. "Don't cry. I'm not dead, and I fucking hate it when you cry."

I punched him on the shoulder, but I didn't stop bawling. "Then don't ever risk your life like that again. You knew you were coming to try to get me away from a madman, and you did it anyway."

"No promises," he answered stubbornly. "If you're ever in danger, I'm right there with you."

"Why do you have to be so damn bullheaded?" I asked.

"I thought you liked my cantankerous personality," he teased as he pulled my head against his shoulder gently, making sure he didn't touch my torso or my ribs.

"I do," I muttered reluctantly. "Most of the time. But that was before I knew you were still doing badass things like you did in special forces, although I'm glad that you're usually just monitoring and running operations remotely now."

He caressed my hair soothingly as he said, "I was Delta Force. I guess I forgot to tell you that. Brock was one of my team members. I was the team leader."

Delta Force?

"Aren't those super-secret groups that nobody knows much about?"

I'd heard of Delta Force through books and social media, and I was also aware the public never saw their faces.

"Yes. I was an Army Ranger first, and then I went to Delta Force. Our identities were kept anonymous, and our missions were shrouded in secrecy. We had a code of silence, and we honored it. You're never going to see a real Delta operator out in public taking credit for any mission. Most of the former members aren't even going to admit they were Delta to anyone who doesn't need to know."

"So you never got credit for any of the dangerous things you did?" I questioned curiously.

"We didn't need credit for them," Wyatt said, his tone sincere. "That wasn't why any of us were there."

"I'm glad you told me," I said with a sigh.

He kissed the top of my head carefully before he replied, "I think you needed to know. No more secrets. I'm so damn sorry if I hurt you with my stupid comment that night. I shouldn't have expected blind trust when I'd done nothing to deserve it. I should have told you about Last Hope before that situation came up."

"I trusted you," I confessed. "I think it was a ghost from my past that crept into our relationship. I shouldn't have asked for reassurance about that."

"If you need it, ask," Wyatt instructed. "You'll never get that reaction again. There isn't now and there won't be another woman in my life, Shelby. The only woman I even see is you, and I think you're probably the only female who would put up with my unromantic, sorry ass."

My heart somersaulted with happiness. "That comment was incredibly romantic. Well, not the one about me putting up with your unromantic ass. The one about me being the only woman you see," I teased. "You do and say a lot of romantic things, Wyatt Durand, and I don't always need the words. Your actions tell me everything. God, what woman could have a badass who would risk his own life for hers and not know that he cares?"

"A completely selfish act," he said lightly. "My life would suck without you, and I doubt very much whether anyone else would have me."

I snorted. "Only every other single woman on the planet if they knew what an incredible guy you are."

"There's a problem with that, beautiful," he drawled. "None of those women are you."

I let out another long sigh.

For a guy who claimed to be unromantic, he said some things that made my damn heart melt into a puddle.

Maybe Wyatt was a grumpy enigma to most people, but I knew the heart that laid under that broad chest of his, and it was beautiful.

He wasn't a *words* guy; he was a man of action.

He'd reinforced that opinion by running into a dangerous situation to rescue me without a damn thought for his own safety.

He could be hurt, and I had hurt him when I'd questioned his feelings for me and his loyalty to our relationship.

I didn't need reassurance anymore.

I just needed…him.

I started to turn my body instinctively so I could kiss him, and then moaned.

Dammit!

I was so twitterpated that I'd forgotten about my stupid injuries.

Wyatt frowned. "You're hurting. I'll get you something for the pain."

I shook my head as I leaned my head against his shoulder again. "I'm okay. I just have to remember that some movements don't work well with beat up ribs. All I wanted was to kiss you."

He moved slowly, and I moved my head.

Wyatt shifted his massive body until he'd turned himself around and he was facing me.

His beautiful gray eyes were swirling with emotion when they met my gaze.

He tipped my chin up with a light touch of his finger, and slowly lowered his head.

The kiss was gentle and light, but there were so many emotions in that simple touching of our lips that it moved me.

Adoration.

Devotion.

Affection.

Reverence.

Everything a woman could savor when she wasn't capable of a passionate embrace.

All of the emotions that proved that there was so much more than just a physical attraction between us.

Wyatt and I were connected, even when I looked like a train wreck physically.

"Better?" he asked huskily when he'd lifted his lips from mine.

"Much better. I think I needed that," I told him as I watched him turn around again so he was next to me.

That kiss had gone a long way toward wiping away the memories of Ted trying to assault me.

Wyatt threaded his hand into my hair carefully and nudged my head against his shoulder again, gently stroking my scalp in a comforting motion.

"Don't you guys usually have nicknames when you're on a special forces team?" I questioned.

He shrugged. "We did. We dropped them when we got back into the civilian world. We were ready to live normal lives, and assimilate back into the nonmilitary world. That's not easy to do when your friends still call you by a nickname. Brock's nickname was Eagle. It would be an odd name for a civilian."

"What was yours?" I asked curiously.

"Arctic," he answered readily.

Arctic? Really?

"Why? There must be a reason for that one."

"There is," he told me. "I didn't have a nickname going into Delta, so I got the name Arctic because I could always direct a mission unemotionally and logically, even when everything turned into a shitshow. I had a talent for compartmentalizing, even when a mission went to hell. To some extent, I still have that ability except when I'm with you. You're one hell of a distraction."

"And you think you're not?" I said with mock indignation. "I had absolutely no problem avoiding sex or relationships until I met a very hot, very irresistible man who was impossible to ignore. You annoyed the hell out of me in the beginning, but I still wanted to tear your clothes off."

I was running out of energy, and I suddenly yawned. The hypnotic motion of Wyatt's fingers rubbing my scalp were getting to me.

"You're more than welcome to do that anytime you want as soon as you're completely recovered," he said hoarsely.

My lips turned up slowly as my eyes grew heavy.

I didn't answer, but I fell asleep with a smile on my face.

Chapter 34

Wyatt

"This place is absolutely amazing," Shelby commented with awe in her tone. "It's obvious now how you can manage to run complex operations from here. It really is high-tech."

I'd spent the last hour showing Shelby around our Last Hope headquarters.

She'd wanted to get out of the house after spending over a month recovering from her ordeal.

She looked beautiful in a white sundress that was splashed with a dark navy, floral pattern. It had a halter top, which worked because it was an unusually warm, early fall day, and the hem ended right above her knee. It was modest compared to some other warm weather dresses, but it didn't matter. My cock had gone harder than a rock just from looking at her in that damn dress.

Hell, lately, my dick got hard when Shelby was around for no apparent reason, too.

It had taken three weeks for her bruises to fade, and I'd been there to watch as they changed color every damn week.

She might be pain free now, but it had killed me to watch her slow, painful movements as she was healing.

The only thing that was still visible was a healed cut on her cheek that had needed a few sutures, and it was a reminder of everything she'd been through every time I saw it.

Mentally, Shelby was strong. She'd started intensive counseling almost immediately. The trauma counselor had come to the house nearly every day for a few weeks, but the psychologist had slowly cut back on those sessions. She'd said that Shelby was adjusting to what happened to her just fine.

Taylor, Harlow, Tori, and Savannah had been a big support to Shelby, which was something I was grateful for, and it had seemed to draw the women even closer together now because Shelby knew everything.

I'd been pissed when the counselor had told Shelby she should be fine going back to work, but my woman had gotten in my face at that point and insisted she *could* work.

She'd also been adamant about the fact that she was fine being home alone, and she'd practically kicked me out of the house to go back to my offices.

Okay, maybe I'd been a *tiny bit* overprotective, but I couldn't fucking help it.

All I could think about every time I saw her was the fact that she'd nearly died.

We ended our headquarters tour in the meeting room, where I'd motioned for her to have a seat.

She sent me a questioning glance, but she sat as she said, "Wyatt, I'm completely healed. You don't have to baby me anymore. I'm not exactly a fragile flower. I've been back in the kitchen for a while now. I am capable of standing for hours at a time."

"It's probably better if you don't remind me that you're working," I grumbled, wishing she'd given herself more time to heal.

"I think if you had your way, I'd end up locked inside the house forever sitting on the couch doing crossword puzzles or something," she teased.

"Don't think I haven't thought about that," I said unhappily.

The only thing I could think about was ways to protect her right now and make sure she never knew another moment of pain or fear. I'd seen enough of that while she was recovering, and I'd hated every moment of it.

"I suck at crossword puzzles," she said with a happy laugh.

"Knitting?" I suggested hopefully.

"Nope," she quipped. "Aunt Millie tried to teach me, and I'm hopeless at it. You're going to have to deal with the fact that I like to be outside and a little more active."

Yeah, well, my rational mind understood that I couldn't keep her in a protective bubble forever, but my primitive instincts said something entirely different.

"Shit!" a male voice sounded from the doorway. "I thought you two were already gone. I'll come back."

I turned to see Marshall standing at the entrance to the meeting room.

I'd known that he was up in his office, even if it was a Saturday. The guy never seemed to take a day off when it came to Last Hope business. But his office door had been closed, which meant he was working on something and he didn't want to be disturbed.

"Wait!" Shelby insisted, which made Marshall halt his hasty retreat. "Are you Marshall?"

The older man nodded. "I'm assuming you're Shelby."

Shelby shot out of her chair, raced to Marshall, and in her typical, upbeat Shelby fashion, she threw herself into his arms without thinking about her actions.

"I'm so grateful that you saved my life," Shelby said enthusiastically. "Thank you for designing that special GPS device, and helping to get me back. I'll always be grateful."

I watched as Marshall stood there for a few beats before he raised his arms and hugged Shelby back.

For several seconds, I thought about how unusual this moment was, and how I'd never seen a woman throw herself at Marshall for a hug.

Our Last Hope leader was an intimidating guy, and he was usually all business.

Other than Tori and Harlow, he probably intimidated most females because it was rare that he even cracked a smile.

Of course, she'd never been intimidated by me, either, so maybe it wasn't actually a brave move for her. She was used to assholes with no sense of humor.

"You don't have to be grateful," Marshall said in a milder voice than I'd ever heard from him in the past. "Rescuing kidnapped victims is what we do at Last Hope."

Shelby stepped back and looked at Marshall earnestly. "You took a risk with Last Hope by rescuing me, and it saved my life. That's a big deal to me. It's not much, but I made you some cookies. I left them near the door because I wasn't sure I'd see you. Let me get them."

She rushed out of the room and went to grab her bag of cookies.

"I wondered what was in that bag," I said wryly to Marshall. "I want you to know that had I known about the cookies, they never would have made it here to headquarters."

Marshall smirked. "You're possessive about her cookies?"

"Once you try them, you'll know why," I replied gruffly.

"She's a good woman, Wyatt," Marshall said grimly. "Don't fuck this up."

I wanted to ask him what the hell he meant, but Shelby came rushing back through the door. "I wasn't sure what you'd like, so I made a variety. Chocolate chip, snickerdoodles, peanut butter, and oatmeal raisin."

"Wait a minute!" I barked. "There's three of those that I haven't tried yet."

Marshall took the bag and actually winked at Shelby. "I like them all. I haven't had homemade cookies in a long time. I'll let you know how much I enjoyed them, Wyatt. Thank you, Shelby."

I had no doubt Marshall *would* rub it in later, when Shelby wasn't around.

"You're welcome," she said and beamed at the older man. "If you think it would help, I'd love to volunteer to come in and feed everyone when you're running a mission. You do have a kitchen, and I'm sure you need to eat after it's over."

I opened my mouth to protest, but Marshall cut off my words with a quick reply. "I think everyone would appreciate that. They're usually starving. Sometimes they go out to grab pizza and bring it back or stop for food after it's over."

Marshall didn't bother to mention that we always invited him when we stopped for food, but he'd always passed.

Shelby wrinkled her nose adorably. "I think I could do better than pizza, and it will be ready here as soon as you're done."

"I'm sold," Marshall said as he actually smiled at Shelby.

"Thank you," she said appreciatively. "It will make me feel better if I can help in some small way."

"No volunteer contribution is ever small," Marshall corrected.

I liked Marshall, and I respected him, but it was starting to grate on my nerves that Shelby had not only thrown herself into his arms, but that she was smiling at him, that dimple in full view, like she adored him.

Hell, she'd even baked cookies for him that I'd never tasted.

It had been so long since I'd touched Shelby myself in any other way but a gentle caress that I'd probably be annoyed by anyone getting more attention than me at this point.

Not that Shelby hadn't tried to toss her gorgeous body into my arms, but I'd gently set her away from me, concerned that I'd cause her more pain.

She'd needed more time to heal.

She still did.

The last thing she needed was a big guy like me manhandling her.

I strode across the room and took Shelby's hand possessively. "The tour is over. Later, Marshall."

"Later, Wyatt," Marshall said, his tone amused. "Thanks for the cookies."

I gritted my teeth because I knew the older man was trying to needle the hell out of me.

I let Shelby and I out past the security measures in place.

Once we were outside, she said, "God, he's really hot. He's nothing like I pictured, I guess. You said he was medically retired years ago. I guess I envisioned someone older and pretty fearsome. He's also really…nice."

"He is older," I informed her stiffly. "He's still a legend in the military, even though he did medically retire years ago. And he's not…hot."

She shrugged. "I think he is, and he's not *that* old. Maybe early to mid-fifties, he's in great shape, and he's got that gruff, mysterious kind of aura about him. I mean, *I'm* not physically attracted to him. I don't want to jump his bones or anything because I've already got the only man I want, but he is attractive. I'm surprised that he doesn't have a woman he wants to spend time with on a Saturday."

I relaxed because Shelby had just stroked my ego enough to curb my jealousy.

Hell, I'd really never thought about Marshall's love life, but… "As long as I've known him, I don't think he's ever had a real date or a woman in his life. He's fond of Harlow's mom, but I don't think that went anywhere romantically. As far as I know, they're just friends. He destroyed his leg during an op, which is why he had to retire."

Shelby shrugged. "So what if he has a limp? He is obviously a highly intelligent, attractive older man, and he's dedicated his life to helping people."

We stopped at the truck, and instead of opening her door, I put one hand on each side of her body and backed her up against the vehicle. "I'm a little envious of the fact that he got your cookies," I rumbled, only half joking.

I didn't put my arms around her for fear of crushing her ribs, but she sent me a sensual smile and wrapped her arms around my neck as she purred, "Do you really think I didn't keep some at home for you? I baked a lot of cookies. I've been more than a little frustrated lately."

I swooped down and captured her plump, irresistible lips, and I had one hell of a time not letting the embrace get heated.

The damn physical chemistry between the two of us was always there, even though there was so much more to our relationship than just my desire to fuck her until she begged for mercy.

I needed her, and I'd been fighting the desire to get inside her gorgeous body for so damn long that I felt like I was going to lose it.

She'd made me crazy from the very beginning, and she still did, except it was even more intense now because I worshipped the ground this woman walked on.

It took an almost superhuman effort to raise my head, step back, and open her door.

Compartmentalize, Durand. Compartmentalize. Shelby's health and well-being come before your dick.

As I closed her door and moved toward the driver's side of the truck, I knew I was losing my supposed legendary ability to keep my emotions in check.

If I didn't pull my shit together, my reasoning ability was going to war with my caveman instincts, and I wasn't sure which one was going to end up victorious.

Chapter 35

Shelby

I'd tried subtle hints.
I'd tried suggestive comments.
Hell, I'd tried everything to get Wyatt to tear my clothes off.

I'd even tried to wear something prettier than my normal jeans and a top for my tour of Last Hope headquarters today, and nothing was working.

Did I really have to bang Wyatt on the head to make him realize that I wanted him, and that I was more than ready to beg him to fuck me senseless?

Throughout my recovery, our emotional connection had grown deeper, even stronger than it had been before.

I was so crazy in love with him that I could hardly breathe, but the way he kept backing away from me was driving me insane.

He treated me like I was fragile, which I probably was in the beginning of my recovery, but I was healthy and my body desperately wanted Wyatt's.

I'm going to have to seduce him.
It wasn't like the physical chemistry between us had gone away.

I knew Wyatt wanted me. He was just afraid to touch me because he didn't want to hurt me.

While I adored his possessive, protective instincts, I was tired of being treated like an invalid.

There was no reason for it.

I'd been medically cleared for *all* activity, and that included hot, sweaty sex.

I also wanted to tell him that I loved him. Not saying those words out loud was getting torturous.

I was no longer worried about voicing my emotions too soon. After what I'd been through, I really didn't want to avoid those three little words any longer, even if Wyatt couldn't say them.

Maybe it was too soon for him, but I knew how much he cared for me. He'd been there every step of the way during my recovery, both emotionally and physically.

He'd taken care of me when I was vulnerable. The problem was, he was *still* taking care of me like I was that injured woman he'd hauled out of that cabin weeks ago.

I'd almost died at the hands of a serial killer, and I wanted him to know how I felt.

Tomorrow was never guaranteed. I'd learned that the hard way. After I was kidnapped, wondering when I was going to die, one of my most frequent thoughts had been ones of regret over never telling Wyatt how I felt.

I was just tossing a casserole in the oven for dinner when Wyatt came through the patio doors. He'd taken Xena out for a short, potty walk, and I watched as the pup went for her water bowl, and then headed for her bed in the living room for a nap.

My breath caught as he came into the kitchen. There would probably never be a time when I could look at Wyatt and still not be amazed that he was my guy.

Even in a pair of jeans and a faded T-shirt that hugged those glorious muscles of his, he was every woman's fantasy.

My body literally ached to have Wyatt inside me, and I wasn't sure how much longer I could be close to him and not appease that longing.

Wyatt frowned before he kissed me on the forehead. "You didn't have to cook."

"I wanted to cook. It's nothing elaborate," I replied with a sigh. "I'm perfectly capable of making an easy meal, Wyatt. I'm starting back at The Friendly Kitchen next week."

He shot me a steely, disapproving glance that would probably make most people run for cover, but I ignored it.

"Not happening," he said gruffly.

"It's absolutely happening," I said as I smiled at him sweetly and crossed my arms over my chest stubbornly. "I'm completely healed, I work at home, and not getting out in the world again is making me crazy."

He ran a frustrated hand through his hair. "Have you already forgotten that you were nearly killed by a psycho from that soup kitchen?"

"I don't think that's something I'll forget anytime soon," I said softly. "But I also can't hide from the world because it happened. It was a fluke, Wyatt. One bad person out of many. I could meet a psycho anywhere in this city. It just happened to be there."

I could see the tension in his body, even though we were a few feet away from each other. But I had to stand my ground on this one. If Wyatt had his way, I'd never leave the house again, and I'd be surrounded by a legion of his security. I couldn't live a normal life that way.

He had to understand that the danger was over. Ted was dead. Life had to go on, and I didn't want to continue to see him stressed out like this.

I also couldn't stand it when he treated me like I was easily breakable when there was absolutely no reason for it.

"No," he rumbled, his features set like they were made of stone.

My temper flared. Never once had Wyatt told me what to do except in the bedroom, where his bossy in bed thing was pretty damn hot.

This, however, was not hot, and he was pissing me off. "Give me one good reason why I shouldn't move on with my normal life?" I said in a heated voice.

He started to pace the kitchen as he growled, "Because I fucking love you more than life itself, and just the thought of seeing you be someone's target again makes me completely insane. Do you have any idea what it felt like to know that you were in the hands of a murderer and that I wasn't sure I could get to you before you were dead?"

I swallowed hard and shook my head. I wasn't afraid of this Wyatt who had completely lost control.

I was mesmerized.

He stopped pacing, trapped my body against the counter with his larger form and put a hand on the counter on each side of my body.

"I'll tell you exactly how it felt," he said hoarsely, his beautiful gray eyes filled with remorse and pain. "That was the moment when I realized that you were my whole fucking world, and that I'd cease to exist in this world without you in it. I wouldn't be me anymore without you, Shelby. You turned my world upside down from the moment we met, and I've discovered that I love it that way. I like having someone who isn't afraid to challenge me, someone who actually sees me, and someone who accepts me exactly as I am. I love you so much that the thought of being without you scares the shit out of me. The thought of you ever being hurt again scares the shit out of me. The thought of you being unhappy is unacceptable to me. Maybe I'm no Prince Charming, but I want that damn fairy tale, Cinderella. I want us to live that happily ever after, but we can't do that if you're hurt or dead."

I put one hand on his heaving chest and the other around his neck, tears streaming from my eyes. It was killing me to see him so tormented, but his impassioned, uncontrolled speech had reached straight into my soul. "I'm not dead, Wyatt. We're both alive. Do you really think I wasn't just as terrified when I realized you'd gotten shot rescuing me? I love you, too, and you're *my* everything now."

As implausible as it might seem, Wyatt Durand and I were soulmates, and we'd probably always been meant to be together. For a time, I'd stopped believing in soulmates or happily ever after. Being with Wyatt had changed all of that for me.

"You love me?" He grumbled the question.

Our eyes met, and I melted down.

Totally.

Completely.

There was no holding back at all for me anymore because I could see the way I felt reflected in his gaze.

"I think I have for a long time. I just wasn't sure you were ready to hear it," I confessed. "And I'd really like the fairy tale, too, please."

He ran a finger down my cheek with the small scar, and then tucked an errant lock of hair behind my ear. "I don't think I'll ever be able to live up to the Prince Charming thing, but I want to make you happy, Shelby. And I can't control the caveman instinct to make you mine and protect you. It's fucking impossible for me."

I smiled up at him as I ran my palm along his stubbled jawline. "Love me. Make me yours because I desperately want you to be mine, Wyatt. Protect me. I can compromise. Just don't expect me to live like a bird in a gilded cage. I won't thrive that way."

"Fine," he said unhappily. "Go back to The Friendly Kitchen if that's what you need to do, but I still want security on your gorgeous ass. At least for a while."

My heart squeezed inside my chest. That was a compromise for Wyatt. "One person," I insisted. "A single bodyguard would work for me, and I think you'll eventually cave in and let me go places on my own."

"Don't count on that," he said grimly. "And I think I'll want to be the one to guard your body whenever possible."

I just smiled wider.

God, I loved this man so much.

Eventually, Wyatt and I would recover from what happened weeks ago. It was still so fresh for him that he was ultra-protective, but I could live with that until those memories faded.

Would he ever be totally relaxed when it came to keeping me safe? Probably not, but he wouldn't be this uptight about it, either.

There was a big part of me that loved his caveman instincts, as long as he didn't go overboard.

I'd never had a man who really cared about my well-being and my happiness, and it felt good, even when he was a little overbearing and bossy about it.

I could handle him and his caveman attitude, and I'd never be afraid to call him on it if it became oppressive. His desire to make me happy was just as strong as his protective instincts, and he'd back down when he was being completely unreasonable.

I pulled his head closer until I could feel his warm breath on my lips. "I wouldn't mind if you decided to get all bossy on me right now," I whispered.

I held my breath. God, I wanted him, and I needed him to realize that I wasn't breakable.

"Shelby," he said in a deep, growly, warning voice. "What do you want from me?"

"Nothing. I just want...you," I said in a needy voice as the hand I had on his chest wandered down to the very large erection underneath the denim of his jeans. "I need you, Wyatt."

"Fuck!" he cursed before his mouth slammed down on mine.

I moved my hand, stroking the outline of his huge cock as he ravaged my lips like a man who was famished.

It wasn't sweet.

It wasn't tender.

And it definitely wasn't gentle.

We devoured each other's mouths with the voracious hunger of two people that had been deprived of what we wanted for way too long.

I moaned against that marauding mouth, desperate to be as close to this man as I could possibly get.

My core clenched in anticipation, and heat flooded between my thighs, my entire body feeling like it was being incinerated.

"Wyatt," I gasped as he let me breathe, his mouth wandering to my neck, my shoulders, and the top of my breasts. Anywhere his wicked lips could touch bare skin, and there was a lot of it with this particular dress I was wearing.

"Your ribs—"

"Are completely healed," I interrupted. "Fuck me, Wyatt. You're not going to hurt me. We both need this so badly."

He pulled my adoring hand away from his crotch and lifted the hem of my dress.

He used brute strength to tear my panties and get to my pussy.

Obviously, he'd reached the end of his patience, and I relished the completely neanderthal behavior.

The feel of his fingers sliding into my wet heat with a relentless purpose made my entire body shiver with need.

"You're so damn wet," Wyatt growled next to my ear.

I gasped as his finger stroked hard on my clit, and then I moaned as he did it over and over until I thought I was going to lose my mind.

"Is this what you need, babe?" he rasped.

"Yes," I whimpered. "Make me come, Wyatt. Please."

I'd wanted him to touch me for so long that I could already feel my orgasm building.

I moved my hips, literally riding his hand, my body pleading for release.

"Oh, God, Wyatt!" I called out as my legs trembled and I imploded.

He held me as I melted down, gripping my ponytail and tilting my head back so he could see my face.

"You're so fucking beautiful when you come," Wyatt said right before he kissed me.

I sighed against his lips, but my hunger for him wasn't even close to satisfied.

I clawed at his T-shirt, needed to feel our bodies skin to skin.

He obliged by yanking off his shirt and tossing it aside before he jerked my dress over my head. I was braless, and the covetous look in Wyatt's eyes undid me.

"I'm probably going to hate myself for this later," he rasped as he threw my dress to the floor and shucked his jeans and boxer briefs. "But I need my cock inside your wet, hot pussy right fucking now."

He picked up my nude body, and the moment my back met the wall, I knew I was going to get *exactly* what I needed.

Chapter 36

Shelby

"Tell me what you want," Wyatt demanded. "You want my cock, babe?"

I speared my hands into his hair and jerked. "I *need* your cock. Inside me. Right now. No fucking around, Wyatt," I panted.

I didn't have the patience to wait any longer.

I was done.

As though he knew I was at the end of my rope, he didn't hesitate. One forceful thrust of his hips and he was buried to his balls.

My head thumped back against the wall. "Yes! Fuck me like you mean it."

"Holy shit!" Wyatt said with a groan. "You feel so damn good, and I always fuck you like I mean it, because it's always just like this."

He was right, but I couldn't handle the teasing today.

My emotions were raw, covetous, and I wanted everything he had. Knowing that he loved me had completely set me…free.

I needed to feel our bodies joined together. I wanted to savor the feeling of him pounding inside me like a wild man because he wanted to claim me.

That was what I needed right now.

"I love you, Wyatt," I breathed into his ear.

"Love. You." he said, his voice gravelly with emotion as he pulled back and thrust into me even harder.

He set a pace that was almost savage, and his fierceness satisfied the longing in my soul.

"You're mine, Shelby," he rasped. "Say it."

"Yours," I moaned. "And you're mine."

"Always," he rasped as he pommeled his cock into me over and over again like he couldn't stop the frenetic motion.

I tightened my legs around him, lost in the erotic, sensual beat of our bodies coming together over and over again.

I loved this man and the way he could arouse my body like nobody else ever could.

I arched my back against the wall, my body beyond ready to climax, but I wasn't there yet.

My heart was racing, and I was panting like I'd done a morning run with Wyatt.

"Touch yourself," he demanded. "I want to feel you coming around my cock, and I won't last long this time."

I slid my hand between our bodies and stroked my clit just as hard as he was fucking me.

I squeaked as he squeezed my ass, one of his fingers sliding between the cheeks. The tip of his finger barely penetrated, and it wasn't painful, but the added sensation set off a powerful climax that shook my entire body.

My orgasm gripped Wyatt's cock in hard spasms that ripped a raw groan from his throat as he pounded into me until he found his own release.

My forehead dropped onto his muscular shoulder as I fought to catch my breath, my emotions totally exposed, every feeling sitting right on the surface.

I panted for a minute before I could breathe normally again, and then I lifted my head to look at Wyatt.

My eyes filled with tears as I saw the same vulnerability in his expression.

"I feel the same way," he said huskily as he reached behind my head and pulled me in for a kiss.

The embrace was full of love, and it soothed me.

Wyatt got me, and he was always tuned into my emotions, just like I could read his.

Complete and utter trust was hard for both of us, but we'd finally found it in each other.

"Did I hurt you?" he asked with concern once he'd released my lips.

I smiled at him. "Do you really think I could come that hard if I was in severe pain? I'm fine, Wyatt. That was…" I fought for a way to describe what had just happened.

"Orgasmic?" he suggested with a wicked grin.

I snorted. "Exactly."

"I think after that much physical exertion, we could use…a nap," Wyatt said nonchalantly.

He was so full of it. Wyatt didn't take naps, and neither did I, but I was more than willing to let him take me to bed. I was eager to make up for lost time. "Wait!" I said urgently as he started to walk out of the kitchen still carrying me. "The casserole."

He stood close to the oven and I turned it off before he proceeded to haul me upstairs.

He dropped me gently on the bed, but I was surprised when he strode into the walk-in closet for a few seconds before he joined me on the bed.

He opened his hand, and there sat a small, velvet box.

"I've been carrying this around since I gave you the earrings," he said solemnly. "I had them both made at the same time. Even then, I knew what I wanted. I just wasn't sure that you did. Hell, I don't know if you're ready now, but I'm willing to take that chance."

I took the box, and sent Wyatt a quizzical look as I opened it.

My breath hitched as I saw the gorgeous and very large engagement ring inside.

It was beautiful, classy, and sat low in the setting so I wouldn't catch it on everything, and I knew Wyatt had done that intentionally because I was a chef.

The large oval diamond was surrounded by smaller accent diamonds, and there were two emerald accents on each side nestled between the diamonds.

I instantly knew he'd included the tiny emeralds because he thought they matched my eyes, just like the earrings.

The ring was the most beautiful thing I'd ever seen.

Even though the carat value was probably outrageous, it wasn't so ostentatious that it was too large to wear every day.

"Marry me, beautiful," Wyatt said hoarsely. "I don't need a rushed wedding like Chase had if you're not ready, but I need to see that ring on your finger so every man who sees you already knows that you're mine."

For the second time in a few hours, I started to cry, huge tears dropping onto my cheeks as I stared at the ring in my hand.

"You hate it," Wyatt said flatly. "Or it's too soon."

"No," I said, choking back a sob. "It's beautiful. I just can't believe you just asked me to marry you with this incredible ring."

"I wanted something bigger, but I know that's not your style."

"It's plenty big already," I teased. "Are you going to put it on my finger? I want to marry you. It is part of the fairy tale."

He took the ring and tossed the box aside. "This isn't the way I planned on doing this, but you know I'm not the romantic type. And if you don't love the ring, we'll get something else."

I swiped tears from my eyes as he carefully placed the ring on my finger.

God, this man had no idea how romantic it was to propose because he couldn't wait another moment to ask.

I didn't need a fancy restaurant or flowers. I'd much rather have that kind of eagerness for a commitment from the man I loved.

"I love it," I said softly as I admired the way it looked on my finger before I leaned forward and kissed him. As I pulled back and looked into his gorgeous eyes, I added, "But not nearly as much as I love the man who just gave it to me. I think I'm probably the happiest woman in the world right now."

"Don't get used to it," he said drily. "You know I'm likely to piss you off."

I shrugged. "Maybe you will occasionally because you're bullheaded sometimes, but you'll eventually compromise."

"I'd still like to lock you up in the house," he said, sounding like he was only half joking. "I meant what I said, sweetheart. I think you took twenty years off my life when you were kidnapped by a serial killer." He reached up and touched the small scar on my face. "Are you sure that you're okay."

I beamed at him. "Never been better. The man I love asked me to marry him today."

Right now, I felt like I could fly.

It wasn't too soon for me.

I knew what I wanted.

And he was right in front of me, completely naked.

"And exactly how long is that man going to have to suffer before we set a wedding date?" he asked as he flopped back on the pillow and pulled me down until I was sprawled on top of him.

I was so happy that I just shrugged. "I'm not really picky about the wedding. I don't need something horribly formal."

I'd been married once, and that marriage had meant nothing. I couldn't care less how I married the right guy.

"You're not getting out of having the wedding you deserve," Wyatt drawled.

"We'll work on it together," I promised him.

"We're doing the honeymoon of your dreams, too," he warned me.

I could live with that. I didn't really care where we went. I'd already have the groom I wanted. "There's so many places I'd love to go."

"Then we'll do an extended honeymoon," he said obligingly.

Was there anything this man wouldn't do to make me happy?

Having been married to a total jerk, I could appreciate the fact that I'd gotten so damn lucky this time.

I'd found a love that I'd always hoped for but never thought I'd actually find.

"What can I do to make you happy?" I murmured as I lowered my forehead to his. "You've done so much for me."

He flipped our bodies over until he was above me, trapping my body beneath his.

"Keep on loving me?" he asked hopefully. "And make sure I get to keep all of the cookies next time."

I snorted as I wrapped my arms around his neck. "Are you always going to be this greedy about my cookies."

"Yes," he said, deadpan. "I'm always going to be an asshole and completely greedy and selfish when it comes to you. Even about your cooking or baking. Get used to it."

I laughed and pulled him closer. "I wouldn't mind if you wanted to show me how greedy and selfish you can be right now."

"I plan on it," he said with a shit-eating grin on his face.

I sighed against his lips as he kissed me.

Sometimes a little bit of greediness wasn't a horrible thing at all.

Epilogue

Wyatt

Six Months Later...

I nursed a glass of whiskey as I leaned against a sturdy tree, watching my bride chat with all of the wedding guests.

We'd been married under a shade tree at a back-country location in San Diego County, a compromise that had suited the two of us.

I'd wanted a gigantic formal wedding.

She'd wanted to get married with absolutely no fanfare and very few guests.

We'd ended up finding this location that was less formal, embraced the outdoors, but was still high-end.

We'd lucked out with great weather, not too hot, which was fortunate because I was wearing a tux.

I'd agreed to keep it small, with closer friends and family.

She'd agreed to a wedding planner, a caterer, and letting me hire one of our designers to make her the perfect dress.

Fuck! She looked stunning in her A-line empire gown that fit her perfectly. She'd nixed wearing pure white because she said it leeched the color from her skin. Instead, she'd chosen an ivory color with accents of baby blue, embroidered with just enough crystals to make her look like she sparkled in the sunlight.

She'd gotten her makeup and hair done professionally, and I loved the fact that she left her hair down in a similar style to the one she'd chosen for the charity gala.

My eyes swept over her again, and they landed on the ring on her finger.

Mostly, she looked like she was mine right now, which made me a very happy man.

A lot had happened in the last six months.

Shelby's popularity had grown enormously, her cookbook was a huge success, and she was already planning the next one.

We'd visited Montana again two months ago, and she'd banished all of the ghosts of what had happened to her there. Thank fuck that it had been an uneventful trip this time.

Last Hope had run a few missions since Shelby had found out about the organization. She'd dropped in to cook every single time, and everyone had been so thankful for a good meal after the op was over that our group would probably complain incessantly if she wasn't with me on every mission.

And me? Hell, I was still an asshole, but I was probably the happiest asshole that ever existed.

I'd changed some, but that was all because I was with a woman that made it impossible to look at the world the same way I had before I'd met her.

I watched her as Shelby started to look around, and I knew she was looking for me.

My chest got tight simply from knowing that she'd search me out in a crowd, just like I'd always be looking for her.

Her eyes lit up the moment our gazes locked. She smiled that radiant, dimple exposing grin that always made me feel humbled that she belonged to me.

It always would.

My instincts were always right, and my gut told me that there was never going to be a day that I took this woman for granted.

"What are you doing over here all by yourself," she asked when she arrived by my side.

"Watching you," I said honestly before I drained my glass and put it on a nearby table. "It's one of my favorite hobbies."

I wrapped my arms around her, and she wound her arms around my neck as she said, "It was such a beautiful wedding. Thank for such a perfect day."

There it was. The gratitude again.

Hell, I wasn't going to complain because I was feeling pretty damn grateful myself right now.

I actually understood that feeling now.

She continued, "Everyone I love is right here in the same place."

Shelby turned her head and eyed all of our family and friends.

Because the wedding was small, we'd only had Chase and Tori stand up for us as best man and matron of honor, but everyone else was here. The Montgomerys, Savannah, my former Delta team, and Shelby's entire family.

Shelby sighed as her eyes landed on her three cousins and her aunt. "I wish my cousins would find the right partner for them. I'd like to see them as happy as I am right now, and it would make Aunt Millie ecstatic."

I chuckled. "I think they've all done everything possible to escape those matchmaking attempts of hers. I don't think any of them are looking for a lifelong partner. They're as jaded as I was before I met you."

She turned her gaze on me, and my chest tightened up again as our eyes met.

"You found someone," she pointed out.

I grinned at her like a lovesick idiot. "I did, so maybe it's not impossible for the same thing to happen to them."

"They just haven't met the right women," she insisted.

I groaned. "You're starting to sound like Tori. She used to say the same thing about me."

"She was right," Shelby reminded me.

"She was," I conceded. "But I don't think matchmaking is going to help. I think they'll find that woman when they're not expecting it."

"Do you think so?" Shelby said hopefully.

I shrugged. "That's the way it happened for me, but today is your day, sweetheart. Are *you* happy?"

"I think you already know that I am," she murmured. "Are you?"

I gave her a shit-eating grin. "I am, but I'll be even happier when I can strip off that cock teasing dress you're wearing."

"Is that what it is?" she asked in a sensual voice.

"You know it is," I accused. "I think you had it designed to drive me insane all day. You're always beautiful, but you look especially beautiful today."

"You look especially hot yourself, handsome," she teased.

My hard cock twitched as I lowered my head until my mouth was near her ear. "What time do you think we can get out of here and start our extended honeymoon. We've eaten a fantastic dinner and the cake. There's only one more thing I want to taste today."

She raised a brow. "Me, too."

Christ! Was she trying to drive me completely insane?

I lowered my head and kissed her, trying not to let the embrace get too heated in front of our entire families and all of our friends.

Her lips and mouth were sweet like the cake we'd eaten earlier, and my head swam from the taste of her mouth.

All I wanted was to get the hell out of here so I could take her home and show her just how glad I was that she was now my wife.

She looked dazed, happy, and hungry for something other than food when I finally let her up for air.

I nearly picked her up and carried her out of the venue.

"There's one more thing you need to do today," she said, sounding almost disappointed that we couldn't start that honeymoon right away.

"What's that?" I asked huskily as I toyed with a fiery lock of her hair.

"The music is starting. I think we're going to need to dance, Prince Charming. I know it's not your favorite thing to do, but it would complete this fairy-tale wedding," she teased.

"Do you want to dance?" I asked.

"Yes," she said breathlessly. "I'm always going to want to dance with you."

I dropped an adoring kiss on her forehead before I answered hoarsely, "Then dance with me, Cinderella."

Hell, I wasn't going to complain about an activity that would keep her in my arms for an extended period of time.

"I love you," she whispered before she stepped back and took my hand with a huge smile.

I swallowed the lump in my throat before I said, "I love you, too, beautiful."

I'd probably never get used to hearing those words from her or seeing her this happy.

My dick could just wait until she'd gotten every bit of enjoyment that she could from our wedding.

I wrapped my arm possessively around her waist and headed for the dance floor.

I didn't think a cranky asshole like me could ever be Prince Charming, but as long as she loved me, I'd let her continue to think anything she wanted.

~The End~

Please visit me at:
http://www.authorjsscott.com
http://www.facebook.com/authorjsscott

You can write to me at
jsscott_author@hotmail.com

You can also tweet
@AuthorJSScott

Please sign up for my Newsletter for updates, new releases and exclusive excerpts.

Books by J. S. Scott:

Billionaire Obsession Series

The Billionaire's Obsession~Simon
Heart of the Billionaire
The Billionaire's Salvation
The Billionaire's Game
Billionaire Undone~Travis
Billionaire Unmasked~Jason
Billionaire Untamed~Tate
Billionaire Unbound~Chloe
Billionaire Undaunted~Zane
Billionaire Unknown~Blake
Billionaire Unveiled~Marcus
Billionaire Unloved~Jett
Billionaire Unwed~Zeke
Billionaire Unchallenged~Carter

Billionaire Unattainable~Mason
Billionaire Undercover~Hudson
Billionaire Unexpected~Jax
Billionaire Unnoticed~Cooper
Billionaire Unclaimed~Chase
Billionaire Unreachable~Wyatt
Billionaire Unexplained~Kaleb

British Billionaires Series

Tell Me You're Mine
Tell Me I'm Yours
Tell Me This Is Forever

Sinclair Series

The Billionaire's Christmas
No Ordinary Billionaire
The Forbidden Billionaire
The Billionaire's Touch
The Billionaire's Voice
The Billionaire Takes All
The Billionaire's Secret
Only A Millionaire

Accidental Billionaires

Ensnared
Entangled
Enamored
Enchanted
Endeared

Walker Brothers Series

Release
Player
Damaged

The Sentinel Demons

The Sentinel Demons: The Complete Collection
A Dangerous Bargain
A Dangerous Hunger
A Dangerous Fury
A Dangerous Demon King

The Vampire Coalition Series
The Vampire Coalition: The Complete Collection
The Rough Mating of a Vampire (Prelude)
Ethan's Mate
Rory's Mate
Nathan's Mate
Liam's Mate
Daric's Mate

Changeling Encounters Series
Changeling Encounters: The Complete Collection
Mate Of The Werewolf
The Dangers Of Adopting A Werewolf
All I Want For Christmas Is A Werewolf

The Pleasures of His Punishment
The Pleasures of His Punishment: The Complete Collection
The Billionaire Next Door
The Millionaire and the Librarian
Riding with the Cop
Secret Desires of the Counselor
In Trouble with the Boss
Rough Ride with a Cowboy
Rough Day for the Teacher
A Forfeit for a Cowboy
Just what the Doctor Ordered
Wicked Romance of a Vampire

The Curve Collection: Big Girls and Bad Boys Series
The Curve Collection: The Complete Collection
The Curve Ball
The Beast Loves Curves
Curves by Design

Writing as Lane Parker
Dearest Stalker
Dearest Protector
A Christmas Dream
A Valentine's Dream
Lost: A Mountain Man Rescue Romance

A Dark Horse Novel w/ Cali MacKay
Bound
Hacked

Taken By A Trillionaire Series
Virgin for the Trillionaire by Ruth Cardello
Virgin for the Prince by J.S. Scott
Virgin to Conquer by Melody Anne
Prince Bryan: Taken By A Trillionaire

Other Titles
Well Played w/Ruth Cardello

Printed in Great Britain
by Amazon

38095666R10162